To Ann and Derek

B

Paris Hide and Seek

Also by Tony Barnard

"The Sheffield Avengers"

"High Five in Jerusalem"

"Pebbles in the Pond"

Paris Hide and Seek

by

Tony Barnard

Copyright © 2020 Tony Barnard

Cover design by DSM Design Ltd.

ISBN: 9798654574619

PublishNation
www.publishnation.co.uk

For Tom

*"You're not supposed to be so blind with patriotism
that you can't face reality.
Wrong is wrong, no matter who says it."*

Malcolm X

Prologue

Paris in May 1968 was congested with both students and traffic. The availability of adequate housing and transport in all of the great cities of the world make life in them nasty and brutal for the disadvantaged. But it is the progressive destruction of available amenities by the seemingly unstoppable invasion of the automobile that is perhaps the most striking sign of a society that spends too much on individual consumption and not enough on societal investment. This was certainly the view of the burgeoning number of students in the French capital who came to denounce the situation as the *'Societe de Consomation.'*

Student numbers in Paris had grown significantly, partly because there had been a marked increase in the birth rate after the Liberation which had resulted in gross overcrowding in universities but it was not just as a result of the 'baby boom' when couples believed that it was now safe to start a family and the hardships of war and depravation had started to ease. At the heart of the problem was the French 'open door' policy to university admission which meant that anyone who scraped through the *'Baccalaureat'*, the summit of the secondary school system could go to university. The result of this was that libraries, laboratories and university administrators were completely swamped and student- teacher relationships had totally collapsed.

Despite a six-fold increase in state spending on education in the previous fifteen years, the record was one of 'too little and too late.' Planners had decided to build huge residential campuses on the outskirts of Paris and these big decentralised campuses developed on the American model, were supposed to have been the remedy for the intolerable overcrowding situation.

These problems of overcrowding and under-administration had been exacerbated by the relentless progress of centralisation and bureaucratisation within the education system. This ensured that virtually no powers were in local hands at a university level and all administrative decisions, all budgetary allocation and all staff appointments were the prerogative of a distant and faceless bureaucracy.

Nothing typified this situation more than Nanterre. Built at speed in the early 1960's, it was intended to relieve the pressure that existed in the Latin Quarter. Its first buildings were opened in 1964 when two thousand students were admitted. By 1968 however, this figure had mushroomed six-fold. Intended by the Ministry of Education as a blueprint for the universities of the future, it became a blueprint for something else completely. These institutions had the effect of isolating students form the rest of the community in the same way as some workers had become isolated in American 'company towns.' The student body led by the Nanterre Sociologists therefore developed the same sense of lack of identity and facelessness as an industrial proletariat, with the its own grievances, its own leaders but with it a growing sense of its own power demanding to live within a community with individual expressionism and not a barracks. They wanted the same social and sexual freedoms which they had witnessed in America and Britain and an end to repression and conservatism. French youth wanted to share in the contemporary counter culture typified by popular music and art and embodied in the influential Beatles Album '*Sgt. Pepper's Lonely Hearts Band*' released the year before.

The centralisation process that had pervaded all elements of French government, not just education, meant that when the students took on the university authorities and the police, they were directly challenging the authority of the state and the whole fabric of French society. Despite living in a period of great prosperity French students had come to detest the society that was being prepared for them. They were ashamed of the Algerian war and appalled by what was happening in Vietnam. The Vietnam War was particularly poignant to the French student protestors, many of whom viewed the American involvement as a continuation of France's own violent imperialism in Southeast Asia as Vietnam had been a French colony for nearly a century from 1858 to 1954. Many protestors sympathised emotionally and ideologically with Ho Chi Minh, the Communist who led the fight for Vietnamese independence from the French and now symbolised North Vietnam's struggle with the South and the United States.

Gradually a profound politicisation of the French youth had taken place, undetected or ignored and as such their anger turned towards their overcrowded universities which they regarded as badly run factories churning out fodder to feed the system and maintain the status quo. Change was taking place across the western world epitomised by the title track of Bob Dylan's third album *'The Times they Are a-Changin'* which became an anthem for change and a youth culture which would not be suppressed. Dylan's music was like nothing that had ever been heard before — not just the twangy, nasal voice, but the lyrics, too. Coming from a conservative Italian family, whose values he was starting to question and that questioning became infectious amongst discontented and alienated youth politicised by the anti-war and the civil rights movements. That discontent had crossed the Atlantic and taken root first in Great Britain and by 1968, in France. For this generation of students, neither the French Communist Party nor orthodox Marxism held many attractions. Instead, its idols were Che Guevara, Ho Chi Minh, and Mao Zedong and it was images of carpet bombing, napalm attacks, and the massacre of civilians by

3

U.S. forces in Vietnam seen on the nightly news on television and in newspapers, that dominated their discussions and view point.

These underlying social and cultural changes were taking place against a political background of stability but also stagnation. In May 1968 France was celebrating the tenth anniversary of a regime which had given her stability, public order, a buoyant economy and a popular foreign policy of anti-Americanism. But this buoyant economy had not translated its way into job creation and unemployment was still at unacceptably high levels. Moreover, the ten years of alienation from a political regime was now taking an effect because throughout this period the political system had been associated with one man- de Gaulle. For too long, many had started to think, political decision-making had been in the hands of an aloof and paternal, if not authoritarian President. Parliament and the intermediary organs of government had been by-passed. Despite all the efforts to decentralise and establish a dialogue between the decision-making government elite and those responsible for implementing the substance of those decisions at the national, regional and local levels, the dialogue had just not materialised. An aloof President, a Cabinet subordinate to him rather than to parliament and a highly centralised civil service continued to rule.

However, in just a few short weeks, a student movement in a modern, capitalist and highly organised and prosperous western society was able to bring the government to its knees. Subsequently administrators who had been in charge of administering 'everything' were exposed to have a real grasp of 'nothing.' Planners who had previously planned 'everything' were unable to have their plans accepted by those for whom they had been designed.

So, in the Spring of 1968, the scene was set and for all of the foregoing reasons, French universities and the Sorbonne in Paris, in particular had now become a powder keg.

Chapter One

Chateau Grand Vue had been in the Dufort family since the middle of the nineteenth century. It was situated in the appellation d'origine contrôlée of Saint-£milion, a commune in the Gironde department in Nouvelle-Aquitaine in south-western France. Saint-Émilion is probably the oldest active wine producing appellation in the Bordeaux region with a history that dates back to the times of the ancient Romans. Numerous Roman ruins are scattered all over the Saint-Émlion appellation and the area takes its name from a Benedictine Monk who was known as Emilian.

In the first classification of St Emilion wines in 1955 by the local Syndicat Viticole, based on quality and not price; Chateau Grand Vue achieved the status of a Grand Cru Classé. This status had been maintained through the re-classification in 1965 and which takes place every ten years. This was a matter of some enormous pride to the Dufort family. The vineyard was situated on gravel terraces towards the bottom of the slopes that surround Saint-Émilion and it is this limestone that is a large part of what creates the distinctiveness of Saint-Émilion wines. The limestone soil offers good drainage in the wet years acting like a sponge, soaking up the water retaining it and then releasing it when needed as the weather turns dry.

The vineyard had been bought by Jean-Pierre Dufort in 1855 and who, with great enthusiasm and physical effort started to extend and build the property culminating in

1914, when his son, Guillaume, won a gold medal at the International Exhibition of Lyon. Jean-Pierre managed to assemble a motivated and closely-knit team ensuring that throughout the year, the many needs of the vineyard were met with a shared vision of producing quality wines whilst still respecting the environment. For over one hundred years since that time, the Dufort family had built up their reputation and expanded the production of the silky rich red wine which was a blend of Merlot, Cabernet Franc and Cabernet Sauvignon grapes. The wine had consistently been able to deliver earthy, spicy flavours with notes of tobacco and truffle and because of the limestone in the terroir, a strong sensation of minerality. As result the Dufort family had become part of the 'Saint-Émilion establishment 'and had amassed a considerable amount of wealth and the current owner Phillippe Dufort had been both proud and delighted that he had been invited to join the prestigious brotherhood of *the Jurade* in 1960. He was one of one hundred and thirty *Jurats* or members who came from all backgrounds but had included royalty, clergymen, political personalities, celebrities, men and women from the world of art, cinema, theatre, sport and business as well as wine professionals and connoisseurs.

The history of *the Jurade* dated back over eight hundred years with its mission to preserve the reputation and integrity of Saint-Émilion wines and promote them all over the world. Benoit had been only twelve years old when he and his sister Monica, who was two years younger than him, had stood with their mother and watched his father parade through the town wearing his traditional red caps and robes decorated with white ermine on the third Sunday in June. After attending Mass, the *Jurats* had walked to the cloister of the Collegiate Church, near the Cardinal Palace or the Monolithic Church to perform the traditional ceremony. Then, after lunch, they had solemnly announced the *'Judgement of the New Wine.'* It had all been very formal.

Nineteen-year-old Benoit Dufort was the great grandson of Jean-Pierre Dufort and he was now in his second year at the Sorbonne in Paris studying Sociology having achieved top marks at his school for the *Baccalauréat économique et social.* He was tall at one point nine metres with light brown hair, blue eyes and broad shoulders. His passion ever since being a young boy had been photography. He had graduated from simple cameras with an eight-photograph exposure film to much more sophisticated equipment.

"You definitely have an eye for it" people would say when they viewed his prints. He was fascinated originally with black and white photography and how light and dark and shadow could affect the image to convey mood and subtlety. He then moved on to colour photography using the money that he had earned working in the vineyards grape picking and doing other general duties that his father had paid him plus generous allowances for birthdays and Christmas.

He had been unable to contain his delight when his parents presented him with a brand new, state-of-the-art Bell & Howell eight-millimetre cine camera, projector and screen for passing his Baccalaureate with such good marks. Now he could become a movie director perhaps even trying to emulate the great French directors of La Nouvelle Vague (New Way), a movement which had emerged in the 1950's and early 1960's with such heroes for Benoit as Jean Luc Goddard, Claude Chabrol and Jacques Rivette. For weeks he practiced with the camera ensuring as he had learnt to keep the camera still and let the subject or subjects provide the motion and only panning the camera very slowly when necessary; otherwise the result as he had discovered, was a rapid blur when playing the film back and an expensive disappointment.

As always over the summer before leaving for university, he had worked in the vineyard but he had put in extra shifts this year working from dawn till dusk and using the money to buy the development and editing equipment that he needed so that he could develop and produce his own films without incurring the significant expense of sending them to a laboratory to be processed. He enjoyed working in the vineyard, driving tractors and collecting large trailer loads of grapes and working in the fields or in the cellars or the cavernous fermentation room which held the giant vats during harvest time. Periodically the juice was pumped over the floating mass of skins, pips and stalks and sometimes this cap or 'chapeau' was pushed down in a process called 'pigeage.' The purpose of this was to combine the colour-retaining components with the must, equalise the temperature and assist the release of colour, tannin and extract from the skins. One of Benoit's jobs at this time had been to join the team of those responsible for assisting in the 'pigeage' process. This involved using a long stick with a metal X fixed on the end to push down the 'chapeau' that rose to the top of the vats during the fermentation process caused by the carbon dioxide that was being released.

This year he would miss the harvest because it usually took place late in September when he would already have left for Paris but there was plenty of work to do on the estate prior to the crucial point of the actual harvest. Benoit had always liked the head winemaker, the vintner of Chateau Grand Vue very much indeed. His name was Didier Arnaud and he had been working at Chateau Grand Vue for over thirty years and was his father's most valuable employee and as such was granted the use of a lovely old cottage on the estate where he lived with his wife, Dominique. Benoit had been in the cottage many times as a boy. They had not been able to have any children and so Dominique always made a fuss of Benoit. It was a lovely house with shuttered windows either side of a large front door and you entered into one large room which was completely covered with dark red ceramic tiles. To the left was an enormous fireplace and sitting area, straight ahead was a galley-style kitchen and to the right there was a dining area with an old oak farmhouse table with two straw-covered oak chairs on one side and old oak bench on the other side where he and his sister Monica used to sit when Dominique sometimes made them some early evening supper.

It was only as Benoit got older that he started to understand why his father respected Didier so much. It was his responsibility to take into account so many different factors many of which were out of his control and at the whim of Mother Nature such as rain, frost, sunshine, humidity and temperature but he also learnt that when you harvest is just as important. It was his expertise that knew when the combination of factors was just right. These involved measuring the sugar content, taste, look, feel and pip colour were all had to come together in the right way at the right time and once again the only factor out of Didier's control was the weather. Benoit knew that all of that took place before he took into consideration the way the grapes were picked, crushed and fermented. It was this skill that Didier had learnt from the previous vintner, Michel, whom he had worked under for twenty years before Michel had finally retired and Didier was given the top job and the responsibility for maintaining the reputation of Chateau Grand Vue.

Monica, who was two years younger than Benoit helped out too but she had always made it plain that she did not want any part of the vineyard in the future as she wanted to study medicine at university and become a doctor which her parents were very keen for her to do. It had always been understood that Benoit, as his father's only son would one day take over the running of the family business and continue the Dufort tradition in Saint-Émilion but for now his father was quite happy that he should gain the best education he could and some life experiences first. He was however, more than slightly perturbed that Benoit had selected the Sorbonne University in Paris.

"Why do you want to study Sociology" he had asked *"Why not economics or Business Studies which will be useful to you in your working life?"*

"Because father Sociology is the study of society – how it works, why it works, and how it could change. It's a fascinating subject that covers all aspects of modern life and I want to be part of that change so I need to understand"

His father had simply shook his head and walked out of the room.

"This Sociology thing is just leftwing nonsense" he had said to his wife later that evening over dinner.

However, he had been quite taken aback when Brigitte, Benoit's mother reprimanded him when she said:

"Remember Philippe the alleged saying of the English Prime Minister, Winston Churchill when he said 'If a man is not a socialist by the time, he is twenty, he has no heart. If he is not a conservative by the time, he is forty, he has no brain.'"

So, it was in September 1966 that Benoit entered the Sorbonne University in Paris. All through the summer as he had worked in the vineyard, he thought he had prepared himself for the student life in the capital city but the onslaught of noise, traffic and people were almost overwhelming to him at first. It did not take him long to realise that the population of Paris which numbered about two and a half million was far more eclectic than that which he was used to. There were very few immigrants indeed, if any in Saint-Émilion but here there were North Africans, West Indians and South East Asians as well as those derived from both Southern and Northern Europe.

Diversity was not so present in the student population. There were very few students of ethnic origin. There was a roughly equal gender split but the majority of students came from either middle class or lower middle-class backgrounds from all across France. It was an eclectic mix of people with differing views and very different life experiences. Some students were older than Benoit and had already travelled quite extensively , hitch-hiking or travelling by train across Europe, Some had been even more adventurous and inspired by the backpacker phenomenon that had emerged out of the countercultural explosion, originally in America and then later in Western Europe, had journeyed overland eastwards out of Europe across Turkey, Iran and Afghanistan to Nepal and India. Benoit was to discover that they had gone in search of not only excitement and adventure but also to seek spiritual enlightenment and cheap drugs. These people seemed to Benoit to exist in a parallel universe that was as far away from his experiences in Saint-Émilion as they possibly could be. Despite having had a few interesting conversations in the student bars, he had never been able to gel with anybody in this grouping. He had had similar experiences with the fashion-conscious and trendy set and also those whom he regarded as the 'social whizz kids' who went around talking to every group of people and seemed to know everyone and were omnipresent at every party or social function. He had also so far avoided the far- left segments of the student body of which there were many. They were always attending meetings and discussion groups and pinning up posters or distributing leaflets around the campus protesting about this and that usually the Vietnam war, American imperialism, capitalist exploitation of workers and those in the third world

Benoit had made a number of acquaintances with regular students of both sexes with whom he would always sit next to in seminars and lectures. However, one evening having returned to the dormitory after a few beers in one of the student bars on the campus, he realised that he did not have any of the following. He did not have a 'best friend,' he did not have a 'close circle of friends' and regrettably he very much did not have 'a girlfriend.' It was not that he was a loner in any sense of the word. He didn't prefer his own company to the company of others at all, it was just that sometimes he found it challenging to make what he called 'easy conversation.' Maybe he came across as too deep and serious he thought. He knew he was bright and engaging and he had always had a very good sense of humour so that when people got to know him, they usually liked being around him.

So, in the summer term he decided that things had to change. He started to relax more, be less intense, engage in casual conversations with people he did not know and just be himself. He surprised himself at the result. He started to become a more popular figure in the bars and people sought him out to talk to, he found himself being invited to more parties and getting involved in far more social events at the university. Most importantly of all he didn't think of home anymore and certainly not the stifling traditions of the Chateau and the life that went with it. He may be a product of 'the establishment' but he didn't have to be part of it.

He was not about to become *'really groovy'* but he also was not going to be taken *for 'a square'* either. He would establish his own space, his own identity and above all be himself and be content and happy within his own skin. He was looking forward to the second year at the Sorbonne and he was determined that it was going to be in the parlance of some of the more *'far out there'* students; *'a gas.'*

Chapter Two

Benoit had met Genevieve at the start of the second year of his course at the Sorbonne University. He had seen her a few times the previous year in the coffee bars and at functions and she was on the same course as him, so she was often in the same lectures and seminars. She always sat at the same table in the student restaurant that was consistently lively. The same group of both sexes met meal after meal, some of them pulling chairs from surrounding tables and doubling up. Benoit noticed that the prettiest girls in the place were among them and she had caught his eye on several occasions but he had never had the opportunity to talk to her and he didn't think that she would be interested in him anyway. The group gathered too, in the café next to the restaurant, which was an extension of it. She was tall with long blonde hair and distinctive cobalt blue eyes which she always accentuated with mascara make up and she often wore skirts with a wide leather belt that accentuated her perfect figure. To Benoit she was part of an impenetrable clique and all he could do was to admire her at a distance.

But all that changed one night in the first week of term. There was a discotheque in one of the bars on the campus and the highlight of the evening was a live band which had started to gain quite a reputation and following in the Paris youth community. Benoit wanted to see them so he went in to the bar at about the time that they were scheduled to appear. He had usually avoided the discotheque as it really was not his thing and he would leave again after the band had finished their set. He had however, underestimated how popular the band had become and the venue was packed out. Everywhere there were groups of students talking animatedly over the loud disco music. He pushed his way through the crowd towards the bar and shouted his order for a beer – 1664 his favourite. Having paid for the beer he turned away from the bar and scoured the crowd looking for anyone that he knew but just then someone brushed past him knocking the glass out of his hands. Benoit immediately bent down to pick up the largest fragments of glass and as he began to stand up, he heard:

"I am so sorry. It was my fault. Let me buy you another."

He looked up and he saw the smiling face of Genevieve and he immediately felt an involuntary flutter in his stomach.

"No – it's OK. Please don't worry" Benoit replied quickly almost stammering.

"Nonsense. I insist" and she manoeuvred her way into a position at the bar.

A few minutes later they were seated on a bench in a crowded booth but with a good view of the stage both drinking the same beer.

"Aren't you with someone else?" Benoit enquired

"Yes, I was but I was starting to get bored of their company. They just talk politics all of the time and are very negative about absolutely everything. I am all for change and there definitely needs to be change in my view but I also want to enjoy my time at university."

Two hours passed quickly and the band really were very good and in between tracks they had been chatting which had surprised Benoit as it was such a relaxed situation. At the end of the set before the onset of the disco once more, Genevieve stood up and said:

"Do you fancy something to eat? Let's go the café and get some food. I fancy an omelette mixte with some frites and mayonnaise."

"Sounds good to me" Benoit replied.

It was well past midnight and everywhere students were still chatting, smoking and drinking coffee. Benoit now knew that she was called Genevieve Legrand, the only child of Pierre and Celeste. She was from Toulouse in the south of France where her father worked as an engineer in the aerospace industry. He was a committed socialist and trade unionist; a member of the CGT, the very left-wing Confédération Générale du Travail Unitaire. When Genevieve was still quite young, Pierre had suffered an industrial accident in the workplace. He had inadvertently left a chuck key in situ when he had switched on a lathe that he was working at. The key had struck him in the face smashing some teeth and leaving fractured cheekbones which had required some reconstructive surgery. He had been denied full compensation because it was decided that there was a degree of personal negligibility in the case due to the fact that he was culpable for leaving the chuck key in situ. This was despite the fact that every chuck key should have been attached to the lathe with a red lanyard which in this case it was not. The effect of this incident had hardened Pierre's opinions still further in that he felt that *'there was one rule for some and another for others'* and for him life was simple it was about *'us and them.'*

It was obvious to Benoit that he and Genevieve came from very opposite ends of the political, economic and social spectrum. He had not revealed too much of his background as he didn't want to appear as being 'posh, 'rich' or 'privileged.' They parted and walked their separate ways back to their residential blocks after agreeing to meet for a coffee *'sometime soon.'* Benoit presumed that this was just Genevieve being courteous and that this was just a polite 'brush off' which would be quite devastating for him because he had looked into those deep blue cobalt eyes and become transfixed but he was also a realist. They had very different backgrounds, they talked and dressed differently and whilst Benoit had some friends, she was obviously one of the most popular figures not just on their course but on the whole campus.

However, he need not have worried. Two days later he met her walking in the opposite direction in the corridor and she said to his great surprise:

"Are you still on for that coffee?" she said, her deep blue eyes penetrating his *"I am just off to the library but I'll see you in the café at four if you like."*

"Yes – that would be great" Benoit replied almost stammering and there it was again that feeling in his stomach like a butterfly flapping its fragile wings. Benoit turned to watch as she walked away noticing that her blonde hair was tied in a pony tail that seemed to bounce as she walked along. He felt breathless.

One rendezvous turned into many and Benoit became more and more relaxed in her company. She introduced him to her friends and to Benoit's surprise once more, he was instantly accepted into the group and its social scene but he was always careful not to reveal too much of his background as he just wanted to blend in with the others. They all met frequently not just in the student restaurant and the but in a café in the nearby Place Maubert just off the rue des Écoles, called 'Chez Henri.' It was situated across the main thoroughfare of the Boulevard St. Germain where the open-air market took place every Tuesday, Thursday and Saturday. It was one of the oldest markets in Paris and on market days the place was full of people buying fresh bread, fish, meat and vegetables all sorts of beautifully grown or prepared produce.

Unsurprisingly, the owner of the café was a man called Henri Leblanc who was about fifty years of age, a round shouldered man with the beginnings of a paunch and with thinning black hair and a ubiquitous Gauloise cigarette draping from his mouth. He ran the café with his wife Veronique and her eighty-year-old mother who never left the kitchen and had a face that could have been carved from an old piece of wood. Parisian cafés have served as a centre of social and culinary life since the seventeenth century. They were not just a meeting place, a neighbourhood hub, a rendezvous point, a place to relax and refresh oneself but they also acted as the social and political pulse of the city. There was a time when the best thinkers of France, in both arts and politics, were to be found around such café tables in particular places across the city.

Chez Henri was always busy and lively, quite small with about six tables seating six patrons per table inside and about the same outside but it had become a favourite of Genevieve's group. Over the last few weeks there had been no other topic of discussion but politics and how that related to economics and the social life of Parisian students. Perhaps in this way, although many of the city's cafes were no longer part of the city's intellectual life, Chez Henri was continuing a centuries old tradition.

Many of the group were committed Socialists some Marxists and some Trotskyites and none more so than Bruno who came from St Malo in Brittany. He was a large character in every sense of the word. He had long brown hair and a shaggy beard and liked to be known as an intellectual authority on Marxism and he therefore, tried to adopt an elevated position on all political discussions.

"What did you think of that lecture by Professor Jacques this morning" said Nancy a petite brunette and close friend of Genevieve's.

"Totally boring and a waste of time" chipped in Pierre blowing a plume of cigarette smoke out of his mouth as he spoke *"He just read from his notes, I don't think he looked up at us or changed the intonation of his voice for a whole hour."*

"Yes, and then he just passed round some handwritten notes that had been produced on one of those Banda spirit duplicator machines so the handwriting that was difficult

to read in the first place becomes an illegible scrawl of purple ink" sighed another.

"Ah that is because the whole programme has been designed to benefit the capitalists" interrupted Bruno completely matter-of-factly. *"Their whole objective is to prepare you to be fodder to feed the capitalist economy. They do not want discussion, independent thought or debate just to follow like sheep."*

"But isn't that the same as in the Soviet Union and that is a Communist state with a Socialist society so what is the difference?" remarked Antoine, a serious looking young man with short blond hair and an earring stud in his left ear lobe.

"Exactly" replied Bruno rather smugly. *"The Soviet Union is not Communist. It is a repressive regime, an example of State Capitalism which in my opinion is worse in many ways than private capitalism."*

"So, what is the solution?" mused Nancy, a student from the Basque region in the south of the country.

Bruno seized upon this opportunity to exert his perceived intellectual authority *"Well I can see the way ahead quite clearly…"*

Just at that moment Genevieve looked at her watch and said *"Benoit we have time for one more coffee before we go to the library and work on our assignments because we only have a few days left before we have to submit them. I will get them. I am having a grande crème – what about you?"* She had obviously heard this speech many times before Benoit thought as she left the table,

He shouted after her *"La meme chose pour moi. Merci"*

The conversation, however, continued after she had left the table.

"It depends upon where you stand" Said Antoine

"What do you mean?" Nancy asked

"Well is change best effected from within or without the system?" Antoine replied

"The system is corrupt and what is required is revolution. It is the only way to eradicate that corruption." Bruno declared

"I am not so sure" Benoit added quietly *"Not everything is wrong with the society that we have built. Sometimes you do not need to knock down a wall to repair it because the foundations are still strong"*

"I hear what you say" interrupted Antoine *"But that is why change is so difficult and complicated. In my view you cannot change the system from within because if you are in it you are part of it. You end up with a stake in it and your vision is compromised"*

"An interesting thought" Benoit mused.

Genevieve returned with the two coffees and Benoit lit a cigarette and decided to sit back and just listen to the debate raging around him.

Bruno was becoming more intense now and finally he stood up and said;

"Listen my friends. The debate over revolution or reform has been one that has plagued this country which is why we have the malaise that we now find ourselves in. It is simple in my view; societal and economic reform is inherently revolutionary"

"It needn't be" Nancy chipped in

"Yes, it does. If the system is rotten then it cannot be reformed because the rot will set in once again. We have seen this so often throughout history."

"It depends upon your definition of revolutionary" Antoine said thoughtfully as Bruno sat down heavily in his chair *"Being revolutionary does not necessarily indicate a wish for drastic action. The principle of desiring revolutionary reform can be a response to political, social and economic hierarchies that deny basic human rights, prevent fairness and equal opportunities for all."*

There was brief period of silence around the table as everyone tried to absorb Antoine's interjection. After a few moments Benoit leaned forward in his chair and said:

"I agree up to a point Antoine but you make the assumption that in order to get a satisfactory result for all stakeholders it would require a united purpose amongst the masses. I can see this in the removal of a brutal dictator or a grossly unfair policy but in the aftermath, history has also shown us that when they come together to define the future, factionalism and ego always come to the fore."

Around the table a few heads nodded in agreement and Genevieve turned and looked at Benoit and a slight smile appeared on her face, she had never heard him speak so profoundly before and she felt internally proud. A while later most of the group broke up and went their separate ways leaving Bruno and a couple of others to continue the discourse.

There was undoubtedly a growing frustration amongst the student population in Paris that had been building for some time; an undercurrent of general dissatisfaction that had as yet not managed to express itself. Indeed, if pressed many could not point to a single feature of this malaise. Despite the overall rise in prosperity and levels of education, De Gaulle's France was a quietly oppressive place. The general wanted a modern, dynamic France but rooted in an old, conservative and non-dynamic social system. It was this stifling, controlling environment that had begun the unstoppable momentum of exasperation amongst the Parisian student community. It appeared to many that France was suffering from a dangerous political malady – boredom. Initially sparked by the so called 'bedroom revolt' of the previous year when Nanterre students demanded access to each other's dormitories and rooms resulting in sit-ins by boys in the girls' residencies and vice versa in which the police and fire service were called to expel the 'invaders'.

This was an issue that was not going to go away for the mass body of the student community. Across the western world, students were protesting about wars, particularly that of Vietnam and fundamental liberties. Here in Paris the protest was initially about sexual freedom, which could be regarded as a rather limited conception of human rights but not so limited if you are French, aged twenty and the sexual revolution was well underway in the United States and even in supposedly reserved Great Britain.

Benoit was still a virgin and quite sexually inexperienced when he had met Genevieve. She had had two sexual encounters whilst at school and a relationship for a few months with a male student in her first year. She was much more avant-garde and confident whilst Benoit was more conservative and reserved. He could not however, resist Genevieve's advances and was taken in by those cobalt blue eyes and blonde hair. He remembered their first night together in her dorm had not been that successful. She had managed to smuggle him past the beady eyes of the concierge by disguising him in one of friend's coats with the hood up but he was so anxious that he might be discovered and that the university authorities would then inform his parents and his lucrative allowance may then be cut or suspended. As a consequence, the physical encounter had been clumsy at best. He often grimaced at the memory of embarrassment after Genevieve had said to him:

"It is better to be the slow commuter train than Le Mistral n'est pas"

Benoit knew that she had been referring to the flagship train of the French rail national railway (SNCF) which ran the express train between Paris and Nice and had been named after the strong wind that battered the French coast around the Carmargue region.

But as the weeks passed by, they became more physically compatible and totally absorbed and content with one another's company, sitting next to each other in lectures and seminars and spending almost all of their spare time together. Benoit had taken her shopping and asked her advice on some new clothes and he had decided to wear his hair longer. His mother would not have approved but 'so be it' he mused. They had attended student meetings and political rallies that seemed to be becoming more and more frequent. Change was in the air. They could both sense it but what change? What did it mean and would it be for the better of for the worse? They both had no idea but they felt, like many others, that they were being swept along by an irresistible undercurrent which somehow felt positive but daunting and slightly dangerous.

"Tonight, I am going to cook you a special meal" exclaimed Genevieve one morning in the Café *"It will be a classic French peasant dish for a rich French boy"* she said teasingly.

"I shall look forward to it" he replied not rising to the bait.

Genevieve had been invited to cook at her friend Marie's apartment in the Latin Quarter called as such because Latin was the language that had been spoken in the area during the Middle Ages.   Marie lived there with her Italian boyfriend Marco whom she had been together with for just over a year. Marie and Marco were both in the year above Genevieve and Benoit and they had met the previous year at a fashion event at the university. Benoit had been told to arrive at seven thirty that evening and he made his way to the apartment having ridden on the Mètro to Cardinal Lemoine station on Line 10. He then made his way south down Rue Monge and then turned left into Rue des Boulangers.

He found himself in a cobbled street with pavements on both sides of the road. At the top end, near where the street branched off from Rue Monge, the buildings were very smart with external black iron railings and balconies set against clean cream-coloured stone. But as Benoit walked further down the street the tall buildings that faced each other were not so well maintained and also at this point the road narrowed making the ambience quite dark and gloomy even though it was still light in the early evening.

Benoit found the number 71 that he was looking for. The building had a more sandy-coloured stonework and some external plaster was peeling off in places. He opened the front door and entered into a lobby area which was quite dark and the atmosphere was tinged with stale cigarette smoke. There was no concierge desk and the open-grilled lift had a handwritten sign on it saying *"L'ascenseur ne fonctionne pas"* so he took the stairs up to the second floor and found the apartment number that he had been given. Music and muted conversations were coming from all of the apartments on that level. He knocked on the white door which also had peeling paintwork and it was opened almost immediately by Marie and he was then greeted by Marco whom he had not met before.

"Genevieve is in the kitchen" he said *"But she has told me not to let you in so just sit here and have a glass of wine"*

The apartment was small with an old two-seater sofa and two armchairs that had seenbetter days. Under the window that looked down on to the street was a small table which had been decked with a red and white checked table cloth and two empty wine bottles with lit candles in them. An old record player was playing the Rolling Stones track '*19th Nervous Breakdown.*' Benoit put his wine glass on the stained carpet and picked up the record sleeve that was lying there, it was a copy of *'Strange Days' by The Doors*. Near where he was sitting on the sofa lay the empty record sleeve of '*Big Hits (High Tide and Green Grass)*' and he looked through the list of tracks and then gazed around the room. Posters were adorned to all the walls, Jimi Hendrix, Che Guevara, Jim Morrison and the Doors, the Grateful Dead and a 'Make Love Not War' anti-Vietnam War placard which must have been used on a demonstration recently. Joss sticks burned from a tall vase in one corner filling the room with incense and together with the cigarette smoke, music, flickering candlelight and a wax lava lamp gave the whole place a sort of mystical ambience. Marco explained to Benoit that he had spent some weeks in the early summer living in London with his elder sister who worked for an Italian fashion company that had established a base in the city. He had gone over as soon as his exams had finished and the next day May 23rd his sister, Louisa, had taken him to the Marquee Club in Wardour Street in the Soho district where he had seen Cream in concert and Ginger Baker had performed his magnificent lengthy drum solo on the track *'Toad'* as the last song of the set before *'Spoonful'* was played as an encore. He had never seen or heard anything like it. He remembered the heady mixture of sweat, patchouli oil, cigarette and marijuana smoke that pervaded the venue. He absolutely loved it. For the next few weeks Louisa had introduced him to Carnaby Street and the 'Swinging London' scene even buying the wax lava lamp that was now in the apartment at the popular Kensington Market. By contrast he said that on returning to Paris he had found the youth culture to be much more restrained and conservative which probably explained why there was such a momentum for change now.

Just as Marco had finished speaking Genevieve came out of the kitchen wearing an apron and her blonde hair tied back into a pony tail:

"Welcome to Gennie's Bistro" she exclaimed and kissed Benoit on both cheeks.

"Please sit down at the table and open some more wine" she said *"You are having my mother's recipe – good honest Toulouse working man's food my father calls it"*

They all agreed that it was indeed good. 'Cassoulet de Toulouse' with pork, vegetables, haricot beans, garlicky Toulouse sausage and fresh herbs.

"My mother always told me that the secret is in the duck fat" Genevieve said as they sat round the table having finished the meal, smoking and drinking red wine. Benoit put his hand under the tablecloth and squeezed Genevieve's knee without looking at her.

As they sat drinking and chatting in the flickering candlelight, a strange sensation came over Benoit, one that he had not experienced before and one he could not put his finger on at the time so he just dismissed the thought. Marco picked up his acoustic guitar that was leaning against the wall and started strumming it gently. He took a large drag of his cigarette and then expelled the smoke in one long plume and then placed the rest of the burning Gauloise between two of the strings at the neck of his guitar. Without any hesitation he launched into a perfect rendition of Bob Dylan's *'The Times They are a-Changin'*

It was a few hours later when Benoit was lying awake on his back in his bed in the male student dorm that he realised what that sensation was that he had experienced earlier in the evening. It was envy, pure and simple jealousy. He had never had anything to be envious about in his whole life, he had always had everything he wanted but it was always the way his parents wanted it to be. Suddenly this evening and over the last few weeks with the developing relationship with Genevieve something had changed. Now he wanted his own place, a place to call his own, his own space that was not tied to the past with obligatory traditions and rituals. He wanted it to be modern so that he could express himself in his own way in tune with the changing times. To dress the way he wanted, to play the music that he wanted, to have the art that he wanted and to love when and how he wanted. Content with these thoughts he rolled over and drifted in to a deep sleep.

There was no doubting it. Benoit was loving his second year at university in Paris. For the first time in his life he felt free. Free of the overbearing shackles of a paternalistic old family and the overbearing and suffocating atmosphere that he had grown up particularly in his teenage years. He had felt the weight of expectation on his shoulders and the constant control of his parents demanding his subservience and obedience. Of course, he had lived a privileged life so far. He had many possessions that other students could not dream of such as his beloved cine camera and equipment but it had felt like a gilded prison; until now. Obviously so much of this change was due to Genevieve. Deep down he still could not believe that he would ever have had a girlfriend like her. Stunningly beautiful, intelligent and extrovert and with a wonderful free spirit that just carried him away when he was with her. Why him? He often asked himself. Genevieve could have had the choice of boys in the faculty and he had often noticed how many of them stared at her when they thought that he was not looking. There wasn't a single day that Benoit did not pinch himself hoping that he was not dreaming and that he would awaken with overbearing and crushing disappointment.

"Carpe Diem" he said to himself *"Seize the Day"* as his old Latin master had used to say.

One such day was 29th January, a date that Benoit, Genevieve, Marie and Marco would never forget. Marco had managed to get hold of four tickets for the Jimi Hendrix concert that was playing at the L'Olympia Theatre, a concert venue in the ninth arrondissement of Paris that night. With building anticipation, they had met up at Chez Henri and shared a few beers with their friends before heading off to the Metro and to the venue. The excitement grew as they exited the Metro at Madeleine and were swept up in the crowds making their way to the venue. The air was dense with the smoke of marijuana and Marco noticed that some of the concert goers smelt strongly of patchouli oil which was not something he had come across in Paris before though it had been a common occurrence during his stay in London the previous year.

27

Over two thousand people were inside the venue when Hendrix took to the stage but it was when the band played *'Foxey Lady'* and *'The Wind Cries Mary'* that the crowd started to go wild. By the time that Hendrix started to play the opening riffs of *'Purple Haze'* the whole venue was in the palm of his hands and the concert-goers were in ecstasy. Later outside they waited until the crowds had thinned out before attempting to enter the Metro. They stood and smoked in a doorway and watched the people pass. Marie clasped her hands to the side of her head saying:

"My ears are still ringing."

"Mine too" said Genevieve

"Remember this moment" Marco said *"Because you may never experience it again."*

Genevieve had not really known what to expect when Benoit, a few weeks later, had invited her to spend a weekend with his parents in Saint-Émilion. She now knew that he was from an old, grand and wealthy family whom her father would have called the 'class enemy' but she was not interested in such definitions and boundaries.

"I am a modern woman" she often told herself *"I will make my own decisions about people, life and the way that I am going to live it."*

Having left Paris and the traffic congestion behind they had travelled for just over six hours but they had taken their time and were in no hurry and they were now approaching the outskirts of St Emilion in Benoit's old blue Citroen Deux Chevaux. It had been his mother's car for a number of years but she had upgraded to a new one that had two different colours and some 'sporty stripes' and other accessories. The Dufort family had bought into the Deux Chevaux concept from the outset. Although it had surprised many when it first appeared because it was a car that had been stripped down to basics in the extreme and looked old fashioned with its added-on headlights but the Dufort family like many others fell in love with this simple and

28

very French car. It soon achieved great popularity particularly in the rural areas of France because of its go-anywhere suspension. The car soon acquired numerous nicknames like 'the canard' from the Hans Christian Anderson story 'the ugly duckling' or the 'tin snail' which referred to its maximum speed of a modest eighty-five kilometres per hour. In Benoit's last year of school the family had hosted an English exchange student for a few weeks over the summer holidays and he had named the car 'John West' in reference to a popular brand of tinned sardines in England, But Benoit loved everything about it from the springy suspension to the push-me-pull-you gear stick and not least the fact that it could travel twenty kilometres on a single litre of fuel.

It was a mild autumn afternoon when Benoit drove in to the centre of the small town of Saint-Émilion and then parked up the car. Taking Genevieve by the hand he said:

"Come on Gennie. I know a great little café where we can have a coffee and a cigarette before you have to face the ordeal of the Dufort family and their inevitable interrogation into you and your life"

Genevieve smiled and squeezed his hand gently thankful for this kind and thoughtful gesture. Maybe Benoit had noticed that she had gone increasingly quiet as they had approached their destination and she had become noticeably more tense and nervous.

Genevieve had never travelled to this part of France before. She marvelled at just how pretty the town was and she gazed upwards at the historic golden-stone structures with many old well-preserved buildings with bright terracotta roofs and numerous medieval monuments. They stood for a while and watched in silence as swallows darted between church spires which were silhouetted by a pale but warm afternoon sun. For ten minutes they strolled hand in hand down sloping cobbled streets lined with bakeries, cafés and bars and staring up at the clusters of golden-stone medieval structures.

"This is the place" Benoit suddenly said as they stopped outside a small café with two tables on the pavement covered with blue and white checked tablecloths held in place by what looked like wooden clothes pegs. They sat down and ordered two coffees and smoked a cigarette.

"It really is very pretty and peaceful here" Genevieve said

"Yes, it is. I was very lucky to have been brought up here but it is also quite a stifling place to be young as it is so stooped in tradition. So very different to Paris!"

"It is also very different to Toulouse but diversity is a good thing. Wouldn't it be so boring if everywhere was just the same?" she mused.

Thirty minutes later they left the town behind and drove through narrow lanes that criss-crossed the vineyards with just rows and rows of vines as far as she could see. Occasionally they came across a white post with various signs with names of different chateaux pointing in different directions; some of the names of which she had heard of before. But Benoit ignored them as he expertly navigated his way through the narrow lanes that all looked the same to Genevieve. Suddenly as they were heading up another lane with just enough room for the car, two large German Shepherd dogs came bounding towards them barking loudly and then they started to jump up at the little Citroen startling Genevieve but Benoit just patted her knee gently with his right hand and drove on slowly. After a couple of minutes, he pulled through some enormous black wrought iron gates and into a small gravelled courtyard with a central fountain feature. Benoit stopped the car and turned off the engine and the dogs were now bounding all around the car and Genevieve became increasingly apprehensive and decided not to get out. Benoit however, leapt out of the driver's door and immediately raised his left hand in the air and then spread his fingers and held it there. Then he slowly lowered his arm until his hand with the outstretched fingers was flat and immediately the dogs stopped barking and just lay down quietly in front of him. Genevieve had never seen anything like it in her life as these once fiercely intimidating dogs were now acting like docile puppies in front of their master. Benoit called to her to get out of the car and come over and stroke them. She approached them gingerly and stretched out her hand and the dogs just rolled over allowing her to pat and tickle their undersides.

"Well you've been accepted by the two who matter most" laughed Benoit as they walked towards the large and imposing front door. But before they could reach it, the door opened and an elderly well-dressed man opened the door wide for them.

"Welcome home sir" he said dipping his head deferentially.

"Thank you, Charles," Benoit replied and turned towards Genevieve.

"This is Genevieve" adding *"Charles has worked for the Dufort family for over fifty years as did his father before him."*

"You are very welcome Mademoiselle"

Charles closed the door behind them and Benoit led Genevieve down a long dark wood-panelled hallway and stopped in front of a half open door.

"OK here we go" he said as he breezed through the door with Genevieve in tow.

As she entered the drawing room Genevieve immediately noticed the heavy drape curtains at the tall windows, the wooden oak flooring, the large gilt mirror hanging above the fire place and the frescoes painted on to the walls and ceiling. She had never seen anything like it in her life. Benoit sensed her feeling of awe and for the second time that afternoon, had stretched out his hand, not telling her that three years ago his father had spent one million francs restoring this magnificent room to its original glory. A man dressed in a burgundy velvet jacket and mustard-coloured cravat leapt out of a very large wing-backed armchair stubbing out a half-smoked black Sobranie cigarette in a silver ash tray and shook his son's hand firmly, gently embracing him before turning to Genevieve and kissing her gently on both cheeks.

"Welcome to Chateau Grand Vue" he beamed, making her instantly feel at ease. Turning to his left he waved a hand at an elegant lady also smoking a black Sobranie cigarette who was sitting on a dark blue velour chaise longue.

"This is my wife Brigitte"

Brigitte got up and she too kissed Genevieve on both cheeks and said:

"How lovely to see you dear. You must be tired after such a long journey. Benoit will show you your room and Charles will bring up you bag. Dinner will be at seven thirty but we will meet in here for an aperitif at seven fifteen. It is your favourite Benoit locally shot pheasant."

"That is wonderful mother" Benoit replied and led Genevieve out of the room.

As they departed Brigitte looked towards her husband and nodded her head in an appreciative gesture.

He just shrugged her shoulders replying *"Peut-être"*

Benoit's parents were already in the drawing room when he and Genevieve arrived at seven fifteen. They sat on a large sofa and Benoit pulled out a crushproof packet of 'Disque Bleu' cigarettes and offered one to Genevieve.

"Oh Benoit. Put away those dreadful things. You are not at university now. Have one of these" and Brigitte stood up and handed over a sliver cigarette box containing some Russian Black Sobranie cigarettes with the distinctive gold tips.

Just at that moment Charles entered the room carrying a sliver salver with four wine glasses and a clear glass wine bottle which Genevieve noticed was obviously chilled because there was condensation on its outside and the wine inside looked slightly pinkish. Charles poured out four glasses and handed them round and then withdrew from the room.

Philippe raised his glass in a toast saying:

"Welcome once again to our home Genevieve. Now let's see what you know about wine. This is…….."

But before he could say anymore Benoit quickly interrupted him:

"No father! Please do not subject Genevieve to your party trick" and he turned to his side saying:

"What he was going to do was to see if you could recognise the nose and developing palate of the Grand Vue wine through this blush which is made by fermenting the skins of the grapes for just twenty-four hours. It is quite alcoholic and very refreshing – enjoy!"

Philippe looked sternly at his son but they all raised their glasses in a communal toast.

Fifteen minutes later Charles was ushering them all in to the dining room up the wood-panelled hallway. The dining room was equally elegant as the drawing room. Two large chandeliers hung from the ceiling over a very long mahogany table that had twelve chairs with gold brocade seats around it. Paintings hung from the walls, a mixture of portraits and landscapes which blended well, providing what some could have regarded as being an environment that was a little austere but with the fragmented light from the one lit chandelier and the flickering large candle Genevieve thought that the set up was very formal but also very convivial.

This evening, only the top half of the table was laid up with just a single large silver candlestick and a few flowers as decoration. As promised by Brigitte, the cook had produced Benoit's favourite dish as the entrée – braised pheasant with Normandy cider, cream and fresh thyme. It was as Genevieve was to say later *'absolutely delicious'* and matched the Grand Vue ruby red wine perfectly that Philippe poured out into large glasses from a silver-topped cut glass claret jug perfectly.

"1964 – a very fine vintage indeed"

Benoit and Genevieve spent the rest of the weekend exploring the estate, walking in the woods with the dogs and enjoying each other's company in the countryside in the late autumn sunshine. Suddenly Genevieve stopped as they walked by a stream on the edge of the woods and turned to face Benoit her deep blue eyes smiling at him.

"It is beautiful here. Just so peaceful. Just you and I and a far cry from the craziness of Paris."

Then she drew him closer to her and kissed him full on the mouth and they fell on to the ground and locked in a passionate embrace making love as the skylarks flew high above them, the wind gently rustling through the trees causing a cascade of russet-brown and golden-coloured leaves to float down to the ground, the two dogs lay quietly with their muzzles down just a few metres away and the sound of a tractor could be heard faintly in a distant field. A serene pastoral scene that was a world away from the storm clouds that were gathering back in Paris.

Chapter Three

Most people in France in 1968 would agree that all students were 'bolshie' or deliberately combative and that students of Sociology were almost certainly more uncooperative or 'bolshier' than most. If this observation was true anywhere, it was most certainly the case at Nanterre and the Sociology department. By its very nature, Sociology, makes those who study it critical and questioning about the society in which they live. In addition, hanging over the department was the grim prospect of graduate unemployment. In France there were extremely few established opportunities for Sociology graduates. It was not surprising, therefore, that it was in the Sociology department that the first stirrings of unrest had been formulated; objections to the way teaching at Nanterre was done, the content of the curricula and to the old irritant of overcrowding.

"I think that I might have made the wrong decision in choosing to study Sociology" Benoit said to Genevieve one evening as they sat at a street-side café drinking a carafe of red wine and smoking.

"Why" she enquired

"For a few reasons" Benoit replied. *" Firstly, there are clearly far more students of Social Sciences than there are jobs outside for them after qualifying even allowing for the weeding out of those who fail to pass their examinations. Secondly, there would appear to be a significant number of students on the course who don't have any chance of passing their final exams and are purely here to cause agitation and disruption for a whole variety of reasons. That's Ok with me but the disruption will have a knock-on*

effect to others who are trying to be successful whatever that means"

Genevieve studied him closely before replying:

"I thought you wanted things to change"

"Of course I do Gennie. There is so much that is wrong. Yes, I am all for modernisation and change for the better but I am not sure that Sociology is the way forward. It would appear to me that all modern French Sociology is just imported from America where disruption and dissatisfaction amongst students of Social Science is far greater than it is here. You know there is some truth in what Bruno and one or two others said at Chez Henri the other day that the sociology we are being taught is a means of controlling and manipulating society, not a means of understanding it in order to change it."

Genevieve shrugged her shoulders and said *"What would you have rather done then?"*

"I've been thinking about that. Certainly not Business Studies like my father wanted me to do. Perhaps Politics and Economics"

"Why?"

"Because I think the knowledge would allow me to effect the changes that I want to see in the real world rather than this 'sociology bubble'"

"Why don't you see if you can change course then, I am sure that it is not too late if that is what you want to do"

"I will make some enquiries when all this trouble settles down as long as we can still be together in the same faculty" and he leaned forward and kissed her on the cheek

"More wine" she said

"Why not?" he replied.

It had not been difficult for Benoit and Genevieve and those in their social circle to notice the growing groundswell of dissatisfaction growing. There were more meetings, discussions and constant murmurings in the bars, cafés and lecture theatres. Then suddenly it just erupted. It was the issue of sexual freedom that produced that initial spark. On the fourteenth of February, St Valentine's Day, a rebellion in favour of 'free circulation' between boys' and girls' hostels and dormitories spread like wildfire throughout France. In nearly every student residence, males stormed the female residential blocks to protest about segregation. This was a fire that would not be quenched which was not realised by the dithering and out-of-touch government who tried pathetically to cobble together some concessions about females having the right to enter male blocks up to a certain time but not vice versa.

"They just don't get it do they?" Genevieve said to Benoit and a group of friends who were gathered at the café at Place Maubert smoking and drinking coffee.

"No, they absolutely do not" replied a red-haired student in the Sociology department.

Benoit did not particularly like the rather outspoken, cocky far left German student called Daniel but tolerated him because Genevieve thought he was 'politically savvy' and at the forefront of change. He was not a regular visitor to the Chez Henri group but dropped in now and again. He was part of a different political clique who regarded themselves as more elitist and at the vanguard of the progressive student movement at Nanterre.

The group of students turned towards the red head and he continued:

"They don't get it because they think that this is just about access to each other's bedrooms. Well it is and it isn't. That is just a symbol of our desire to be treated as adults. We want the freedoms enjoyed by the rest of the nation, political freedoms such as those of association, information, expression as well as sexual freedom."

The others all nodded in general agreement with Daniel adding further:

"And it is not just about getting rid of the restrictive dress code either. There are fundamental issues at stake representing the future of our society and our role in it."

"I agree" added Marco *" "But I still don't see why they insist we should all dress like mini capitalist businessmen in jackets, shirts and ties. When I was in England male students were wearing flared purple trousers, which looked great"*

There was general consensus on Marco's remarks and a great deal of laughter when Marie stated firmly:

"There is no way I am going to be seen with you wearing purple trousers!"

Benoit got up saying:

"That's told you my friend. Come on Gennie we have got to go if we are going to view that apartment." He disliked the way that the group seemed to defer to the red-hired German student and clearly the feeling was mutual because when they were out of earshot Daniel said to no one in particular:

"I really like Genevieve but I don't understand what she sees in that bourgeois stiff."

Marco just turned to him and gave him a hard stare but decided against saying anything.

Over the next few days Benoit had made the decision that he wanted to rent his own apartment. The dormitory in the residential block had been fine for the first year at university but now he wanted his own space. He believed that he could afford it through the allowance that his parents sent him each month and he had told his mother that he wanted the space to be able to work more without being interrupted and to get more sleep because it was so noisy in the dormitory. He did not tell her the real reason, of course, which was he hoped that Genevieve would move in with him and they would not have restricted access to each other and he could spend so much more time in her company.

He had viewed a few apartments but none of them seemed suitable. They were either too expensive or too cheap and tatty and he was starting to give up hope when he was given another address by the Letting Agency for a flat that had just become available. The apartment was in the student quarter not that far away from Marie and Marco's flat in Rue des Boulangers where they had had dinner a few weeks before. It was located on the Rue de la Clef and located in the district of Jardin des Plantes in the fifth arrondissement of Paris. It was on the third floor of the building with a one room lounge/ dining room and one bedroom and a small galley kitchen and a shared bathroom with the adjacent flat off the landing. Benoit had been particularly excited to discover that the flat also had access to a small enclosed attic space which he thought would be perfect for his photographic dark room. He had also managed to negotiate a reduced rate for a long-term rent of a single car parking space in an underground car park in Rue Gracieuse which was a five-minute walk from the apartment in Rue de la Clef where he could park the old Citroen Deux Chevaux safely off the road.

Genevieve had not hesitated for a second when Benoit had asked her if she would like to come and live in 'their flat' when Benoit had made the suggestion when they were alone at Chez Henri's café. She smiled broadly and stood up and through her arms around his neck.

"I have been waiting for you to ask me" she said *"I know that we will have a very limited budget but we will make it beautiful. Our own special place."*

It was the third week of March when they finally moved in. Benoit's parents had given him the money for a new bed and mattress and they had visited a magasin de meuble d'occasion – a second hand furniture shop that had been recommended by someone at the university. They had selected a black corduroy sofa, a large cream rug that had a few cigarette burns on it but was clean and otherwise had been well looked after. They also bought a dressing table for the bedroom and some table lights and a coffee table and two old arm chairs for the lounge which had slightly threadbare arms but were otherwise OK. The pride and joy for Genevieve however, was a chrome coffee table with a glass top which must have been really expensive but the previous owner or a guest must have dropped something on it and there were two large fractures across the glass and the owner of second hand shop had advised against putting any weight on it as he did not know how long it would be before it shattered but glasses and coffee cups should be 'Ok' he had said. Furthermore, he had promised that all the items would be delivered on the day that they were moving in. Benoit just hoped that the lift in the apartment block would be working that day. The propriétaire of the apartment had promised them an electric cooker which he said was not new but it was very clean and in good working order and that too, would be delivered to the flat on their moving-in day. Genevieve had decided that she would not tell her parents about moving into the apartment at this stage, after all they had not even met Benoit yet although she had told them that she did have a new boyfriend of whom she had become very fond.

It was strange in a way Benoit thought, how accustomed he had become to living in Paris and was now about to embark on having his own place. He had grown to love the hustle and bustle and the comings and goings of so many people. It had a vibrancy all of its own, a smell, a sense and a noise. Even the ghastly congested traffic added to the background ambience. But most of all he had come to love the Métro. For Benoit it was a symbol of the city. Something that Parisians take as an everyday experience was almost magical to someone like Benoit having been brought up in the countryside. He adored the uniform architecture and unique entrances influenced by the Art Nouveau movement. This styling was also adopted by the green station kiosks widely becoming known as 'le style Métro.' But it was the trains that mostly fascinated Benoit particularly as they rushed into the stations on their rubber tyres and suddenly dozens of people reached for the door catches to swing the double carriage doors open before pouring on to the platform. It was mesmerising but not in the rush hour or 'heure de pointe' – this was definitely a time to be avoided when travelling Parisians could be at their rudest and most aggressive. Umbrellas, briefcases and even newspapers became weapons to leverage advantage along a crowded platform in order to board a train. Benoit had learnt to avoid these times or to just walk to destinations. It was safer and better for one's sanity he thought.

Benoit and Genevieve worked hard on decorating their apartment. Their budget was limited but it was remarkable how two coats of brilliant white matt emulsion on the walls and ceilings could transform the previously slightly gloomy space into a much brighter and seemingly more spacious environment. They had decided on a black and white theme probably inspired by Marco's description of the Biba style that he had discovered in London. The centre piece was the chrome and glass coffee table which stood on the cream rug in the middle of the room and on the table was a new white porcelain martini-logoed ash tray that Henri had given them as a flat-warming present The centre light had a black raffia-style lampshade and the table lights had matching small black lampshades. The bedroom walls were decorated with some black and white charcoal drawings which Benoit had mounted into black picture frames. The drawings had been done by someone Genevieve knew from Toulouse who was attending art college in the city and had been an old school friend. Benoit had never asked but he suspected that the 'old school friend' might have been a former lover. The bed was covered by a large black and white Zebra-striped throw which she had found in a small shop in the rive gauche and two small table lights either side of the bed with small black lampshades and another central ceiling black raffia-style lampshade completed the look.

One afternoon Benoit had come back early from the university and told Genevieve not to come home till after six that evening. He spent the afternoon displaying a dozen of his black and white photographs that he had had enlarged at a specialist shop on the west bank. He had hung them in identical black frames symmetrically across one wall and they were picked out by two wall mounted spotlights on the adjacent walls. The effect, he thought to himself, was quite dramatic.

When Genevieve returned later that evening she exclaimed:

"C'est magnifique Benoit" as she studied the twelve prints carefully arranged on the wall. They were all images of Parisian life taken over the last few weeks, boats on the Seine, the Mètro of course, Notre Dame, the Eiffel Tower and the Arc de Triomphe but the shading of light and shadows was what made them so dramatic and interesting.

"I shall call this series of photos 'life in contrast'

"But why have you produced them all in black and white?"

"Because *I have always thought that black and white photography is more symbolic in that it can portray feelings and emotions through the use of light and shadow rather than relying simply on colour"* he replied. For an afterthought he added:

"Also because they were cheaper! No only joking!"

They sat together on the sofa and opened a bottle of red wine and just sat and drank looking at the photos on the wall with the only light being provided by the two spotlights.

Genevieve turned to look at *Benoit* and kissed him gently on the cheek saying *"It is our private gallery"*

Benoit looked at her and just smiled.

The previous weekend Benoit had gone back to his parents to collect all his photographic developing and editing equipment to set up in the dark room in the attic of the apartment. Whist he spent the night back in Saint-Émilion his father had said over dinner:

"I hear that there is trouble brewing at the university. Do not get involved Benoit. You are there to study not to get involved with hotheads and a bunch of lunatic socialists and communists confronting the police and the university authorities. No good can come of this. You could get injured or end up with a criminal record which you will have for the rest of your life."

Benoit had said nothing but just nodded his head in acquiescence. He left on the Sunday morning to make his way back to Paris with his Citroen loaded up with not only his precious photographic equipment but with pots and pans, kitchen utensils, crockery and cutlery that his mother and the cook had said that they no longer required and would be perfect for his new flat. She had also provided him with bed linen, bath and hand towels and other things that she thought might prove to be useful. Just before he left his father came out of one of the outbuildings followed by Charles and each of them was carrying a case of Grand Vue wine because Benoit could see the writing on the side of the cardboard boxes.

"1966" he said *"A little young yet but very drinkable. I am sure that you and your friends will enjoy it to celebrate your new home"*

"I am sure we will father" Benoit said as he stacked the cases into the car. He then embraced his mother and shook his father's hand shouting: *"Au revoir"* through the open driver's window of the blue Citroen as he pulled out of the small gravelled courtyard with the two large German Shepherds running beside him; one on each side.

Upon his return he spent the next few evenings and time when there were no lessons constructing the makeshift dark room in the attic. When he was happy with it, he called down to Genevieve who was preparing some food in the galley kitchen of their apartment:

"Gennie come up here and see what you think"

Genevieve managed to climb up and clamber into the small attic room space which was very dimly lit with a dim red safe light attached to the wall and the whole space smelt strongly of different chemicals."

"Developer and fixer" Benoit said as he noticed her smelling the air *"Necessary I am afraid in the photographic process."*

"Very clever Benoit" Genevieve said and she embraced him tightly in the confined space. Benoit could feel the warmth of her body against him and the rise and fall of her breasts as she breathed and the slight hardening of her nipples through the T shirt that she was wearing. He stroked her long blonde hair and stared into her cobalt blue eyes finding himself getting increasingly aroused. In just a few moments Genevieve had undone her belt and let her skirt drop to the attic floor and reached out for the top of Benoit's Levi jeans. Then with great acrobatic and athletic ability they made love in the cramped space despite the harsh chemical smells that caught them in the back of the throat but basking in the soft red glow of the safe light.

Meanwhile the situation in Nanterre was becoming increasingly tense day by the day. They could all feel it and sense it. Something was going to happen and it was going to happen soon Benoit said To Genevieve that evening. It happened the following day on 22nd March. Student activists and radicals who had become known as the *enragés,* were joined by several hundred other student demonstrators and they stormed and occupied an administration building at Nanterre; led by Daniel Cohn-Bendit. Genevieve was one of those caught up in the swell

44

of instant emotion as the word went around like wildfire as to what was about to happen.

"The atmosphere was electric" she told Benoit later that evening *"What had started as a protest about a few students being arrested at the anti-Vietnam war protest a few days earlier just suddenly developed into an outpouring of all our grievances."*

"The university administrators called in the police quite soon" replied Benoit

"Yes, I know" she replied *"We left soon afterwards having stated our grievances"*

"I have heard that the university disciplinary committee have summoned Daniel and a few others to meet them tomorrow and they may be threatened with expulsion. Whilst I believe that it is right that we should all get involved, I think maybe you should distance yourself a bit from them Gennie. They are hotheads and can mean trouble"

"You are probably right" she replied *"I am not sure what the genuine motives of that faction are but I am certain that they go a long way beyond university reform. I saw some of them damage the building and spray graffiti on the walls before they left. They are now calling themselves the March 22nd Movement."*

Over the next few days Nanterre became a cauldron of political discussion. Conspiracy theory was layered upon conspiracy theory.

"There are plainclothes policeman everywhere" someone told Benoit in the Café

"Trust no one unless you know them" said another

"The police are starting to round up and detain those they regard as the main agitators" chipped in another.

As with all things there were elements of truth in all of these claims and rumours but although Benoit was determined to be part of the movement for change, but at the same time, he also wanted to distance himself from being in any way regarded as an agitator or 'agent provocateur.' Restraining Genevieve might prove to be more difficult he thought. She had been brought up on left wing politics and agitation. It was in her blood. He had not yet met her family but from what he already knew he and her father Pierre were not remotely close either socially or politically. In fact, they were poles apart. Benoit knew that Pierre would be actively encouraging his daughter to challenge authority and the status quo. Whilst Benoit would not think of restricting her strong independent spirit and free will he had to keep her out of trouble but at the same time not jeopardise his relationship with her in anyway and he already knew that in the coming weeks that may prove to be a significant challenge.

Disruptions led by the enragés continued every day, small in scale but constant and eventually on 28th March, the exasperated Nanterre faculty President made the decision to close the faculty for three days. This only resulted in a larger protest which involved over five hundred students and was eventually broken up by the police. Genevieve had encouraged Benoit to come along and join in. She was chanting and singing but Benoit was relieved that she and her friends had remained in the middle of the student throng and were not at the front where he noticed two things had changed. Firstly, the police were photographing all of the leaders of the disturbance and secondly, he saw the presence of members of the riot police; the infamous CRS. Coming from a rural middle-class town Benoit had never seen any members of the (CRS) but he had heard all about their reputation over the last few days at the university which had started to dominate conversations amongst the students.

"Who exactly are the CRS?" Benoit asked the group who were sitting outside Chez Henri the following afternoon.

"They are fascist pigs, capitalist lackeys and the attack dogs of the bourgeois elite" Bruno said almost spitting out the words with real venom.

Benoit ignored him and looked at Antoine without repeating the question.

Antoine thought for a minute, took a large gulp of Coca-Cola that he was drinking and then said:

"Without going into too much detail, the Compagnies Républicaines de Securité or CRS is run by the Minister of the Interior. It was created in December 1944 as an elite unit to safeguard the Republic amid fears of a Communist insurrection. Its remit was expanded three years later to deal with the growing unrest throughout the country caused by food rationing, a poor harvest and coal shortages. In the autumn of 1948 the CRS, acting on the orders of Jules Moch, the then Minister of the Interior, was ordered to bring thousands of striking miners to heel. It did so with bullets, killing several and wounding hundreds. So began a history of violence and repression. Because one of its primary roles is the maintenance of public order in the face of serious unrest, in other words crowd and riot control, it has inevitably given rise to controversy and criticism of the excessive use of force and lack of discipline. They are easy to identify because of their black round helmets, long black coats and large batons"

"Thank you, Antoine," Benoit acknowledged *"You are very knowledgeable."*

Marie shivered as she sat alongside Genevieve at one of the tables they had pulled together outside the café:

"Not nice people"

"No, they are not" replied Antoine *"We will all need to be very careful indeed."*

A few days later Genevieve and Benoit, Marco and Marie found themselves at a party. Someone Genevieve knew had a friend with very rich parents who were out of town. It was being held in a large apartment in an upmarket neighbourhood near to the Champs-Élysées. There were numerous balconies with superb views of the river and the city. It was a chilly April evening but the weather was clear; typical of this time of year in Paris. Benoit looked over the railing on a balcony smoking a Disque Bleu cigarette and staring at the majestic sights of the city. The Eiffel Tower, the cathedral of Notre Dame and other distinctive landmarks; some of which illuminated against the night sky. This was a world away from the quiet backwater of Saint-Émilion and somehow the scene had an enchanting effect on him and he just soaked it all in as he drew on the cigarette which glowed bright red in the darkness. He stared out at the vista before him. So much had changed in his life over the last eighteen months. Once again, he marvelled at how he had come to love the vibrancy of Paris. The lights, the sound, the music and conversation coming from hundreds of street cafés or the delicious smells that wafted out of restaurants from the most expensive to a humble family-owned bistro. He had even come to accept the traffic – it was all part of living in this city. He now had a place of his own, felt a sense of belonging and the ability to express himself without restraint or the necessity to conform to given protocols or etiquette. Above all he now had Gennie. He often pinched himself just to check that he was living in real life and not is some fantasy world.

It was only a couple of days after the news of the assassination of the black civil rights leader Martin Luther King in Memphis, Tennessee and everyone was talking about his murder and the subsequent riots and protests that had engulfed America. Benoit had always admired Martin Luther King despite his father calling him a '*troublemaker and a rebel rouser.*' Benoit liked not only his oratory but his sincerity and deep thinking. He had read avidly a pamphlet that had been distributed at his school which he hid from his parents in which King had advocated his theories of non-violent protest and the equal rights of all human beings having being created as one by God. In particular, one phrase had stuck in his mind and for some reason it came to him now as he leant over the railing staring at the distinctive shape of the church of Notre Dame and thought about the riots now being carried out in his name in America:

"The old law of an eye for an eye leaves everyone blind"

A tap on the shoulder brought him out of his reverie. It was Marco, the Italian boyfriend of Genevieve's friend Marie. He held out a bottle of cold 1664 which Benoit took gratefully.

"You are deep in thought mon ami" he said

"Yes, I was just thinking about Martin Luther King" Benoit replied. *"He was a good man and I admired him"*

"Yes, he was. Unfortunately, racism, bigotry and reactionary conservative authority is spread widely across the western world." Marco said with a sigh.

"France is sadly reactionary" Benoit said without much thought before adding *"Even my own father is probably part of it."*

"I have a real concern for the future. Everyone here in Paris is very optimistic and that real change is in the air which I share but I am also fearful for us. History tells us that real change always comes at a price. Perhaps the wisdom of Martin Luther King can guide us when he said 'The time is always right to do what is right' or something like that but we must all be careful and look after each other."

They both stared in silence at the Paris skyline without saying anything for a few moments and then Marco said:

"Come on, let's find the others inside."

Genevieve had just finished talking to a group of people and was moving away to find another drink when Marie approached holding two glasses of wine and gave one to her.

"Thanks" said Genevieve *"That's just what I was looking for"*

They talked for a while mostly about other people in the room and who was seeing who and so what when Marie suddenly said:

"I've been meaning to ask you for a while now. What first attracted you to Benoit? I just wouldn't have thought that he was your type"

"What's my type?" Genevieve replied

"Oh I don't know. Someone pretty trendy and the life and soul of the party sort of thing"

"You obviously don't know me as well as I thought you did Marie. There was a time that that was the case but I've moved on. Are you saying that Benoit is boring?"

"Good Lord no!" blurted out Marie *"Not at all. Now I have got to know him I really love him and Marco really respects him and values his friendship. It's just at first I thought he was just a little cold perhaps?"*

"That's just the way he is but he is not like that at all. It is just a form of social shyness."

"Well I know that now"

"I must admit he didn't cross my radar at all until we met by accident really. But he was just so polite and different and interesting from what I thought he would be. And you know what Marie, he is one of the few boys that I have known that have not tried to get me into bed at the first opportunity. Above all Marie, he makes me happy and makes me laugh."

"Well you cannot ask for more than that."

Across the other side of the room Benoit and Marco re-entered into the throng of the party from the balcony as the Leonard Cohen track *'Suzanne'* was playing quite loudly. Its melancholic and haunting vocals and rhythm seemed to absorb them both instantly and Benoit noticed that even though the room was full the noise level of conversation had dropped as everyone was listening to the music.

"I love this song" Benoit said:

"So do I" replied Marco *"Marie and I play it a lot. Did you know he wrote it a couple of years ago in Montreal? Suzanne was the wife of one of his best friends called Armand and they made a very attractive couple. There was no intention on Cohen's part of any impropriety at all which is why he used the phrase of touching her perfect body with his mind in the lyrics or something like that"*

Over the next few weeks Benoit had decided that now he had set up his dark room photographic laboratory in the small loft space above their apartment he would make a short film about Genevieve and their life in Paris. He took his cine camera out on numerous occasions as they travelled around Paris on the Métro stopping to film at La Place de la Republique, Notre Dame, Sacre Coeur, from the top of the Eiffel Tower and from a boat cruise along the River Seine at night with all the sights of Paris illuminated on the riverside. For a few evenings he secreted himself away in the loft space forbidding Genevieve to enter in case she 'spoiled' the film whilst he was developing and editing it. Eventually one evening he said *"C'est finis"*

The following evening Benoit and Genevieve invited their friends Marie and Marco to their apartment for some drinks and for the 'premiere' of the silent movie. They had arrived at the door of the apartment with a bottle of red wine and an object wrapped with paper and a red ribbon tied into a bow on it.

"This a flat warming present from us both" Marie said handing the object over to Genevieve

"Oh thank you so much. That really is very kind of you" and she sat in one of the old armchairs and carefully unwrapped it and then held it up for Benoit to see.

"Oh wow! A lava lamp. That is absolutely brilliant. Thank you both so much."

She got up and carefully placed the lamp on a small table in the corner of the room and plugged it in. The lamp immediately lit up in colours of turquoise and red.

"You have to let it warm up" Marco added *"and then it starts to work properly. The warmed wax rises through the surrounding liquid, cools, loses its buoyancy, and falls back to the bottom of the glass vessel in a cycle that is visually suggestive of lava hence the name. I saw them in London last year and I was fascinated by them".*

"How trendy" exclaimed Genevieve excitedly.

"We cannot thank you enough" Benoit added *"That really is very generous of you both."*

Earlier on Benoit had shifted all of the furniture in the small apartment into one half so that he had just enough space to erect his screen and he mounted the projector on to the dining table and pointed it at the screen. Three of them were now squeezed on to the small sofa with Benoit standing by his projector. Genevieve passed round a bottle of wine so that everyone could top up their glasses and Marco offered everyone a cigarette. Benoit turned off the room light and then switched on the projector and the shaft of bright light shot across the room hitting the screen illuminating the twirling cigarette smoke in its wake. There was a moment of anticipation and then Benoit said *"OK here we go. Lights, camera, action!"* and he pressed the start button and the film spools started turning.

Benoit had edited the film well and it opened with Genevieve introducing herself to the camera in a close up and then the camera panned away as she made her way across La Place de la Republique as Benoit followed her past magicians and musicians and small protests about this and that and someone reciting from a book. The Place de la Republique, which borders the 3rd, 10th and 11th districts is one of the largest squares of Paris at more than thirty-three thousand square meters. It is located at the site occupied in the fourteenth century by the stronghold of Charles V's Porte du Temple enclosure. Benoit knew as he allowed his camera to take a panoramic view around the square that not much had changed over the centuries. Decorated in 1811 with a fountain called the *'Château d'Eau',* it took on its present appearance during the Second Empire, in the nineteenth century, with the creation of Avenue Magenta, Avenue de la Republique, and Boulevard Voltaire. But it was now as it always had been; a meeting place for discussion and gatherings, a place that belonged to everyone. The film then cut to Notre Dame and then the Seine riverbank at night until it was over about three minutes or so later.

"Fantastique" exclaimed Genevieve and Marie together and they clapped their hands in delight.

"Well done mon ami" Marco said as he stood up and slapped Benoit on the shoulder.

"Lets' watch it again" shouted Genevieve excitedly but let's have another drink first.

So Benoit rewound the film and they watched it again and then again a third time before he switched the room light back on again and rewound the film for the last time and then shut the projector down, careful not to move it until it had cooled otherwise he knew that he risked damaging the expensive bulb.

"Do you know what Benoit" Marco said as they sat and opened another bottle of wine and he passed round his cigarettes once more *"You have a real talent Benoit. I think you should use your skill to make a film diary of the events that are currently happening in Paris. We are living in turbulent times and you never know your films could be of historic significance in the future."*

"That's a brilliant idea Marco" Genevieve replied.

Benoit thought for a moment and then said:

"Yes Marco that is a good idea. I will buy some more films tomorrow. You never know they could become part of some sort of historical archive."

"C'est bien."

Chapter Four

On Thursday 2nd May the situation in Paris changed significantly. Firstly, the Prime Minister Monsieur Georges Pompidou departed on a lengthy foreign visit which deprived the French government of the one man who might have been able to contain the boiling pot of unrest before it was too late. He had appeared to be the only man who had wrested some executive authority away from the President and was not just another of his fawning servants. Student protest was not something for the haughty President to get involved with which had left a dangerous vacuum.

Secondly, following weeks of conflict between the students and the authorities at Nanterre, the administration had taken the decision to shut down the university. The following day as Benoit and Genevieve and the usual crowd were gathered at Chez Henri, the atmosphere was even more animated than usual with everyone having an opinion on the current situation and all trying to express their opinion at the same time. It was noisy interactive chaos. Bruno was having a heated and animated discussion with Pierre and he was waving his arms in the air and after a few more minutes he got up quickly from the table, knocking over his chair and shouted *"You just don't understand the big picture"* and walked off mumbling to himself.

"No. It is you my friend that do not comprehend the wider issues at stake here. Your world view is just too narrow and simplistic" Pierre said calling after him and calmly blew a plume of smoke into the air from the cigarette he had just inhaled from.

Benoit just looked at Genevieve and shrugged his shoulders and said *"What would like to drink?"*

A few days later on 6th May there were larger than normal groups of people sitting or standing at the tables outside Chez Henri that morning. Apart from the usual crowd of Antoine, Pierre, Bruno, Nancy, Marco, Benoit, Marie and Genevieve, there were a lot of other students that Benoit did not know but he had seen most of them in and around the university and there were also some that he had never seen before at all. For the last ten minutes a discussion had been taking place about the police and their tactics and their increasing resort to violence and aggression. With the university now closed, Chez Henri and many other cafés like it around the Sorbonne, had become the alternative debating chambers and informal seminars were taking place all day every day now. In this way they were once again fulfilling their historic tradition of acting as the political and social pulse of the city.

"They are just the weapons of an oppressive bourgeois ruling class" stated Bruno

Two students who had been sitting nearby suddenly walked up to the group and said:

"We have been listening to what you have been discussing. Can we join you?"

"Of course" said Antoine and so they dragged two chairs across and sat with the rest of the group gathered around two café tables that they had pulled together.

"I am Thomas Laurent and this is Etienne Dubois. I am a third year Politics student and he is a third year Psychology student and we are both studying here at Nanterre. We are particularly interested in your discussion about the police"

"In what way?" followed up Antoine

"I am doing a dissertation this year on the Police psyche and why they think like they do which results in their actions" said Etienne.

"I was interested in your comment that you just made about the police being weapons of the ruling class." Thomas said looking straight at Bruno.

"Oh" Bruno replied

"Because I think that you are partly right"

Bruno beamed a wide smile and nodded and then said *"Partly. What do you mean?"*

"Well" Thomas continued *"I agree that the police in most western democracies have become an agency of societal control in that they represent the established values. However, I also believe that the police, particularly in crisis situations exist not only to control but to divert opposition to the government of the day on to themselves which is a different thing."*

"They act as a sort of buffer between the governing elites and the masses." Chipped in Etienne

"This is a situation that we are experiencing right now here in Paris" stated Antoine

"Exactly so" replied Etienne

"So, the police are actively being used on the streets of Paris to deflect anger and disaffection away from the government and on to themselves" Benoit said after clearly thinking deeply about what had just been said.

"Yes, and in that way, they are the recipients but also the source of the current political resentment in terms of both verbal and physical abuse." Thomas added.

"This is a continuum of social life. The maintenance of public order has become one of the prime functions of the police in western liberal democracies"

"And is this is a deliberate policy and strategy of the ruling elite?" enquired Nancy

"Yes absolutely"

"I had never considered the issues we are experiencing in those terms" Genevieve said quietly

"I think you are giving them far too much credit" Bruno suddenly said *"The police are quite simply the active arm of the status quo and we are seeing them do this with the use of batons, shields and tear gas grenades. Bullets will be next. They are fascist pigs and the enemy of the people and they are all the same"*

"I think it is also important that you look at things from their perspective" Etienne replied *"It is true that the police, particularly in France, do appear to have distinctive cognitive tendencies both individually and as an occupational grouping which portrays them as being conservative both emotionally and in their politics. This is not surprising when you consider that after all their raison d'être is the preservation of public order."*

"Exactly what I have been saying" Bruno smiled *"They are just agents of repression to maintain the status quo."*

"No. I really think that this is too simplistic a view" Etienne replied. *"Liberal criminal reform can often be seen by them to be 'coddling criminals' and even perfectly legal social deviance like long hair worn by men is often viewed as a prelude to potential criminality"*

"This is exactly what we are experiencing now in the University" Marco who had been sitting quietly listening to the discussion whilst smoking a cigarette, added *"Hair style, dress sense and sexual freedom are all being seen by the establishment as an erosion of authority"*

"I agree entirely" replied Etienne *"It is these views that put the police at odds with the those of us who are currently now in dissent and demanding change and reform in France. They simply do not have the capacity to appreciate the reasons for this dissent or demand for change or indeed for any other innovative social behaviour."*

"This is a very interesting line of thought" Benoit added.

The conversation ebbed back and forth with the discussion becoming more and more animated particularly from Bruno and a few other hard-line Marxists with whom he associated. Whilst they all shared a lunch of a huge plate of baguettes filled with brie and ham; this group tried to dominate the conversation by speaking louder than the others. Eventually Bruno stood up and said *"Listen the situation we are currently witnessing is classic in terms of class struggle...."*

But before he could continue Benoit announced *"Something's going on."*

Everyone looked away from the table. Groups of students were shouting and running across the Place back towards the university.

"What's happening" someone shouted to the nearest student running past.

"There is a massive demonstration happening at the Sorbonne right now" he replied without stopping.

Benoit turned to Thomas and Etienne saying *"We meet here most days. I would be really interested in continuing this discussion"*

"So would I" Nancy and Antoine both said at the same time and a number of others who were gathered around the tables all nodded.

All at once they all got up leaving money on the table for Henri knowing that if it was

short they would 'settle up' with him later or the following day. They joined the growing crowd of students making their way in the direction of the Sorbonne. Police sirens wailed as they heard someone was shouting through a megaphone. The crowd started to walk faster as though responding to increased tension in the air. Benoit noticed more people with megaphones, some wearing motorcycle helmets trying to keep the crowd moving in one direction and establishing some kind of order. Up front he could see that other protesters had started to build make-shift barricades with anything they could lay their hands on. Suddenly a loudspeaker blared out:

"Disband by the order of the President of the Republic. All those who do not disband at once will be treated accordingly"

Immediately there were shouts of *"Fuck you"* from the massed crowd.

As they neared the main entrance of the Sorbonne Marco suddenly shouted *"Look over there"* and he pointed ahead to his right. The others followed his outstretched arm. Cordons of police with helmets and riot shields had started charging into the arriving students waving batons and arresting people at will on a completely ad hoc basis. In response some of the demonstrators started to remove 'les paves,' the street cobble stones by leveraging them up with iron bars. They were massive, each weighing a few pounds and looked as though they could land a lethal blow. A huge confrontation took place in front of their eyes with cobble stones being launched over the barricades and onto the police who were protecting themselves with large shields and helmets with wire cages to protect their face. When the first volley of cobbles stopped the police retaliated by throwing tear gas grenades at the demonstrators, many of whom had covered their faces with scarves as improvised gas masks.

Genevieve was even more determined to get as near to the front of the protest as she could and she pushed her way through the crowd, leaving Benoit behind to try and take some film footage. When the police fired tear gas, the protesters answered with Molotov cocktails. Demands for the crowd to disperse were continuously made from officers carrying megaphones in the front lines of the police. Apart from the usual hail of obscenities, the police were answered with chants of:

"Long Live the Paris Commune"

Genevieve knew this was an historical reference to the Paris Commune, a radical socialist and revolutionary government that ruled Paris from 18th March to the 28th May in 1871. In recent days they had been numerous debates amongst students, including many at Chez Henri over the policies and outcome of the Commune which many believed had had significant influence on the ideas of Karl Marx, who described it as an example of the *"dictatorship of the proletariat."*

The sight of the CRS en masse was certainly a frightening vision, heavily armed and dressed all in black, wearing shiny helmets and long leather boots, their menacing appearance matching their reputation of often using indiscriminate and excessive force.

Genevieve retreated back through the crowd back towards Benoit. But five minutes later she was fired up again and tried to run forward but Benoit held her back saying:

"Let's avoid this confrontation and get into the university by one of the side entrances" he shouted and they all ran at speed off to the left desperate to avoid being gassed or struck with a baton.

A few minutes later they arrived on to the campus and they could clearly see that the great paved central courtyard of the Sorbonne was crammed with hundreds of students who had starting protesting about the closure of the Nanterre faculty and also about the summons to six of the Nanterre enrages, including Cohn-Bendit, to appear on Monday before the university's disciplinary council. The speeches through the megaphones had all moved on from the familiar themes of overcrowding of the facilities, a

61

mind-numbing curriculum and inadequate training for job skills to police brutality, repression and state authoritarianism and had taken a far more serious and threatening form.

At about 4.45pm a large column of helmeted police armed with rubber truncheons and shields marched through the narrow-arched entrance into the courtyard and surrounded the protesters. Genevieve suddenly surged forward letting go of Benoit's hand and pushed her way towards the police lines and Benoit lost her in the crowded throng. Luckily on this occasion there was no outbreak of violence and after talks; the student leaders agreed that they would leave. The police gradually pressed the mass of students back towards the entrance. However, instead of simply letting the students disperse, groups of twenty or so were cordoned off and bundled into black, shuttered vans that had been parked up close to the walls of the university and were blocking the road. Genevieve was scooped up and forced into a van with a number of others that she did not know. Benoit had caught sight of her as she was being taken and he pushed his way like a mad man to get to her but as he got towards the front of the crowd, he saw the van door slam shut and through the wire-mesh window he just caught a glimpse of her packed tight with others on wooden benches and the van quickly accelerated away.

"Gennie. Gennie" he screamed at the top of his voice but then instinctively he quickly darted to his right using his height and strength in a move that he had learnt on the rugby field at school, to avoid being taken himself in the next batch of protesters being rounded up.

At first there was an eerie silence that suddenly overcame the student throng at the shock of seeing their colleagues taken away but then this quickly became replaced with highly charged emotional outrage. There were jeers and shouts, sporadic at first and then swelling into mass chants of *'A Bas La Repression!'* and then one stone was thrown followed by dozens of others and then pavés some of which hit their targets smashing a van's windscreen and leaving the police driver with blood running down his face. It all happened so quickly, this pent-up rage just exploded like a champagne cork from a bottle as the response was so immediate and spontaneous and it was not even the students with the strongest political convictions who were the first to explode. The students surged up to the retreating police vans hammering their fists against the metal bodywork, others lifted parked cars and turned them over into the road to try and block the procession of vans. Gas grenades started to explode everywhere which drove screaming students with their eyes running and stinging into cafés and doorways and anywhere to seek some sanctuary. Out of nowhere sprayed slogans started to appear on walls and street furniture *'stop the repression'* and *'CRS=SS'*; all hell was starting to break loose.

Benoit spotted Marco and Marie a few yards ahead of him in the road and he ran towards them. Marco was holding Marie's hand tightly as she tried not to vomit after being caught in a whirlpool of tear gas.

"The bastards have got Gennie" he screamed just as another car was overturned to their right and a protester with a motorcycle helmet and with a megaphone in his hand clambered on to it started shouting instructions to the crowd below him.

"Come on let's get out of here" shouted Marco and he crossed the road avoiding the progressing vans and various obstacles and led them down an alley and away from the Sorbonne. After half- running, staggering and walking for ten minutes they stopped and gasped for breath. They saw the Cluny La Sorbonne Mètro station about one hundred

metres ahead and headed straight for it and charged down the stairs with the burning acrid smell of the tear gas following them down. Fortunately, a train had just pulled into the platform as they arrived and they all jumped on and sighed with relief as the doors closed and it pulled out of the platform and back into the dark tunnel.

Two hours later Marie said to Benoit *"You can sleep on our sofa tonight"* as they all sat in their apartment drinking coffee and listening to melodic sound and perfect harmonies of '*The Sounds of Silence*' album by Simon and Garfunkel playing quietly in the background.

"Yes you must as it will not be safe on the streets of the Latin Quarter tonight. There will be groups of riot police out for revenge on anyone that they believe is a legitimate target" Marco had already been out to the shop just down the street to get some food and wine and been told by the shopkeeper that he was closing early as there were groups of protesters and police engaging each other all over the area. Fires had been lit in the roads melting the tar and loosening the cobbles which were then used as missiles, traffic signs torn up and strewn in the road with the police responding furiously swinging their batons coshing the innocent and the guilty with equal ferocity. Pavement cafes were stormed and tables overturned, simple passers-by were rounded up ferociously and taken away in police vans, commuters emerging form Métro stations unaware of the situation above ground were suddenly set upon without remorse.

"What about Gennie" said Benoit quietly with growing concern in his voice as the sad and lonely lyrics of '*I am a Rock*' came out of the record player.

"She'll be OK. Don't worry Benoit" soothed Marie.

"They will keep her overnight with all the dozens of others. They will all be processed and have their details

recorded and they will try and scare her but I suspect that she will be released in the morning with either a warning about future behaviour or potentially she will face a charge of public disorder and be made an example of which will result in a fine."

"Well they can't put the cork back in the bottle now" said Marie as they sat eating some fresh baguette and cheese and she opened a second bottle of red wine which Marco had bought just before the shopkeeper had lowered his shutters early on his shop down the street from their apartment.

"You are right" replied Marco "Even those who were not committed to the protest will now unite behind les enragés and things can only get worse from now on."

Chapter Five

Benoit had spent a sleepless night on Marco and Marie's sofa which was not surprising as it was only a two-seater and his long legs fell off the end uncomfortably. He had kept tossing and turning despite the considerable amount of red wine he had consumed during the previous evening. He just kept thinking of Genevieve in police custody and how she was being treated. Although she presented a very cheerful and confident front to the world, Benoit now knew that behind the facade she was really quite a vulnerable young person. They all awoke and went outside and Marco and Marie went to the shop whilst Benoit made his way to Chez Henri for breakfast promising to contact them later in the day when he knew about Genevieve's situation.

The air was warmer. It was going to be a lovely spring day but there was adrenaline in the air he could sense it. As Benoit walked to the Métro station he was carrying the small back pack that he had bought a few days earlier that contained his cine camera. He had deliberately bought an inexpensive one so that it would not obviously reveal that it had an expensive piece of photographic equipment in it that might then become a target for theft. He was angry with himself because he and Genevieve had witnessed scenes that would have contributed significantly to his film archives that he was making but the film had run out after only about thirty seconds and he had then remembered that he had used much of it up on a previous occasion when he had been filming Genevieve and the opportunity had been lost.

He intended to walk directly to Chez Henri's which was only about ten minutes away straight up the Rue Monge but this morning as he was in no hurry, he decided to take a detour and walked past Place Maubert and then along Boulevard St Germain and into the Place Saint-Germain-des-Prés. The chic Place which is home to expensive shops, eateries, and the medieval Église de Saint-Germain-des-Prés, Paris's oldest church and is normally the city's literary and cultural centre. But the scene that greeted him this morning as he walked into the Place and then into the Rue de Rennes was an appalling sight. Buses with their tyres slashed and windows broken were strewn across the road, cars were upended with their windows smashed, marking spots where the hard core of students had put up a fierce resistance to the police onslaught, who after having been subjected to a full days rioting; clubbed the demonstrators indiscriminately with a sickening ferocity. The scene was one of complete destruction and something Benoit had never seen in his life. The road was torn up in numerous places, shop windows were smashed and the acrid smell of tear gas still seemed to linger in the air mixing with the smell of smoke from numerous small fires. Traffic signal poles had been uprooted to both attack the police vehicles with and as large levers to prise up the cobblestones and many were just left on the pavements and in the road, bent and twisted. He looked around and saw sprayed in black paint on a wall were the words:

"LA SOCIETE EST UNE FLEUR CARNIVORE"

Standing in front of the slogan were a group of street cleaners with their brooms just shaking their heads in disbelief and wondering how they were going to clear up the mess that surrounded them.

Benoit walked back the way he had come in silence, deep in thought and after about fifteen minutes was back at Place Maubert and he made his way over to Chez Henri's. There was already quite a crowd there; many of whom

Benoit did not know but word had spread that this was a place for a good debate with some interesting people. He sat down at a table where Antoine was drinking coffee with a girl he had not seen before. Antoine was reading the paper and pointed out a headline to Benoit and saying:

"Look at this"

"That's interesting Antoine. The police really are isolating themselves from the main body of society by their use of excessive violence."

Evidently a public opinion poll now showed that eighty per cent of Parisians were in favour of the students was printed in all of the newspapers and it was being discussed on news programmes on the radio. Someone at one of the tables had a transistor radio tuned to a news station and three students were huddled over it seeking the latest updates. Benoit ordered a coffee and a half baguette and some brie cheese from a waitress he had not seen before. Apparently, Henri had employed a few students to help him and Veronique out at busy times of the day. One by one members of the group turned up with different stories to tell about the events of the previous afternoon and evening.

Benoit repeated his statement over and over again:

'The bastard flics took Gennie away in a pig wagon, I don't think she was hurt but I am really worried about her."

"I have heard that over five hundred people were taken into custody yesterday" said one *"I am sure that she will be OK"*

"They can't lock us all up" said another

"The tear gas they are using is not the usual stuff. It has got chlorine in it which is the same as the Americans use in Vietnam" said another

Just then Bruno turned up with his head bandaged as a result of a truncheon blow. He was wearing his injury like a badge of honour *"The revolution has started comrades"* he said as he ordered an espresso coffee and a croissant from Henri who just looked at him and slowly shook his head saying:

"This is madness this will not end well. You must talk. Fighting is not the answer"

But Bruno was not listening instead he launched into a tirade of class warfare slogans and saying that the teachers were all supporting the student movement now and that they were in a process of unstoppable momentum.

"We must now get our message to the blue-collar workers that it is their struggle as well and that we are their natural comrades in arms"

"But the leader of the Communist party has denounced us this morning as spoiled children of privileged parents" chipped in Nancy

"As has the Socialist party" said Pierre

Henri returned with Bruno's coffee and Benoit's coffee and bread and cheese as another two members of the group arrived and ordered coffee from him too.

"That is their position at the moment" said Bruno as he dipped a part of his croissant into his coffee *"But the situation will clarify when they understand that our grievances are in line with their own aspirations."*

The conversation ebbed and flowed with more people arriving and some leaving. Benoit had been astonished to learn that more than thirty thousand students, teachers and supporters had marched towards the Sorbonne yesterday to confront the police. He knew it had been a large demonstration but not that large and to an extent Bruno was right; the protests were spreading and permeating into other layers of society; not just socialist leaning Sociology students. He decided to wait another hour before returning to the apartment and just then Genevieve arrived with Marie and Marco. She had been released early and had gone to Marie and Marco's flat because she knew that Benoit would be there. She looked tired and dishevelled and she just walked up to Benoit and threw her arms around him and cried gently into his shoulder. He hugged her not wanting to release his embrace but she eventually pulled herself clear and wiped her eyes with a tissue that Marie held up to her. She had been released on police caution and warned that if she was arrested again, she would face a heavy fine or maybe a severer punishment.

After about an hour or so of chatting and relaying tales of the previous day's events with their friends Benoit and Genevieve said *'au revoir'* to their friends leaving them to continue the debate at Chez Henri and took the Metro back to Place Monge and then walked to their apartment stopping to buy some food on the way. They then spent the rest of the day sleeping and resting. Genevieve decided to telephone her parents later that evening, in case they were notified by the police and they walked together to the call box at the corner of the street:

"But why did you get involved Genevieve" her mother said *"You are at university to learn not to get arrested by the police"*

Her father had been more sympathetic however, when she had answered the same question by saying *"Because they are robbing us of a meaningful future papa. I don't want to be exploited or become disposable or a slave to a system that takes away my freedom in exchange for meaningless trinkets."*

She was surprised when he said nothing else but *"Je comprends mais fais attention ma petite."*

The next day Benoit had arranged to meet Marco at Chez Henri. Genevieve had decided to stay in the flat and have a lie-in. It was another sunny day so Benoit decided to walk to Place Maubert rather than take the Mètro. As he walked along, he smoked a cigarette and thought to himself. Over the last few months, he had grown quite close to Marco. He liked him as an individual, they had similar tastes in music and attitudes to life and he valued his opinion on things. When he arrived at the café, Marco was already there

70

talking to Pierre and Antoine and Nancy. Benoit joined them at a table and ordered a coffee and a croissant from the new waitress who arrived almost immediately as he sat down.

"The service is improving here" Benoit said after she had retreated back into the café.

"Yes and it is service with a smile" added Antoine

"Rather than old grumpy Henri you mean" Benoit said referring to the eponymous owner of the café.

"True but where would we be without his sanguine view on life each morning." Marco said laughing.

"Sanguine! You must be joking" added Pierre

"Sorry I was being sarcastic"

A few minutes later Bruno arrived with a petite brunette at his side.

"This is Yvette" he announced to the group as they pulled up two chairs from an adjacent table and joined the others.

"Yvette is part of the Atelier Populaire" Bruno proudly announced. *"She is a student at L'Ecole Nationale Supérieure des Beaux-Arts and they have taken over the faculty. The revolution is spreading my friends."*

"What is the Atelier Populaire" Nancy enquired

"The idea was to keep the effort collective to avoid bourgeois values. We no longer call ourselves Ecole des Beaux Arts but we sign our posters Atelier Populaire, the Popular Workshop. We are producing hundreds of silk - screen printed posters that you are seeing adorned on walls across the city and particularly here in the Latin Quarter" Yvette replied.

"I have seen them everywhere" Antoine interjected" *There are some brilliant slogans. I particularly like the one with the bandaged face an agonised gaze and the text 'A Youth Disturbed too often by the Future'"*

"We have dozens of volunteers who undertake the posting of the posters under the cover of night so that

Parisians can wake up the following morning and see the issue at hand" Yvette said "*The walls of, the Latin Quarter are now the gallery of a new rationality, no longer confined to just books, but democratically displayed at street level and made available to all.*"

"*I would like one for my bedroom wall in the student residence*" Nancy stated casually

In an instant Yvette turned towards her and said with a real venom in her voice:

"*The posters produced by the Atelier Populaire are weapons of the struggle and their rightful place is in the centres of conflict and are not to be used for decorative or aesthetic purposes and should not be displayed in Bourgeois places of culture*"

Benoit turned towards Marco and blew out his cheeks "*pheww*"

Not long after, Thomas and Etienne reappeared at the café and ordered coffee from Henri who was clearing the tables and emptying ash trays. They were greeted with enthusiasm from most of the group that were gathered there but Bruno and Yvette managed just a muted "*Bonjour*"

"*The situation has definitely escalated and evolved since we last met a few days ago*" Antoine said looking at Thomas as he and Etienne pulled up two chairs to join the burgeoning group outside Chez Henri's that morning.

"*It certainly has. The danger is no one seems to know where it is heading and it could take on a momentum of itself and spiral out of control*"

"*What do you mean?*" Marco said

"*Well most policemen are conservative, conventional, upwardly mobile and mostly sourced from lower- and working-class communities.*"

"*So what difference does that make?*" Benoit interrupted suddenly becoming self-conscious of his own origins.

"It starts to become a problem when the police, as they are now currently experiencing in Paris, are faced with young middle- and upper-class students at some of the best universities in the country who are denouncing them as 'pigs' and other verbal abuse together with hurling bricks and pavés at them. This is far more difficult for them to accept than the normal situations of crime"

"The current public opinion cannot help that situation" said Antoine

"You are absolutely right" Etienne replied *"Liberal and moderate Parisians and others in France are demanding that the police act towards deviant behaviour and unrest with restraint and professionalism and that they do not have the right to react aggressively towards provocative acts and no matter what, they should not, as we have all witnessed; lose their self-control and discipline."*

Marco suddenly got up saying *"I need some more coffee"*

Benoit passed him a crumpled ten franc note that he took out of his back pocket and asked Marco to get a drink for both Etienne and Thomas as well.

"I see what you mean about not knowing where it is heading now" Benoit said turning towards Thomas.

"Yes I am fearful for the future mon ami" Thomas replied

"Why so?" Antoine interjected *"The change is needed and it is positive"*

"Oh I agree the change is very much needed but I am worried about how it may be achieved and at what cost."

"It is a sacrifice worth making and is the destiny of all the revolutionaries of the proletariat" Bruno suddenly said as he got out of his chair, stubbed out a cigarette in the ash tray and then walked off towards the Metro station with Yvette following him closely behind.

"What did you mean by 'at what cost'" Antoine enquired of Thomas once more.

Marco returned just at that moment with a tray of four steaming cups of coffee which he placed on the table and then handed over the change to Benoit.

Thomas took a cup from the tray and sipped the coffee allowing it to linger in his mouth and back of the throat before swallowing it; obviously considering carefully his answer to the question.

"I believe that those who rely on the police to maintain order are naïve if they imagine that the police are always going to be content to preserve order as defined by the government. It is very likely in my opinion that, particularly given the situation of their current psyche that Etienne was describing a few moments ago; they could end up defining the kind of order that they are going to impose which naturally will be one that which suits them and their world view best."

Benoit shot Marco and then Antoine in turn a worried glance just before Thomas continued:

"It is true that the police in all political systems are an overtly political force created to subdue dissent and maintain the status quo. As a consequence, the police have always preferred to recruit men into the force who are conventional and can be moulded into a common psyche that will increase their likelihood to moderate or resist change."

"Why should this be an issue" interrupted Benoit

"Simply because the police often have a very difficult job to do. They often see themselves as 'the meat in a sandwich' which calls for sensitivity, fine judgement, the tolerance of both verbal and physical abuse and particularly above all, the projection of a balanced and proportionate response."

"But that is not what we have witnessed over the last few days here in Paris" added Antoine.

"Exactly" replied Thomas. *"There is no doubt in my opinion that effective and responsible policing that is carried out within the framework of the law is completely*

74

dependent on wide ranging public support. However, as we have all seen, that this has not been the case here in Paris and so the police have been acting under stress and duress and that vital relationship has been eroded away. This vacuum then, in my opinion, can only increase the opportunity and the likelihood of a collective overreaction by the police which then creates a vicious circle because this I turn, only destroys public trust still further."

"Your hypothesis would seem to indicate that the worst is yet to come" Benoit said quietly.

"I am afraid so" replied Thomas

The four of them drank the last of their coffee and then they too departed for the Métro station promising to catch up with each other again over the next few days.

Chapter Six

On Friday 10th May another huge crowd had congregated on the Rive Gauche. Barricades had been quickly erected with not just the usual pavés but with materials raided from building sites, scaffolding poles, hoardings ripped from buildings, café tables and chairs and every piece of street furniture that could be obtained. Benoit and Genevieve, together with many of their friends were in the middle of the crowd shouting and chanting *'Libérez nos camarades!'* The massed throng of protesters marched into the Place Denfert-Rochereau, a large crossroads near Montparnasse. The crowd was made up of not only students and their lecturers and teachers but with working class people many in overalls and healthcare workers in white aprons.

Many carried large banners between them holding them aloft with poles on each end with the initials of trade unions or student movements, or anti-Vietnam war or anti-capitalist slogans. or just plain red and black flags. They were led by a hard core of protesters wearing crash helmets and other protective headgear who tried to steer them towards their intended target which was the Maison de la Radio; the centre of the French broadcasting system on the Right Bank of the Seine. However, the riot police had blocked all the bridges across the river with their vans that had been parked bumper to bumper. Prevented from reaching their destination the protesters swept down the Boulevard St Germain but were once again faced with a strong police presence who were trying to force the protesters up the Boulevard St Michel back towards the Sorbonne.

However, the great massed throng of protesters suddenly surged forwards towards the police lines that were a continuous phalanx of giant riot shields. Missiles sailed over their heads towards the police, torn up cobble stones, bottles, cans and a myriad of other objects which bounced off the shields or landed behind the police line. Suddenly a massive ball of flame exploded in front of them and then again as numerous petrol bombs ignited. The police responded with volleys of tear gas from their snub-nosed grenade launchers that they fired from the hip. Clouds of sweet and acrid smelling tear gas swirled around the crowd and filled the void between the front of the protesters and the police lines.

Benoit and Genevieve found themselves caught up in an unstoppable momentum that just propelled them forward like an undercurrent when swimming in the sea, they were helpless to resist it. A girl carrying a placard that just said simply *"Pas Content"* was suddenly crushed back against them. As they were pressed forward once again Genevieve stumbled and she thought that she might be crushed by the weight of the crowd behind her but Benoit reached down quickly with two strong arms and hoisted her back on to her feet as they surged forward with the crowd once more.

Suddenly Benoit noticed an unexpected movement on the left flank of the massed protesters and he caught a glimpse of a detachment of CRS running out an alley where they had been concealed, with their shields raised and their batons swinging mercilessly. They tore into the unsuspecting maelstrom of students and at the same time a similar operation happened on the righthand flank and the massed body of protesters were trapped in a kind of pincer movement. A huge orgy of noise and violence erupted. Benoit pulled Genevieve closer to him with his left hand around her waist and with his right hand he held his camera at arms-length above the crowd and pointed at the attacking detachment of CRS on the left flank. He could not see what he was filming but he just kept his finger on the button and tried to hold the camera as still as was possible in these conditions.

Genevieve tugged at his waist and pointed. Benoit turned his head but kept the camera pointing in the same direction as before. He could clearly see groups of protesters stumble to the ground under the weight of the surging shields and swinging batons. The CRS police seemed to have lost all control and discipline as individual officers just chased after protesters clubbing them to the ground mercilessly. They then launched into indiscriminate baton charges assaulting students, journalists, passers-by, tourists, cinema-goers and elderly couples sitting at café terraces simply watching the spectacle unfold. All attempts at restraint had vanished and they were now out of all control. They were no longer firing gas canisters into the air but aiming them directly at protesters with a view to maiming and causing injury. Time seemed to have stood still as Benoit and Genevieve watched in horror at the events that were unfolding around them.

"We have to get out of here" he shouted, his eyes stinging and streaming with the effects of the tear gas.

Then Benoit felt the button on the camera retract indicating that he had run out of film. He threw the camera strap around his neck and grabbed Genevieve and tried to push back through the crowd which was starting to break up and disintegrate under the massed attack. Then it just happened. The crowd just in front of them the crowd just parted and a clearing developed on the left flank where he had been pointing his camera and Benoit was able to advance forward a few metres for a few seconds of uninterrupted filming. Then the police started to rapidly propel the crowd back from the clearing trying to create a small impenetrable exclusion zone. As they did so Benoit caught a glimpse of two bodies on the floor, face down on to the cobble stones and pools of crimson blood spilling from their open head wounds that were plain for him to see. They were pushed back and riot police started to strike out with their batons flailing in all directions and one of them was pointing directly at Benoit. It was utter chaos and everything appeared to be happening in slow motion but in actual fact it was the complete reverse; events were unfolding before them at lightning speed.

There was a cacophony of sound all around them, shouting, screaming and the missiles kept falling as did the constant 'pop' of another exploding gas grenade. Benoit straightened himself and then harnessed all his strength to drag Genevieve backwards by putting one arm around her waist and holding her close to him so that they didn't t get parted in the crush and melee that had enveloped them.

"Come on" he shouted *"This is our chance to get out of here."*

Genevieve looked up at him, her face ashen and with an expression of terror, she said nothing but just nodded and clung on to his arm tighter than before. Benoit noticed that her eyes were red and swollen and he could not tell if this was the effect of the gas or if she had been crying.

Eventually they were able to get nearer to the rear of the crowded throng of protesters and push towards the side of the boulevard and out of the centre of the road. The crowd had thinned out here and they felt able to breathe a little easier. Finally, after what seemed an eternity of struggling and pushing and stumbling, they managed to escape the main boulevard and ran as fast as they could down a side street. They had become separated from their friends and Benoit and Genevieve just ran with a small group of other people. Suddenly they found themselves in a dead end of a small and very narrow residential street.

"If the police come now, we are sitting ducks" shouted Benoit. Genevieve clutched his hand tighter with genuine panic now searing through her chest. Just at that moment a

woman appeared in a doorway and motioned for them to come inside quickly. Benoit and Genevieve and a handful of others followed the woman through a small passageway that led into a courtyard. They all stood quietly without speaking, breathing heavily and listening to the shouts, the sound of heavy running feet and the noise of gas grenades exploding outside. They stood still, some crouched or sat on the concrete but no one spoke. An hour passed and the sounds of activity seemed to have faded. The woman who was probably the concierge of the building peered out of the doorway and into the street and seeing no one she waved at them, indicating a signal that all was clear and motioned for them to all leave as quickly as possible. Benoit muttered a quick *'Merci Madame'* as they all hurried out of the door and separated; going their different ways.

Benoit and Genevieve started to make their way back to their apartment, all the time looking behind them to check that they were not being followed or pursued by members of the riot police seeking revenge. Benoit never let go of Genevieve's hand and with his other he clung on to his camera having twisted the leather strap around his wrist to prevent it being snatched away from him. He avoided returning to the main Boulevard St. Michel except for a few minutes before he indicated that they turn should go left on to Rue Cujas, a narrow residential street with parked cars on both sides of the road. They walked quickly passed closed shops, banks and other office entrances. There were relatively few people around them at this point but they could hear the sound of running feet and shouts from both behind and in front of them. But mercifully the air was only tinged with the stench of tear gas and not surrounding them in great clouds as it had been earlier. They continued on to the Place du Panthéon and then on to Rue Clovis, a thoroughfare that ran through the Sorbonne district which had very few shops and they passed the old Saint-Etienne-du-Mont church and walked to the end of the street. They then turned left on to the Rue du Cardinal Lemoine which was very near to Marco and Marie's apartment. As soon as they reached the crossroads with Rue Monge, they decided that that they would probably be safer in the Métro as they were now right in the heart of the student quarter and they only needed to travel one stop to Place Monge and then on to the Rue de la Clef and their apartment.

They stood on the platform panting, their hearts beating fast and adrenaline pumping through their veins. The platform was quite busy with a mix of people, some business men, some shoppers, and groups of students, some still clutching placards and many with blood stained faces or with their heads covered in makeshift bandages but they were not shouting now; just talking quietly huddled in small groups. It was quite a surreal sight before them as if this scenario had suddenly become the norm in central Paris.

The fighting continued throughout the night. The protesters were well prepared and petrol bombs were as prevalent as the ubiquitous pavés. Marie and Marco were in the Rue Gay-Lussac, below the level of the Place de la Contrescarpe. It was about 1.30pm when the police launched another concerted attack against a barricade behind which they were standing. Bystanders and students alike caught in their path were beaten as the police protected by gas masks advanced. The air was thick with tear gas and suddenly more police arrived from around the corner behind the barricade. Marie and Marco and the others with them were trapped. Marco and Marie initially thought that they had found refuge in a residential building and they had been delighted to find that the front door was open. They ran in and climbed the stairs which were very poorly lit and then spread out amongst various corridors trying to find a niche or recess or a janitor's cupboard that might provide them with some sort of sanctuary. But the police were relentless now in hunting down the perpetrators of this disturbance and they were making house to house searches, banging on apartment doors with their batons and it was not long before they were discovered, beaten badly and then hustled down the stairs and taken away in a police van.

By daybreak of the second day of fighting, the number and frequency of police assaults became overwhelming and the barricades started to fall and the students fled. Benoit and Genevieve made their way to the Chez Henri café. They were the first of their group to arrive and so they ordered two coffees and two croissants with some raspberry jam and butter.

"Where is everyone" Benoit enquired of Henri when he brought the coffee and croissants to the table.

Henri took the Gauloise cigarette that was dangling from his mouth and blew out the smoke and then just shrugged his shoulders in a typical Gallic gesture and said:

"I have no idea. Perhaps they are in police cells. There has been a huge amount of violence by the police. It would seem that even when the demonstrations were over, the riot police were continuing to roam the streets looking for victims. I have friends who are law-abiding house-holders in the quarter who are being treated like an occupied population. The police were ordering that windows should be closed and if they were not closed immediately, they fired grenades directly through them. This is insanity. The police are supposed to be here to protect the public and maintain order not to be the perpetrators of violence and disorder. The world has gone mad. This government has much to answer for now!" Henri just shook his head in disbelief and took a large pull on his cigarette and then leaned forward and stabbed it out in the ash tray on the table.

Five minutes later Marco arrived showing some serious bruising on his face and two stitches in his forehead and covered in a bandage that encircled the top of his head.

"The bastards chased us into a building and Marie got thrown down a flight of stairs."

"How is she" enquired Genevieve earnestly

"She is OK but she is still in hospital and they will not let her out until they are sure that she is not suffering from any concussion" he replied.

"Sit down my friend and I will get you a coffee" said Benoit as he passed over a crushproof packet of cigarettes across the table.

"They stormed the building that we were hiding in and then they started checking everyone and asking them to show them their hands. Those that had dirt on were assumed to have built the barricades or to have dug up pavés and treated accordingly. They have let me go with a severe caution this time" Marco said *"Probably because the CRS had already beaten the shit out of me. I fucking hate those vicious thugs."*

"I heard that they even threw gas grenades into the infirmary at the Sorbonne last night. There is no end to their savagery" someone else added.

Marco had brought a couple of the Saturday newspapers that he had bought from a kiosk in the street with him and so they spread them out across the café table and they were full of photographs of the previous day and night's rioting in what the media were now calling *'The Night of the Barricades.'* The Rue Gay-Lussac was littered with overturned and burnt out cars. Evidently sixty cars had been burnt out and one hundred and eighty-eight others were badly damaged. The scene looked like one from a war zone and not from the centre of a modern European capital city. There had been sixty barricades built in the Latin Quarter and four hundred and sixty-eight arrests.

"Read this" Marco said to Benoit pointing to the front page of the newspaper. *"The Minister of Education said of*

last night's protesters *'Ils ont ni doctrine, ni foi, nil oi- they have neither doctrine nor faith nor law.'"*

"If you ever needed a reminder of how out-of-touch this government is with reality I think that summarises it rather well."

Henri brought the coffee that Benoit had ordered for Marco to the table and Marco took out a packet of aspirins from his pocket, put two in his mouth and sipped the coffee swallowing them.

"My head aches like hell"

"I am sure it does and unfortunately it will for some time" Genevieve said sympathetically.

Not long afterwards Bruno turned up at the café carrying an old battered motorcycle helmet by its chin strap; its visor completely shattered and hanging loose.

"The revolution has arrived comrades" he exclaimed as he sat down. He was clearly animated and had obviously been up all night. His hair and beard were even shaggier than normal and his face was streaked with sweat and fire smoke.

"There must have been at least sixty barricades around the Sorbonne last night. The ancient symbol of French insurrection has been revived with the help of our working proletariat comrades."

'This was obviously the stuff of dreams for a 'revolutionary' like Bruno' thought Benoit, *'The promised combination of intellectuals and workers in a common anti-bourgeois revolutionary cause.'*

"I was on the Rue Gay-Lussac last night with Pierre" said Antoine who had just joined the group at the table. *"It was utter madness. I would not be surprised if some people got killed"* he said fiddling with the stud earring in his left ear as he spoke.

"That is the price of revolution" Bruno said interrupting Antoine as he spoke *"I was with Cohn-Bendit when he gave the order for dispersal over the radio at 5.30am. This is the*

first salvo of the heroic revolutionary struggle. It is as Trotsky said we are in a state of permanent revolution otherwise impurities form bourgeois corruption and influence will taint the revolutionary process."

Benoit muttered "mmmn" under his breath and Antoine took a large breath and then blew out his cheeks slowly. Benoit didn't doubt Bruno's zeal but he felt it was more youthful exuberance rather than genuine a considered intellectual position. Or was he just being a cynic? A product of his own privileged upbringing? He like, Genevieve and all of the others were caught up in the spirit and excitement of the moment. Who couldn't be? There was atmosphere of adrenaline and expectation. Change was in the air. Perhaps it was the time for French youth to make themselves heard and have a genuine impact on their future lives. He wasn't sure and still had an open mind. But there was something about Bruno that bothered him. Someone had once called it *'The Children of Karl Marx and Coca Cola.'* Reading *'Das Kapital'* well fed in a warm, well-furnished and safe student environment and listening to the latest music from extensive record collections on expensive state-of-the-art stereo systems bought by their parents last Christmas as a present.

Just at that moment Nancy arrived out of breath. *"I have just come from the university and there has been an announcement. The CGT and CFDT together with the FEN have all called on their members to strike and demonstrate on Monday"* she said her face flushed red with the exertion of running.

"It has started and the process cannot be stopped" said Bruno a huge smile widening on his stained face as he spoke.

Benoit said quietly *"The two most powerful union federations in France together with the major teacher's federation that is a game changer. Student revolt to industry and public services is a completely different challenge to the authorities."*

"The state in permanent revolution" Bruno said to no one in particular.

Nancy said *"I think you are right Bruno"* and then she reached into her pocket and extracted a packet of cigarette rolling papers, licked the glued portion of one and then added two others to it, one lengthways and one horizontally. Then she tore a strip of cardboard from a discarded cigarette packet on the table and made a tightly rolled coil at one end to act as a filter. Then she carefully filled the papers with a mixture of tobacco and crumbled hashish and then proceeded to carefully roll the joint and lick the length of the two papers to hold it all together. She lit it and inhaled deeply, holding the smoke inside for as long as she could before expelling it out in a long plume. She closed her eyes and sat back in her chair but not before handing round the joint to the others who all declined except Bruno who accepted it gratefully and he too took a long pull before exhaling the distinctive and slightly floral smelling smoke and then proceeded to take a second drag.

"Go steady" Nancy said opening her eyes *"Wait before you take any more because it can take time before you feel it and you don't want to overdo it as it can creep up on you."*

A half hour later, Benoit and Genevieve started to make their way back to their apartment after inviting Marco to join them for a meal later that evening if Marie was still being detained in the hospital but he had politely turned down the invitation saying:

"That really is very kind of you but if Marie is still being kept in, which I am sure that she will be, I am going to go and spend a few hours in the amphitheatre in the university this evening. It has been tuned into a giant debating centre which they are calling the *'Assemblées Générales.'*

Evidently there are up to five thousand students in there every night."

"*OK*" said Benoit "*But if you change your mind just come around anytime.*"

As it was a pleasant morning, they decided that they would walk back slowly as they were in no hurry. There were no lectures or seminars to attend, no assignment essays to complete so their time was their own. So they sauntered all the way along Rue Monge starting at Place Maubert and ending at the meeting with Avenue des Gobelins, a distance of about twelve hundred metres or so. But first as it was Saturday which meant it was market day in Place Maubert, they wandered around the market stalls piled high with fresh fruit and vegetables and stalls selling fresh bread, and fresh meat and fish. The aromas of roast chicken wafted in the air coming from a rotisserie on another stall run by a man and wife both with chubby red cheeks but with wide and engaging smiles on their faces and these smells mixed with those coming from a man with an enormous frying pan who was cooking cèpes in olive oil and garlic and serving them in pieces of toasted baguette. There was also the ubiquitous crêpe stall selling a variety of pancakes both sweet and savoury that ranged from delicious 'Nutella' chocolate to ham and cheese or spinach and mushroom. There were stalls selling cheeses from all over France which added different smells to the overall market ambience. There were stalls selling charcuterie and fresh flowers and everywhere people were talking and interacting with one another. Life goes on thought Benoit. It was a typically French scene that could have taken place in any street market in any city or town in France.

"*This is lovely*" Genevieve said as she stared around them.

"*Yes. It is*" Benoit replied "*I was just thinking that myself. This is real life. Not what we experienced last night.*

87

There is no violence here. No stench of acrid tear gas, just ordinary people engaging with one another and selecting beautifully grown and prepared products on a sunny spring morning."

"Would you like a chocolate-flavoured crêpe?" Benoit asked

"Yes I would – but only if you have a bit of its as well" she replied looking up at him and smiling.

Benoit ordered the pancake from a lady with neatly tied back greying hair and a smart pinstripe navy blue and white full-length apron tied around the waist in a large bowl. She poured the mixture from a glass jug onto the hot metal plate and patted it down with a wooden spatula. A couple of minutes later she put in a large spoon of *'Nutella'* Chocolate spread from a jar and then expertly folded the crêpe and placed it in a grease-proof paper wrapping and handed it to Genevieve. Benoit paid her the money and they walked away from the stall. Genevieve then asked him to stop a minute and she opened up the grease-proof paper wrapping at both ends and held it carefully with two hands in the middle.

"You start that end" she said *"and I will start from this end and we can meet in the middle!"*

An hour later as they were unlocking the front door of their apartment on the third floor, their neighbour, an elderly lady who lived on her own with her small pet dog opened her door and said:

"There were two men here earlier this morning asking about you. I was just coming home after walking Charles. They obviously didn't know you because they asked me what your names were. They wouldn't say what they wanted and I decided that it was all a bit strange so I didn't answer any more questions and just shut my door."

"Thank you, Madame Charpentier," said Genevieve and then she turned to Benoit and said *"What is that all about then?"*

Benoit shrugged his shoulders and pursed his lower lip and replied *"I have no idea."*

"I don't want to go out of the flat for the rest of today or tomorrow Benoit" "Genevieve had said earlier as they walked towards the end of Rue Monge. *"After everything that has happened, particularly last night I am feeling a little scared if I am being honest and I just want us to spend some time alone together."*

"That is absolutely fine with me" Benoit had replied.

"Good. Then I will cook you a lovely Duck a la Orange dish tonight"

"Fantastic!. That is one of my favourites."

"I know" Genevieve said quietly with a smile.

They had purchased some food and wine on their way home from the small *magasin alimentaire* just further down the Rue de la Clef from their apartment building. Genevieve then set about preparing them an evening meal and Benoit put an LP on the record player.

Over the rest of the weekend an uneasy peace seemed to pervade in the Latin Quarter as everyone, students, police, shopkeepers, café owners and residents took stock and looked at the wreckage still lying in the streets. Nearly all of the detainees were discharged over the weekend but four young men were taken to court and served with a two-month prison sentence each as a deterrent. Benoit and Genevieve stayed in their flat most of the weekend, listening to music and cleaning and tidying and other domestic duties that often get neglected when there is so much else going on. On Sunday evening Benoit had walked around to Marco's flat to enquire about Marie. They had a bottle of beer each and Marco told him about his experience the previous evening.

"it was generally interesting. There are some very genuine and creative thinkers in the university" he said and

then added *"But there are also some genuine lunatics out there who think they are on a different planet."*

Benoit laughed and drank the rest of his beer and left saying that they would catch up together again some time tomorrow.

Chapter Seven

It was a bright April morning in the city of Algiers when sixty-year-old Nassim Haddad opened the door of his grocery shop at 6.00am as he always did and stepped outside to roll up the shutters and start to set out the stalls for the fruit and vegetables outside of his shop. Then there it was – straight in front of him. Nassim just stared at the rusty blue roller shutter. Sprayed on it in white paint in large writing were the letters *'OAS'*. Blatant vandalism was not common in Algiers and Nassim had never seen anything like it nor did he know what it meant. So, he rolled up the shutters and set out his stalls and laid out his fruit and vegetables for sale and decided he would speak with other local traders during the day to see if they knew what it meant. He sat on an old wooden stool and stroked his black beard now streaked with grey, drank some strong sweet black coffee and smoked a hand-rolled cigarette with the strong Turkish tobacco which he particularly liked and watched as the street slowly came to life. Other shopkeepers were opening their shops and setting out their wares for sale. On one side of his shop was an 'Algerian Coffee shop' and on the other was a traditional barber's shop. Across the road and opposite was a café which always opened early in the morning and many of the tables were occupied by men drinking coffee, mostly *Qahwa Maâtra,* a fragrant coffee that is flavoured with cinnamon and vanilla and dates back to the seventeenth century. They were talking animatedly to each other and smoking. A couple of men sitting at one table and on seeing Nassim they raised their hands and shouted *"SabaaH al-khayer – good morning"* and Nassim replied the same and nodded his head.

He rolled another cigarette and lit it, taking a deep pull the end glowed bright red and he held the tobacco in his lungs longer than usual and then expelled it out in a long plume of smoke. He decided that he may not know what the graffitied letters may mean but he had a gut feeling that they could only mean one thing - trouble. For a number of years now he had been leading a double life both as the genial grocer but also as a senior commander in Algiers of The National Liberation Front (FLN) fighting for independence from France.

Nassim's shop front was not the only premises to have been daubed in paint and soon the letters 'OAS' were to be found painted on walls, fences and pavements all around Algiers and the other cities of Algeria in Oran, Contstantine and Bône. On that morning few Algerians knew even what the letters meant. However, soon *'L'Organisation de l'Armée Secrête (OAS)* – the Secret Army Organisation – was to become almost daily news on radio channels and in newspapers throughout the world. In 1961, the three-way conflict between the OAS, the Muslim Nationalists and the French army cost more than five hundred lives and injured over two thousand more. Things deteriorated the following year when in the first two months alone, nine hundred and twenty people were killed and one thousand six hundred and forty-nine were injured. Many of the casualties were innocent women and children who just happened to get in the way of OAS bombs, Muslim grenades or French army bullets. Its motto *'L'Algérie est Française et le restera'* – *often shortened to* just *'Algérie Française'* - *Algeria is French and will remain so* became ubiquitous in the French media.

Jean-Pierre Robert was twenty-three. He had joined the army soon after he had left school. He hadn't done well at school, and had a bad attendance record and found academic studies difficult. He preferred to play truant with a couple of friends and he had carried out minor acts of vandalism, criminal damage and theft which caused him to have a few brushes with the police. His mother had died when he was only ten years old and he had been raised by his father although he knew that his father regarded him as a 'burden' and a 'nuisance.' Consequently, he was sent away to a boarding school in Dijon. The school was for boys only and was run on a military-style strict disciplinarian regime. It was a harsh environment it was not surprising, therefore, that the young Jean-Pierre had learnt to fend for himself. He was not afraid to get into fights and absorbing the punishment either from a stronger opponent or more often from the teaching staff. He quickly found that many other boys liked being around him and saw him as a leader, a role that suited Jean-Pierre just fine. He was a complete academic failure and he had minimal contact with his father over the last few years, returning home for a few short breaks only. His father now had a new woman in his life and it was clear on each visit that he resented the intrusion of his son. At the end of the last school year he was preparing to leave and was having a last 'career discussion' with a sympathetic but exasperated tutor who suggested that he may well be suited to life in the army as ' *it could be the making of you,* ' so Jean-Pierre agreed and a couple of days later found himself in the local army recruitment office and he never returned home again.

Jean-Pierre took to army life straight away. He was used to the discipline and he liked the fact that he didn't really have to think for himself but just do as he was told. He made some strong friendships with others that seemed to have the same world view as himself which was one of extreme patriotism and a scathing hatred of academics, liberals and socialists whom they thought weak and damaged French culture, values and above all pride. He had travelled widely with the army throughout many African states and Indochina as the process of decolonisation accelerated in the late 1950s and into the new decade. Two comrades had served with him all of this time- Jacques Simon and Alain Moreau.

In many ways the three of them were very different but they had experienced very similar traumatic childhoods. Alain had done well at school particularly with literature as he spoke fluent English and had studied Shakespeare and other English literary classics but the death of his mother when he was only seventeen had thrown him off balance as she had been his great sponsor in terms of literature and the pursuit of an academic career. Then he had been forced to live alone with his alcoholic father who beat him regularly and told him to 'man up' and get a job in a factory to bring some money into the household. One night after a severe beating he waited till his father had fallen asleep on the sofa and then he stole all of the money that he could find in the house and made his way the next morning to the nearest French Foreign Legion recruiting centre where he was immediately given free accommodation, food and clothing.

Jacques was different again. He was physically strong and well-built. He had been good at sports at school and had chosen the army as a career from an early age. They called themselves 'the three musketeers' and during a period of about five years they forged a strong bond of friendship and comradeship which had an underlying theme. They were ashamed of what they were doing. At every twist and turn they were being used to gradually dispose of the French Colonies overseas. Jean-Pierre had been glad that he had not played any part in the embarrassing disaster of the defeat by the North

Vietnamese at Dien Bien Phu which triggered the French withdrawal from Indochina. They were the actors participating in dismantling the French Empire, a source of pride that had projected the French language and culture occupying five thousand square miles of overseas territory and a population of over one hundred and ten million people. And now it was being given away and as Alain had said one night as he quoted the two final lines from the T.S. Eliot poem *'The Hollow Men'*:

*"This is the way the world ends
Not with a bang but a whimper."*

For the last year the 'three musketeers' had found themselves in Algeria together with more than four hundred thousand other French troops. They were now part of the First Foreign Parachute Regiment (1e REP) and to them and many others like them, Algeria was where the rot had to stop. With the French government in crisis and the creation of the Fifth Republic in 1958, Charles de Gaulle had returned to power with a strengthened presidency with the significant support of the Algerian colonists and the officers of the French forces who saw in him the strong leader who would quickly crush the Muslim revolt and make Algeria firmly and permanently part of France. However, they were soon to be dismayed and disappointed by de Gaulle, when in his first pronouncement on the Algerian situation he said that he would have to study the situation before deciding on a policy for Algeria. This was a bitter blow to these supporters and to them there was only one clear policy and there was no room for any vacillation on this. However, de Gaulle reinforced his position a little later when he declared:

"Those who believed it possible to create a French Algeria have pursued an impossible dream. It is too late by history's clock for such visions."

To Jean-Pierre, Jacques, Alain and many of their colleagues this was nothing less than a complete 'betrayal' by President de Gaulle and during the night of 21st April 1961 their regiment among others under the leadership of three generals took control of all the strategic points in Algiers. The 'putsch' however, petered out in just a few days because many of the field officers and much of the rank-and-file conscripts remained loyal to de Gaulle but the OAS was born. The 'three musketeers' and their REP comrades were amongst the legionnaires leaving the city of Zéralda Sidi singing Edith Piaf's song "*Non je ne regrette rien - No, I regret nothing*" after hearing that their regiment was to be disbanded.

They soon gravitated towards the fledgling OAS together with several hundred other Foreign Legion and paratroopers from units that had been disbanded by de Gaulle after the April mutiny. They became part of about one hundred and fifty core members of the OAS in Algiers that were divided into thirty squads. Unlike other squads, however, they remained 'underground' in the sense that their identities were never known to the police and therefore they did not have to be in hiding. They did not take part in the overt activities that the OAS was carrying out in its attempt to abrogate the functions of the state like collecting taxes and threatening serious reprisals to those Europeans that paid their French taxes and over-stamping bank notes with the initials OAS. For the next year they hid in 'plain sight' engaged with other jobs but they also planned and committed a range of atrocities across the city. Bombings and targeted assassinations were carried out with a ruthless violence and efficiency and they became infamous as 'l'équipe fantôme - the ghost squad' because they moved undetected under the cover of darkness to deliver death and destruction night after night with the sole purpose of preventing an Algerian independence.

However, the following March, de Gaulle signed the Évian Accords, a treaty between France and the Provisional Government of the Algerian Republic and in a referendum in the following month, the French electorate approved the Accords, with almost 91% in favour. On 1 July, the Accords were subject to a second referendum in Algeria, where an overwhelming majority voted for independence and de Gaulle pronounced Algeria an independent country on 3rd July.

Two months later the 'three musketeers' decided to leave Algeria with complex, deep feelings of disillusionment, loss of direction and purpose. The announcement had led to a significant upsurge in violence but it soon began to dissipate as the proponents realised that their activities were futile and they would not be able to change the direction in which the country was going. *'Algérie Française'* had become a lost cause and the rallying call now fell on deaf ears.

"What has the last few years all been about? Alain said as he and Jean-Pierre leant over the deck rail as the ferry pulled out of the port of Alger on its twenty-hour journey to Marseilles.

"I really am not sure now. I was so certain about life two years ago but now" Jean-Pierre replied and he looked up from staring at the sea with the water whipped to a froth by the engines as they accelerated to move out of the port. He stared up at the whitewashed buildings of Algiers, both modern and old, that seemed to rise up out of the sea and he thought of the last two years they had all spent together. Initially life was simple, he followed orders in the army, there was a reason why the French were in Algeria but all that changed. It became dangerous to wander around the labyrinthine narrow streets of the casbah. Every spice seller or merchant was a potential terrorist, every muted

conversation could be conspiratorial, every push and shove could mean a knife in the back. Then to all intents and purposes he and his friends had become 'terrorists' themselves at least in the eyes of the state. For him though, they had been on the side of the morally just, counter-revolutionaries to prevent the self-determination for Algerians, which would have meant the domination of the European minority by the Muslim majority. There was, however, no denying it, they had committed some serious atrocities and killed and mutilated many people and now it appeared to him that it had all been for nothing and all they had left was their guilt and some nightmarish memories.

At that moment Jacques arrived stirring Jean-Pierre out of his reverie. He was carrying three bottles of cold beer which he handed round, raised a bottle to his lips and said:
"Tous pour un"
And the others dutifully replied *"Et un pour tous"*
They drank the beers in silence as they watched the port slip further and further into the distance until it had slipped below the horizon and all they could see was the Mediterranean Sea.
Five minutes later Alain broke the silence by saying:
"Until now I, like you, have thought that de Gaulle was a 'traitor' and that he had 'betrayed' the French interests in Algeria but now maybe I feel that times are changing not just in France but across the western world. He may not be perfect and he may be a pragmatist but perhaps there is an unstoppable momentum for change and perhaps he is the best bulwark against the unacceptable face of this modernistic change like creeping Communism and Socialism, increased immigration and the breakdown of law and order and respect for what our country stands for.
"
"What do you mean exactly?" said Jacques

"Well look at the trade unions in France and their increasing influence over people's lives and their constant threat to paralyse the workings of the government and the state. Did you know that the Confédération Générale du Travail (CGT) is in bed with the French Communist Party and I wonder where their true allegiance lies? Also, I have heard that the Confèdèration Française Democratique du Travail (CFDT) is planning to drop the word 'Christian' from its title and also all reference in its statutes and programme to the Catholic church."

"You are right Alain. I do not regret what we have done. I firmly believe it was in the best interests of our country and the tricoleur and all that it represents." Jacques replied.

A few hours later as they sat eating Moules Marinère in the café on the ferry, Jean-Pierre dipped a piece of baguette that he had torn off into the hot liquor and said:

"I have been thinking. We have served in the armed forces of our country for a number of years. Our military records are clean. Yes, we were part of the 1 RER that was disbanded but so were many others and we were never implicated of any association with insurrection or membership of the OAS. I have heard that the Police are recruiting ex-servicemen and in particular the CRS and I think that we may fit in there very well. It would provide us with regular and secure employment because I now want to get somewhere to live. I have had enough of moving from place to place with just the things in my kit bag"

Jacques and Alain both nodded in agreement and then Jacques said:

"I am proud of being French. I am proud of our history, traditions and culture which I am passionate about preserving. I do not want to see all that has been achieved be discarded by misguided left-wing socialists, so called modernisers and radicals."

"I think that we have just made a collective decision" Alain added.

Jean-Pierre smiled and took the bottle of Muscadet white wine and topped up their three glasses and raised his in a toast:

"Vive La France et nous"

They all drank the wine in one swallow and each of them knew that in that moment the special bond that had grown over the years between them would never be broken.

Chapter Eight

It was Sunday morning 12th May and Benoit and Genevieve had decided to take a walk back to the scene of the huge demonstration and rioting that had taken place on Friday. They had left their apartment on Rue de la Clef and crossed the Rue Monge and threaded their way a number of small streets until they came on to Rue Claude Bernard and then to the end of Rue Gay-Lussac which took them about twenty minutes or so. As they wandered slowly down the Rue Gay-Lussac it was clear to them that it still carried all the scars of *the 'night of the barricades.'* Burnt out cars littered the pavements, just blackened shells with all the paint burnt away. Most of the pavé cobble stones had been cleared from the road and now lay in huge piles either side of it. The acrid smell of tear gas still seemed to be present in the air even all this time after the event. People were casually walking up and down the street still quite nor believing what had taken place here. These were ordinary Parisians from all over the city who had come to see the scene for themselves having been horrified at what they had heard on the radio or seen in the newspapers. They huddled in small groups talking with other visitors and the residents of the Rue Gay-Lussac itself who were anxious to tell them about their own experiences and how they had witnessed the vicious assaults by the CRS riot police not just on the student demonstrators but on innocent bystanders, residents and anybody who just happened to be in the wrong place at the wrong time.

Benoit and Genevieve carried on walking up the Rue Gay-Lussac and about half way up at a crossroads they could see that a building site had had its wire perimeter fence pulled down in several places. This was where a lot of the material had come from for the barricades – large metal drums, wooden planks and steel girders and stone blocks. Anything that could be taken away and used had been done so.

"This is like the aftermath of a war zone" Genevieve said *"We were very lucky to escape when we did. Things could have turned out very differently if that kind lady concierge had not helped us just at the right time."*

"Yes I know" replied Benoit *"Come on I have seen enough. Let's go for a coffee and breakfast at Chez Henri's"*

They turned right at the intersection onto Rue St. Jacques and then turned right again into Rue des Écoles. The streets were littered with broken street furniture and torn up paves, broken shop windows and graffiti was sprayed everywhere. The biggest surprise of all though however, was when they entered Place Maubert. They just could not believe what they were seeing. The normal tranquil Place with its lively street market on three days of the week was a total mess at the point where it joined up with Boulevard St. Germain; outside the large café Tabac St. Germain; advertising itself as a *'Tableterie', 'Papeterie' and 'Librarie.'* A large barricade had been built across the street made up of pieces of iron railings and iron fencing, old handcarts, rubbish bins and overturned cars and vans. There were holes all over the Boulevard where pavés had been levered up from the street and there were piles of them everywhere lying with improvised tools such as broken street signs and pieces of scaffolding poling.

"What a mess. I can't believe that it happened here too." Genevieve exclaimed.

They walked back into the Place and towards the café and were relieved to see that it had not been damaged apart from having its outside tables and chairs scattered around which Henri was now collecting and setting upright and some of the white china ash trays with the Martini logo on them printed on the three sides, lay broken on the cobblestones.

"I will go inside and get a brush and help you clear up" Benoit said

"Thank you mon ami"

Benoit walked inside the café and ordered two coffees and two croissants from Veronique who was arguing with her elderly mother in the kitchen who had been complaining about hooligans and disrespect for society and the country. As he walked back out of the café carrying a large broom, he noticed that the windows of the café had been plastered with two posters stuck up on an angle in haste. There was the one he had seen many times around Paris with the CRS officer swinging a baton above his head and the letters 'SS' emblazoned on his riot shield but there was also one that he had not seen before, it was a black shadow of de Gaulle holding his hand over the mouth of a discontented student with the slogan:

'Sois Jeune et Tais Toi – be young and shut up.'

Benoit spent the next half hour sweeping up any debris around the café and emptying it into a bin whilst Genevieve had helped Henri re-set up the table and she had just finished wiping them all down when Veronique appeared with the coffees and the croissants and some strawberry jam and butter.

"It is free for you today and merci" she said

They sat for a while and then Antoine and Nancy showed up and started discussing the huge protest that had been planned for the morning.

"I cannot believe the mess on the other side of the Place "stated Nancy *"I hadn't realised that the rioting had reached here."*

"It reached out all over the Latin Quarter" replied Benoit *"The police thugs were on the rampage all night and into the early hours of Saturday morning. They were like packs of wolves hunting down their prey."*

"This wasn't the maintenance of law and order. This was simple and straightforward retribution and the police dishing out their own form of justice." Antoine interjected

"How can this behaviour be sanctioned by the government?" quizzed Genevieve

"It cannot be. It is completely illegitimate but the President thinks that he is a law unto himself."

"It is time for him to go" said Benoit *"We need change, a more modern democratic government and not this blatant benign dictatorship presented as paternalistic governance."* Benoit added *"We will see you tomorrow"* and he got up from the table stretched out his hand to Genevieve and the two of them walked off hand in hand across the Place and towards the Mètro.

The demonstration the next day on Monday 13th May was once again absolutely enormous. On this occasion, eight hundred thousand people had been energised and taken to the streets of Paris. The great swathe of chanting, placard carrying, banner waving humanity marched from the staging point at Place Denfert-Rochereau. Benoit, Genevieve and Marco had joined the march but Marco had left after an hour saying that he was going to visit Marie and hoped that he would be able to take her home from the hospital. They walked along side people from all types of associations and ways of life who had all joined the march at various other staging points along the route.

Benoit had instinctively brought his cine camera with him only to discover later that he still hadn't changed the film which had run out when he had been filming at the protest on the previous Friday so he left it in the back pack. As they marched in the middle of the throng of people Benoit recollected some of the scenes he had witnessed over the last few days. Maybe there was something in what Bruno had been claiming in the café the other day. He had witnessed dozens of local residents of the Latin Quarter, who, completely unresentful of their own discomfort, had dropped sandwiches to the students trapped behind their barricades below and had poured buckets of water from their windows and balconies to dilute the saturating tear gas. In response the CRS had fired gas grenades indiscriminately and deliberately through apartment windows and into crowded cafés that were sheltering the students.

At the front of the march with their arms around each other's shoulders were the student leaders, Alain Geismar, Jaques Sauvageot and Daniel Cohn-Bendit. Trade Union leaders and any politicians were kept further back. No one was under any disillusion that it was the student movement that had managed to galvanise the various interests together and mobilise the hordes on to the streets of Paris. They were to be taken seriously; no longer could they be dismissed as a 'lunatic fringe.' Of the many slogans that were shouted and chanted that day along with the demands for the resignation of Prime Minister Pompidou or the denouncement of President de Gaulle and his use of the authoritarian forces of the state, one was prevalent; *'We are all German Jews.'* This was in direct response to the right-wing press who were criticizing Cohn-Bendit for his German nationality in veiled anti-semitic terms and demanding his expulsion from France.

Near the top of the Boulevard St Michel, Genevieve decided to rest for a while and climbed on top of a wall that was bordering the Jardin de Luxembourg where they just sat and watched for about an hour as row after row of demonstrators marched past; thirty or more abreast. Benoit could see that banners of every kind, size, colour and shape were being carried with both political and non-political slogans. Some banners were covered in vivid symbolism. It seemed to both of them that people from all parts of society, every trade and every workplace were represented. Benoit noted one group of hospital workers all wearing white coats who were carrying a large white banner with red lettering on it which said *'où sont les blessés disparus'* – *'where are the missing injured?'*

They continued to watch in silence and with a sense of awe as a great stream of humanity marched past them. The sun was shining and there wasn't a car or bus in sight and today the streets of Paris belonged to the demonstrators.

An hour or so later, as they were now separated from their friends, they re-joined the march all the way up the Champs-Élysées and on to the Arc de Triomphe. It was a strange and eerie feeling as they crossed over intersections in the road where the traffic lights were still working but for once there was no traffic to control except human traffic which today was not going to pay any attention to a red light. They stood and listened to the speeches at the rally at the end of the march and then feeling exhausted, they decided to make their way back to their apartment. They entered the Métro at Étoile station which was located under the Arc de Triomphe and made their way to the platform for line 6 for the four stops to Châtelet where they would change to Line 4 to Odéon and then change again to Line 10 to Place Monge. Étoile station was busy and packed with demonstrators, commuters, tourists and Parisians all pushing and shoving and remonstrating with one another.

As they edged their way along the crowded platform to where there was more space at the end, Benoit felt a huge tug on his camera strap but he pulled back hard and it came free and he clutched it tight to his chest. He instinctively turned around but his gaze was met by a seething crowd and a sea of faces but he was unable to focus on anyone who was looking directly at him at all. He wrapped the leather strap a few turns around his wrist for a better grip and walked on; not thinking any more of it. Thefts on the Métro were common particularly, pickpocketing which was fast becoming an epidemic.

As the train entered the packed platform the crowd surged towards the doors. Benoit leapt on the train and turned to Genevieve to help her board but he saw that someone had tugged her backwards so he lent forward and grabbed her by both arms and pulled her on to the train just as the doors closed and the train started to pull out of the platform.

"What happened there" he said as they stood in the crowded carriage.

"I am not sure just as I went forward someone grabbed me by the shoulder hard and tried to pull me backwards through the crowd."

"Because they wanted to get in front of you?"

"I am not sure. It just happened so fast."

Benoit just looked at her with a face full of concern and then embraced her tightly.

As Benoit opened the front door of their flat Genevieve said *"Just wait here a minute"* and she knocked on the door of the apartment next door. There was an immediate sound of yapping of a small dog and Madame Charpentier opened the door on a chain.

"Oh it's you dear" she said

"Sorry to bother you Madame but I was just wondering if you had seen those two people who were asking after us yesterday again today?"

"No dear I haven't" she said

"OK thank you" and the door closed and Genevieve heard her chastising the dog for being so noisy.

A couple of hours later Marco came around to the flat. *'Strange Days' by The Doors* was playing quietly on the record player in the corner of the room and the lava lamp now warm, was throwing out vivid colours of red and blue which mixed with the flickering candlelight from the two candles in the empty wine bottles that were on the table.

"Marie is going to be released from the hospital tomorrow" he said as he sat on the sofa and lit a cigarette.

"That's good news" Genevieve replied

"Yes, it is. She will have to take it easy for a while, she is covered in bruises and was lucky that she didn't break any bones but it was the concussion that they were most worried about, I fucking hate those CRS bastards they just ran into the building and chased us up the stairs throwing her down behind them and cornering me and another student. They then bashed us on the head with a baton and then carried on going after the others further up the stairs. They just don' give a shit. All they want to do is to use the maximum amount of violence they can against unarmed students."

"We have witnessed similar events" said Genevieve.

"I don't know where all of this is going" said Marco *"But it is getting bigger and bigger all the time. Everywhere you go in Paris everyone is debating and discussing the events – on the Mètro, in the street, in bars and in cafés. It is moving way beyond student grievances that started in the Sorbonne. Everyone is suddenly talking about politics, society, government and transformation. By the way I love those photographs"* Marco said pointing at the gallery on the wall,

"Particularly the Metro train coming into the station in slow motion. You really are very good you know Benoit"

"I don't know where this is going either" said Benoit *"Or where it might end. We are most certainly living through some exciting but dangerous times. We will have to see – just take care and look after Marie."*

After they had eaten a simple supper of semi-fresh bread, cheese and paté and drunk the best part of two bottles of red wine, Marco said that he had to leave because he had to tidy their place up before Marie came home the following day.

Marco had taken the small cage lift up to third floor pulling the grille tightly closed before it ascended but he decided to walk down the six flights of stairs to the entrance lobby and then he opened the door into the street. As he exited the building, he saw a man opposite leaning against the wall with his hands thrust deep into the pockets of a black leather jacket that was buttoned up to the collar and wearing dark glasses. He was staring straight up at the third-floor window of Benoit and Genevieve's flat which he had just left. When he saw Marco, he looked away immediately, turned up the collar of his jacket and with his hands still shoved into the pockets, started to casually saunter down the street.

The next few days were to see the worst rioting that Paris had witnessed since the Algerian disorders a few years earlier. Both girls and boys masked their faces with handkerchiefs to protect themselves against the clouds of tear gas and they set fire to cars, set up cobble stone barricades and attacked the police with a ferocity of pent up frustration and anger. The main weapon on the demonstrator's side was the pavé. The French cobble stone that weighed about three pounds and which could be easily prized up from the roadway by the determined protesters. Barricades of hundreds of pavés, many at least six feet tall, were erected incredibly quickly by the protesters who had formed human chains which provided almost limitless quantities of ammunition. When used as projectiles they caused some serious injuries to the police particularly when they were received full in the face or chest. These injuries just caused the cycle of violence to escalate with more ferocious baton charges, gas grenades and water cannon which could knock the protesters down and toss them several yards across the street such was its force. This in turn caused the protesters to answer with dozens of hurled petrol bombs or Molotov cocktails as Benoit discovered that they were called. Over coffee at chez Henri, Bruno had told him one morning that the name originated from the Second World War. Vyacheslav Mikhailovich Molotov was the Soviet Foreign Minister. During the early part of the war Finland had refused to surrender some land to the Soviets who then invaded. The poorly-equipped Finns faced Red Army tanks and borrowed an improvised incendiary device from the Spanish Civil War. Like those now being used by the protesters in Paris, these were crude incendiary devices made out of glass bottles filled with petrol and with a wick soaked in alcohol. When the bottle smashed against its target on impact a cloud of fuel droplets and vapour was ignited by the attached wick causing an immediate fireball followed by spreading flames as the remainder of the fuel was consumed.

The situation had undoubtedly started to spiral out of control and the unrest had changed fundamentally in character and started to take on the form of a mass insurrection and civil disorder. Discontent had started to spread out from Paris to other cities in France and support from the public was still very largely sympathetic resenting the show of force by the authorities and the seemingly inept government actions to redress some of the legitimate concerns of the protesters.

Chapter Nine

It was a bright August morning a year after Jean-Pierre and his two comrades had returned from Algeria and the sky was a shade of clear blue as he stepped out of his apartment in the city of Nancy, a large city located in the north east of France in the department of Meurthe-et-Moselle of the Lorraine region. A gleaming Bordeaux-coloured 1936 Citroen Traction Avant with black wings and white ribbons tied from the windscreen to the top of the radiator grille came to a halt at the side of the road. Jean-Pierre walked towards the car with two other men, one on either side of him, all dressed in matching dark blue suits, white shirts and yellow silk cravats.

'*Bonjour*' the driver said cheerily as he got out of the car wearing an immaculate light grey suit and hat and opened the rear door for Jean-Pierre and one of the other men to get in and the third man, who was larger than the other two, sat in the front passenger seat.

The driver started the thirty-six bhp engine and pulled gently away from the kerb. Jean-Pierre sat back in the red leather rear bench seat and looked out of the window as the car purred gracefully through the traffic on its way to l'*Eglise des Cordeliers* situated in the old town of Nancy.

Jacques reached into the left inside pocket of his jacket and pulled out an elegant antique silver hip flask which he had earlier filled with Cognac. It was Delamain. Undoubtedly his favourite, one of the oldest Cognac producers founded in 1762 and was widely regarded as being the benchmark against which other Cognacs are measured. Jacques turned around and passed the bottle to Jean-Pierre who took a large gulp before handing to Alain beside him who did the same. Jacques took the flask back and took a gulp saying:

"Tous pour un"

before screwing the top back in place and returning it to his inside pocket.

"There is enough for one more large gulp each before we enter the church" he exclaimed.

"Très bon" replied Jean-Pierre and he settled back in the seat once again and stared out of the window lost in his thoughts.

"Are you having second thoughts mon ami?" Alain said turning towards Jean-Pierre beside him.

"Non. Not at all."

"She is a beautiful lady. You are a lucky man."

"Yes I know."

"Remember the quote from Victor Hugo mon ami. La vie est une fleur, l'amour en est le miel'- Life is the flower of which love is the honey"

Jean-Pirere had met Camille a few months after returning back to France from Algeria. She had a regular cabaret spot singing in a nightclub called *'Le Chat Noir'* that he had started to attend on frequent basis. She had a wonderful melodic voice that seemed to float across the smokey atmosphere of the club with just the small lights on each table to illuminate the environment. It was an enchanting ambience that had started to mesmorise Jean-Pierre. He wasn't a particular music afficionado but the way she sang in a smokey bluesy voice in the unique zouk style which was characterized by a slow, soft and sexual rhythm, provided him with an inner peace that he had not known before. He discovered that her name was Camille and that she was from the French island of Guadeloupe in the Caribbean and had moved to France with her family about five years ago when her father had been offered employment in the country.

This one particular Saturday night he had been sitting listening to her and sipping beer and smoking. She was singing a few songs that he had not heard before but they all had a similar theme with lyrics all about love and sentimental issues. She was wearing a tight-fitting long white dress which accentuated her shapely figure that was pulled in at the waist. Her hair was a deep brown set in long ringlets and large gold loop earrings hung from her ears and moved and caught the light as he tilted her head with the microphone in her hand. When she had finished her set, she stood for a moment to receive the applause and disappeared back stage. Jean-Pierre got up from his table just before another singer appeared on the small stage and made his way across the club in between tables till he arrived at the stage door at the rear. He knew the doorman, whose name was Aufrey. He was a very large black man from the former French colony of Senegal in West Africa which had gained independence from France about three years ago. Jean-Pierre had drunk some beers with him in the club when he was not on duty and shared his experiences of being stationed in Dakar with the French army for nine months in 1959.

"Can I talk to Camille for a few minutes please Aufrey?"

"You know that no one is allowed back stage monsieur but as it is you Jean-Pierre I can give you five minutes" and he opened the door and then closed it again quickly after Jean-Pierre had gone through.

Jean-Pierre walked along the dimly lit corridor and stopped outside a door which had a paper sign taped to the door which said simply *'Camille.'* As Camille was a resident artist Jean-Pierre thought it a reasonable assumption that she would have her own dressing room. He knocked gently on the door and waited. A few moments later it opened slightly and Camille showed her face in the opening.

"Can I help you?" monsieur?

"Can I talk to you for a moment?"

"You are not allowed back stage. How did you get here? I will call the security"

"No please don't do that mademoiselle. I just want to talk to you for two minutes. "Can I come in?"

Camille recognised Jean-Pierre as a regular attender at the club and she had noticed how he had often stared at her and secretly she had been quite flattered by the silent attentions of a young, handsome and fit-looking man.

"You can come in for two minutes but if you misbehave, I will call for security"

"I just wanted you to know that I thought the songs that you sung tonight were wonderful and so sentimental and I hope that you don't mind me saying so but you also look the most beautiful woman that I have seen you and I have watched you perform here many times."

"Thank you, monsieur. That is very kind of you. I have seen you in the audience many times too."

Jean-Pierre took a deep breath and decided to bite the bullet and said:

"My name is Jean-Pierre and I would be really flattered if you would agree to have dinner with me next week when it is your evening off duty."

Camille looked at him for a while and said nothing. Jean-Pierre could feel his heart beating faster as she looked straight into his face with the most beautiful brown eyes that he had ever seen:

"That would be very nice Jean-Pierre." She said softly.

They had remained married for four years and Camille had given birth to a baby boy called Jean-Baptiste and

Jean-Pierre had thrown himself into his job with the CRS which he had joined with his two old friends six months after returning from Algeria. They had all been welcomed because they had exemplary military records and a wide range of experiences. They had requested that they would like to join the same company but there was only one that was able to accommodate their wishes. This was one of the 'general service' companies which together with the mobile gendarmerie, constituted a highly mobile reserve force for the government. Their purpose was fourfold. To provide security during large public events and mass gatherings. To patrol and secure specific areas. To maintain law and order during demonstrations and full riot control; and to reinforce local police forces in their general security operations. The three of them were all based in barracks near Nancy but, unlike the gendarmes, they were able to live at home when not seconded to a mission which could take them anywhere in the country.

Then one Sunday morning in July 1967 Jean-Pierre had awoken in bed, having slept in till nearly lunchtime because he had been drinking heavily till late the night before. He walked out of the bedroom in their apartment and called *'Camille'* but there was no reply. He walked into the bathroom and opened the cabinet and found a packet of aspirin and put two in his mouth and washed them down with a gulp of water from the tap. He wandered into the kitchen area and there were the remains of breakfast that Camille and Jean-Baptiste must have shared earlier. Jean-Pierre felt the coffee pot and it was stone cold so it must have been a few hours ago. Then he saw it. It was propped up against the milk jug. A handwritten letter in Camille's handwriting. Jean-Pierre picked it up and read it quickly.

Mon Cher Jean-Pierre.

I am writing this to you this morning because I have been thinking of doing so for a while now. I have loved you and I probably still do and I am so grateful for the life of Jean-Baptiste but it is because of him that I have come to this decision.

I cannot tolerate your violent temper and huge mood swings any more particularly when you have been drinking. I am just not prepared to tolerate the physical and verbal abuse that you inflict on me on a regular basis any more. Jean-Baptiste needs a better role model if he is to grow up in the right way and be successful in this fast-changing modern world.

Au Revoir

Camille. X

Jean-Pierre slumped down on to one of the chairs and rested his elbows on the table and covered his head with his hands and wept.

He had decided not to try and find Camille and persuade her to return to him for two reasons. Firstly, he knew that there were many places that she could just 'disappear' in her community all over France and he would never be able to penetrate that community if she did not want it. And secondly, he didn't want to because deep down he knew she was right which had made it all the more painful to bear.

It was just over nine months later, that the 'three musketeers' were travelling in a bus back to their accommodation after spending the whole of the night of Friday 10th May and much of the following Saturday on the streets of the French capital. They were exhausted and preoccupied by something that had happened but they would have to deal with that problem tomorrow. In addition, there was an air of disillusionment among them and the rest of their colleagues on the bus. They had heard on the radio that Georges Pompidou, the Prime Minister, had returned to Paris that morning and that barely three hours after his arrival, he had addressed the nation and single-handedly reversed the current government policy. He announced that the Sorbonne would be reopened and that the Court of Appeal would pronounce on the jailed students.

"It would seem my friends that once again we have been used and then betrayed by our government" Jean-Pierre said to his friends

"He has hung us out to dry" replied Jacques *"He has left us out on a limb in the chill wind of public hostility."*

Just at that moment one of the senior members of the CRS on the bus sensing the mood, stood up at the front of the bus and said through a microphone like a tour operator:

"Comrades do not be dismayed. You are the true patriots not like our current government which is made up of politicians who bend and twist with the wind. They sent us out to not only restore law and order but to protect the values of our country and now only for them to declare that the actions of those we were to oppose were entirely justified. It would seem that the authorities have accepted the foreign flags that they fly now as the symbols of the French university. This will not happen and I have every confidence that our President will restore the natural order of things so keep your heads held high."

"So once again, it would seem that we have to have faith in de Gaulle" Alain said wearily to no one in particular.

Chapter Ten

The streets were remarkably calm that Tuesday morning as Benoit and Genevieve left their flat and walked to the Métro Station at Place Monge. Benoit had instinctively taken his cine camera with him but once again forgetting that he still hadn't changed the film that he had used up four days earlier so once again he left it in the back pack. The shops were open, people were going about their normal daily business, commuting to work, shopping or just sitting at café tables talking, eating and drinking. The streets had been swept and cleaned overnight and it seemed that the only hangover from the huge demonstration the day before was that there were a lot of fresh posters plastered to walls, kiosks and any flat surfaces available. Yvette and her comrades at the *Atelier Populaire* must have been busy last night Benoit thought to himself. One particularly caught his eye that had been plastered to the wall by the entrance to the Métro station, it was a drawing of a riot policeman swinging a baton above his head and with the letters '*SS*' emblazoned on his riot shield. This particular poster seemed to be everywhere in Paris.

He thought back to the conversation that he had had with Thomas and Antoine a few days ago at Chez Henri when Thomas had outlined the dangers of the alienation of the police by the wider society and he realised that this vicious circle that he had described was already taking place. Neither he nor Genevieve had been aware of a man in a black leather jacket smoking and reading a newspaper leaning against a wall twenty metres behind them and as they descended into the Métro station he folded up the paper and walked briskly back the way they had just come.

The platform at Line 7 was quiet and they made the journey of just one stop to Jussieu and then changed on to Line C for the ongoing one stop and alighted the train at Maubert Mutualité station and walked into the Place Maubert and approached a table outside Chez Henri's where Antoine was sitting on his own with a Café Crème and smoking a Disque Bleu cigarette. They could have walked as it usually only took ten minutes or so but they both felt tired this morning after the energy they had expended the day before on the demonstration.

"Bonjour" Antoine said as they sat down

"Bonjour" they replied at the same time

"Were you at the demonstration yesterday" Antoine enquired

"Yes we were. It was amazing. So many people. This whole situation is escalating at a rapid pace. No one could have predicted this would happen or where it will all end up"

"I agree. I do not know where this will end. The workers are getting very agitated now and lots of factories and places of work are being occupied across France."

Benoit looked up and attracted Henri's attention as he was serving at another table. Henri walked over and took his order of two Café Crèmes and a croissant and a pain au chocolat for Genevieve.

"Do you want another cup of coffee Antoine?" Benoit enquired

"No I am OK thank you" he replied.

Five minutes later a taxi pulled up at the kerb on the Boulevard St. Germain and Benoit saw Marco and Marie get out. They crossed the road into the Place and approached the table. Benoit got up and shook Marco's hand firmly whilst Genevieve stood and embraced Marie warmly and Antoine nodded at Marco. Marie looked pale and wan with dark rims under her eyes and her face was covered in purple bruising.

"My God look at you" Genevieve exclaimed *"What have they done to you."*

Marie sat down and the tears just rolled down her cheeks and she buried her face into Genevieve's shoulder.

Benoit walked with Marco into the café

"Is she OK?" he asked his friend earnestly.

"Yes she is very badly shaken up and needs to rest for a few days and take things quietly because concussion can be a nasty business. What kind of thug could do this to a defenceless woman?"

"It is beyond belief" Benoit replied *"The riot police are completely out of all control. They are using arbitrary and indiscriminate force which is completely out of all proportion to the disorder that they are supposed to be monitoring. We are living in very strange times indeed I am very worried about where this may all end up."*

When they got back outside, Bruno had appeared and was telling everyone about how incredible it had been yesterday and how he had been right at the front of the march just behind the student leaders.

"No one can deny that it is the student movement that is galvanising all the various elements of dissent into one enormous and unstoppable momentum. We will go down in history" he exclaimed before recognising some other students he had seen yesterday sitting at another table. They had just returned from the university and were talking animatedly about what they had all seen and witnessed.

Unknown to Benoit, early in the morning the day before, the line of CRS police guarding the entrance to the Sorbonne were discreetly withdrawn. The students moved in, first in small groups, then in hundreds and then later in thousands as the word spread rapidly. Some left the march to return and within a few hours it had been completely reoccupied. The tricolour flags that had been flying were hauled down and replaced with a myriad of black and red flags of all shapes and sizes. Over the next few days, the paved inner courtyard of the Sorbonne became a cauldron of far left and revolutionary politics. Huge portrait posters appeared on the internal walls: Marx, Lenin, Trotsky, Mao, Castro and Guevara. Dozens of stalls sprang up loaded with all kinds of socialist and far left literature. Leaflets and pamphlets by anarchists, Stalinists, Maoists, Trotskyists could all be found there. The courtyard of the Sorbonne had become a huge revolutionary depository for literature that hitherto had only circulated 'underground' or in closed circles. Everywhere there were groups of people engaged in heated discussions about the CRS riot police, the barricades and what would happen over the next few days and weeks.

This physical reoccupation of the Sorbonne by the students was followed by a mushrooming of intellectual activities. Everything was up for debate, there were no restrictions and to emphasise this point numerous copies of one of the posters produced by *the Atelier Populaire* were plastered on the walls saying *' l'est interdit d'interdire' – it is forbidden to forbid.'*

Day and night all the lecture theatres were packed to capacity and a continuous stream of passionate debates took place and soon a noticeboard appeared near the front entrance to the university that indicated what topics were being discussed and where the debates were taking place and at what time. There was an order to the proceedings.

"We are in complete control" Bruno announced to the group.

"Yes we are. We have taken the moral high ground and demonstrated that real academics is about debate and creativism and not about having to swallow pre-packaged

rubbish that is intended to manipulate and control" added another.

Benoit, Genevieve, Marco and Marie sat outside at one of the café tables. Whilst Marie was talking in depth to Genevieve about her experiences that she had endured, Benoit was half-listening to what was being said by the crowd at Bruno's table. After about half an hour or so, Marco said that he was taking Marie home and that he would catch up with them all in a couple of days. Not long after Benoit turned to Genevieve and said:

"Let's go Gennie. We need to get some food because there is nothing in the apartment but first of all I think we should go and see what is happening at the Sorbonne. I have been listening to what Bruno and some of the others have been saying

"But the university has been closed"

"No it was re-opened quietly yesterday morning and the police have withdrawn."

"Really! OK let's go"

After walking around the courtyard in the Sorbonne for half an hour and chatting to a few people they knew they left the courtyard and walked back to the Metro station at Cluny La Sorbonne and made the return journey to Rue de la Clef calling in at the local shop just down the street before they entered the building and took the lift up to the third floor.

"Madame Charpentier will be glad that they have fixed the lift" he said casually as he unlocked the door to the apartment. Then he just stood in the doorway and froze.

"What is it?" Genevieve said.

"Oh my God. What a hell of a mess. What on earth has happened here?" and he walked slowly through the door followed by Genevieve who just shrieked and then put her hand to her mouth before bursting out crying. Benoit closed

the door quietly and surveyed the scene before him. There was glass all over the floor from the broken photograph frames that had contained his 'life in contrast' collection and records and books were strewn everywhere across the room. The sofa had been turned upside down and had been slit open with a knife and much of the stuffing had been pulled out and thrown around. The lava lamp, which had been the much-treasured flat-warming present from Marco and Marie, was smashed and its contents had leaked out on to the carpet. Walking through into the galley kitchen he could see that all the cupboards and drawers had been ransacked. There were bottles and jars all over the floor, some broken with their contents spilled out into a multi-coloured sticky mess which he tried to avoid stepping in. Pots and pans had been taken out of cupboards and then thrown on the floor. Genevieve walked up behind him and as he turned around, she said:

"Why? We have nothing of any value to steal? Why cause this much mess and damage?

"I don't know" Benoit replied *"What is puzzling me is that the front door was locked and there was no sign of damage or a break-in"* He took the cine camera off that had been around his neck and hung it by the strap on the back of the door.

"What does that mean?" Genevieve sobbed

"It would seem to indicate that this was the work of a professional burglar but as you say there was nothing of any value here. It just doesn't make any sense."

They walked into the bedroom and were met with the same scene of carnage. All the drawers had been pulled out and their contents emptied on to the floor. The bed had been stripped and the mattress was on its side against the wall. All their clothes had been pulled out of the wardrobe and just strewn around the room.

Genevieve started to cry once again and said:

"I feel completely dirty and violated. Someone has been through all my things. My underwear and everything. How could they?

Benoit just turned around and went back into the lounge and set the sofa back on its feet and sat on what remained of the cushioned surface. He reached inside his pocket and took out a cigarette and lit it with his lighter and just sat there in silence. After a while he realised that Genevieve had come back into the room and was sitting on the floor with her back to the wall and with her head bowed. The torn slow-motion photograph of the Métro train that Benoit had taken was in her hands.

"How could anyone do this to our special place Gennie?" he said quietly and moved off the sofa to sit down beside her and he kissed her gently on the cheek and she leaned into him and he felt warm her warm tears on his face.

Suddenly he got up and said *"My dark room"* and he raced to the hatch that opened into the small attic space and climbed up. Amazingly everything was exactly as he had left it and it would appear that the burglar had either not discovered the space or had overlooked it in the haste of the intrusion.

"Gennie could you make us a cup of coffee each and I will pack an overnight bag for each of us as I think we should find a cheap hotel to stay in tonight so that we can then clear up tomorrow. We clearly cannot go and disturb Marco and Marie as she will need quiet and rest. I will also contact the police then. There is no point now. If whoever did this could open and close a locked door without damaging it, they would have been clever enough to wear gloves so I doubt that there will be any fingerprints. We will get something to eat and then have an early night and come back here first thing in the morning and clear up. After we have had the coffee, could you just go and see Madame Charpentier and see if she saw or heard anything?"

Five minutes later Genevieve left the flat and was back soon after and said:

"No, she didn't see anything but about two hours ago she heard a lot of banging and the noise of things being thrown around and she just thought that we were having a row. She said that she hoped that she never saw the men who had come previously, again because they were rough and rude"

"Ok" Benoit said *"Let's grab our things and go. There are a number of cheap hotels near the north of the city"* and he took the cine camera from the door and put it in his bag.

They made their way back to the Place Monge Métro station and descended down and after consulting the Métro map made their way down to the platform. Just as the next train was pulling into the platform two men in black leather jackets started to run towards them from the other end of the platform shouting at them to stop but the doors started to close and they could not reach them in time but to Benoit's dismay he saw them get into a carriage further down the train.

"Who were those men and what did they want with us" Genevieve said with concern

"I don't know but I think we should get off soon and change trains"

"Why?" she replied

"Because they got on a carriage on this train just as the doors were closing further down the train"

As the train pulled into the station at Châtelet, a station where many lines intersected, Benoit already had his hand on the door handle as soon as the train started to slow down and he waited impatiently for the hiss of the unlocking mechanism so he could flick it open the minute it was released. They got out of the train and ran along the platform clutching their overnight bags and followed the way to Line D. Fortunately a train was just arriving so they jumped on and stared out desperately hoping that the doors would close quickly. As the train started to pull out of the platform, they saw the two men arrive obviously out of breath from running but they had been just a few seconds too late.

"They were there again" said Genevieve *"They are following us but why?"*

"I wish I knew" replied Benoit with genuine concern in his voice.

They stayed on the train until it arrived at the Gare du Nord where they got out but instinctively turned to watch if they were being followed as they left the platform.

"I can't see them" Genevieve said breathlessly

"Good. Let's get out of here fast" replied Benoit.

An hour later they were sitting outside a café with Benoit sipping at his second glass of beer, 1664, his favourite and Genevieve was drinking a large glass of red wine. They had found a reasonably inexpensive hotel and checked in as Monsieur and Madame Renaud. The room was on the first floor and was simply furnished with a double bed, two bed-side tables with lamps on, a dressing table and stool and an armchair. After unpacking their overnight bags, they had gone out to have a drink and something to eat before retiring to bed early because they were both exhausted and drained by their experiences that afternoon. The café was just around the corner from the large Gard du Nord railway station. It was pleasant and they sat in a chair on the veranda under a blue awning. As he sipped his beer Benoit picked up the menu which was under the ash tray on the table in front of them. After everything that had happened that day, he realised that they had had no lunch and he suddenly felt very hungry.

"I am going to have a steak frites and green salad" he announced looking up from the menu

"Please order the same for me" Genevieve said *"and a large carafe of house red wine"*

Benoit went inside the café and ordered the food. He then returned and lit a cigarette and stared out at the street and watched the people passing by, many carrying large suitcases.

"I wonder where they are all going" he mused

"Trying to get out of Paris probably"

"Do you think so?"

"I wouldn't be surprised. There is talk in the newspaper today about a possible general strike and maybe some people are sick of the violence and damage being carried out in the city."

"You may well be right" Benoit said *"After all it is hardly the city of love, romance and light at this time is it?"*

"Don't worry Benoit. We will restore our flat back to its previous condition as our romantic hideaway" and she leaned towards him and kissed him gently on the mouth.

The next morning, they decided to call in at Chez Henri before going back to the flat to start the process of cleaning up the mess and restoring it back to the way it was the best that they could. To their surprise Marco was sitting at a table on his own with a large plate of jambon et frites in front of him.

"It is my breakfast" he said *"I didn't get a chance to eat last night and I have left Marie on her own to sleep this morning so I did not want to make a noise in the apartment."*

Looking down at their bags he said:

"Where have you been or where are you going?"

Just then, Henri appeared at the table and they ordered two Café Crèmes and a croissant and a pain au chocolat. Then Benoit proceeded to tell Marco everything that had happened the previous day and also about the two men that Madame Charpentier had seen at the weekend.

"I am so sorry" he said *"You had made your flat beautiful and homely. Marie and I both loved it. But now you mention it I have just remembered something. Last night after I left your apartment, I saw a large man in a black leather jacket leaning against the wall across the street and he was staring straight up at your apartment and then he walked away when he saw me.*

"So, we are being watched and followed" said Benoit*" What did he look like?"*

"He was tall, well-built with a rugged face and had the bearing of a military man. He was a very tough looking character."

"But why are they chasing us? What harm have we done them?" Genevieve added with as eyes started to become moist.

"I don't know my friends but I think that you need to be careful, these seem to be very serious people indeed."

Henri arrived at the table with the coffee and the food and they eat an drank in silence.

Suddenly Benoit put the cup down sharply on the glass table top which caused both Genevieve and Marco to look at him directly.

"I don't think that they are after us after all" he said quietly *"They searched and ransacked the apartment when they obviously knew that we were not there because they had been watching it. No, I think they are after something that we have"*

"But what could we possibly have that these people want? They seem to be very dangerous professionals. We do not have anything worth stealing." Genevieve said in reply.

"Well whatever happens you cannot stay at your flat tonight because not only is it still a mess but it will be being watched. You must stay with us" Marco said.

"That is so kind of you" Genevieve replied *"But Marie needs her rest"*

"No, it will be fine. In fact, I am sure that she would like to have the company and I know that she would be furious with me if she found out about your situation and I had not offered our help and support. See you about 7.00pm and I will cook something – just bring some wine" and with that he went into the café and paid Henri and then waved them *"adieu."*

"I have just had an idea" Benoit said when the two of them were alone. *"I know that the flat maybe being watched but we need to go back and get some more clothes and I need to do something. We just have to be very quick about it."*

They paid their bill to Henri and raced to the Metro station and caught the two trains back to the apartment. At every stage they kept looking behind them to see if they were being followed. They also stopped at a tobacconist kiosk and whilst Genevieve bought some cigarettes, Benoit doubled back to see if he could see anyone acting suspiciously. His eyes scanned the street looking for anyone appearing to be watching Genevieve, or staring into a shop window or hiding behind a newspaper; anything that looked out of place. But he could see nothing that caused him any concern. So he changed his gaze to the opposite side of the street and repeated the process. Still nothing. He hurried back to Genevieve and they walked quickly to Rue de la Clef and into their apartment block. The lift had broken down again so they took the six flights of stairs and Benoit gingerly opened the front door not quite sure what he was expecting to see this time. But the same scene of wanton destruction met them as it had done the day before. Nothing had changed.

"Gennie please can you pack two suitcases or clothes and anything else we may need. I will be up in the attic."

Benoit hurriedly opened the trap door into the attic space and carrying his cine camera he climbed in and turned on the special red lighting. He closed the trap door, put on his cloth apron and safety goggles and then carefully emptied the film out of the cine camera. He knew that developing a cine film was a delicate operation and that great care needed to be taken to be sure that it was carried out correctly. He had to work quickly but not with haste. Fortunately, he had done this process many times before. He loaded the film into a spiral holder and then in turn loaded it into the processing tank. The film was then processed in the tank using the correct concentration of developing solution which he had added previously and he set the timer. Whilst the film was being developed, he set up the piece of delicate drying equipment and then after the required time had lapsed, he added the fixer agent to the tank and reset the timer for four minutes turning the spiral holder every thirty or forty seconds.

"Nearly ready" he shouted down to Genevieve without opening the hatch.

Once he was happy that the film was dry enough, he carefully inserted one end of the film into a slitter and pushed it through until it came out the other side. He grasped the newly slitted end and pulled the remaining length of film through the slitter. He then

spliced the two ends together and placed it on to a spare reel, ready for projection or editing.

"OK Gennie" he shouted *"You can come up now"* and he turned off the special red light and turned on small spot lamp. There wasn't the time or space to set up the projector and screen so he loaded the spool onto the editing machine with the small screen and they both crowded around it in

the cramped attic as he slowly turned the handle of the machine to move the film forward. A thought suddenly came into his head, it wasn't that long ago that he and Gennie had made love in this cramped space but now all that seemed a distant memory. The film spool started to revolve and the film passed through the editor and onto the empty spool on the other side. Images started to come on to the screen. These were the images that Benoit had taken when he and Genevieve had been in the middle of the mass demonstration the previous Friday. They had started the march from the Place Denfert-Rochereau, the huge crossroads in Montparnasse but they had been prevented from crossing the River Seine by the police who had blocked all of the bridges. As a result, the protesters had turned and swept down the Boulevard St Germain but suddenly they had been faced by a strong police presence whose intention it was to force the protesters up the Boulevard St Michel back towards the Sorbonne.

That was when the great massed throng of protesters suddenly surged towards the police lines. The film started to run a bit jolty now as Benoit was jostled and pushed in the crowd as he attempted to hold the camera still, above his head but his height had provided a good view of the scene and clearly captured the moment that the CRS detachment ploughed straight into the crowd with batons swinging indiscriminately. And a second detachment of CRS officers running out of an alley on the left flank of the protesters ambushing them and catching them in a pincer movement. The film continued and although they couldn't hear it, they both remembered the cacophony of noise, screams, obscenities and shouting, but the film clearly showed the pushing, punching and the explosion of petrol bombs and clouds of tear gas that sometimes obscured the images on the scene for a few seconds.

Then all of a sudden, the camera caught the moment that a small group of riot police attacked two people on the ground who had stumbled and fallen as the main group had retreated. As they lay on the cobbled street, they were set upon by two members of the CRS who rained repeated blows to their heads as they just lay there motionless. Blood could clearly be seen to be pooling on the ground from the open wounds on their heads. The camera then captured the sight of the crowd starting to part and the police pushing them away to create an exclusion zone around the two bodies on the ground and in that second, one of the officers who had beaten the protesters, looked up and his face was perfectly framed in the middle of Benoit's camera lens.

Genevieve put her hand to her head and muttered *"Mon Dieu. Do you think that they are dead?"*

Benoit stopped revolving the handle on the editor machine and looked at Genevieve and said:

"One of them certainly is. I am not sure about the other but I wouldn't be surprised if they have both been killed. We have just witnessed a murder and at the very least a very serious violent assault which may be being attempted to be covered up. No wonder they are after us. We are the only ones who know what really happened and more importantly who did it."

"What do we do now?" Genevieve replied as the gravity of the situation had suddenly sunk into her *"Well we obviously cannot go to the police."*

Benoit hurriedly rewound the film all the way through the editor and on to the spool on the other side and then removed the spool and put it in a metal film tin.

"Come on Gennie" he said *"We need to go and go now!"*

Genevieve climbed back down out of the attic space and waited by the front door with the two suitcases as Benoit shut down all the equipment and grabbed the editor machine and the film canister and climbed down and joined her. He zipped the film tin into the inside pocket of his jacket and squeezed that editing machine into his suitcase and they both left the flat closing and locking the front door behind them.

They quickly climbed down the six flights of stairs and when they arrived into the entrance hall Benoit said:
"Wait here a minute while I look outside"
He slowly opened the exterior door, half expecting to see a man in a black leather jacket leaning against the wall opposite staring at him but there was no one there. He looked furtively up and down the street and seeing no one, he then waved Genevieve out to join him and they hurriedly walked down the Rue de la Clef, the opposite way to the Métro station at Place Monge. At the end of the road they turned right on to Rue Daubenton passing the cinema La Clef on the righthand side.
"Are you alright carrying that suitcase" Benoit said a little breathlessly as they had been walking quickly
"Yes. No problem" she replied *"It is not heavy as I only put a few clothes in it.*

They carried on walking the short distance to the Rue de MIrbel and then crossed over the Rue Monge and entered the Métro station at Censier Daubenton on Line 7. Benoit looked up at the large clock in the ticketing hall of the station. It was two in the afternoon. He took Genevieve by the hand and guided her over to the large Métro map on the wall.
"Pretend to be looking at the map" he said *"Guide your finger along one of the lines as if you are looking for a particular station"*
He then put down his suitcase and started to scout the two entrances to the ticketing hall of the station. His eyes darted everywhere in search of men in black leather jackets or faces that just didn't look right or looked threatening but

he saw nothing that caused him any alarm so he returned to Genevieve and they descended down the stairs to the platform.

"Where are we going" asked Genevieve *"We are not due to visit Marco and Marie for another five hours and I do not want to arrive early."*

"I agree but we can hardly wander around Paris with our suitcases either and mine is quite heavy with the editing machine inside. I know where we can go and lie low for a few hours and where we will just blend in. Come on we need to cross over onto the other platform that is going southbound"

They only had to wait two minutes for the next train but Benoit was anxiously looking up and down the platform for any sight of their pursuers. The train was heading to Villejuif Louis Aragon.

"We only want to go two stops and then we will change lines" Benoit said as they climbed into the carriage. They got out of the train at Place d'Italie station and once again Benoit pulled Genevieve to one side and waited till all the other passengers had alighted the train before he was confident that they were not being followed. They walked to the platform for Line 9 and made the four-stop journey to Denfert Rochereau. It was ironic thought Benoit but this is where they had arrived to join the demonstration only four days ago which had now caused their lives to be turned upside down.

They found the platform for Line B and took the train to Antony station where they alighted and got a shuttle bus into Orly airport. The airport was undergoing construction of a new West Terminal which had started earlier that year. They walked into the area for flight departures and found a café conveniently situated in the corner and sat down at an empty table, putting their suitcases by their side. They blended in perfectly as a young couple about to make a departure to some destination with their luggage.

"Good choice" said Genevieve *"Wouldn't it be nice if we could actually fly off somewhere?"*

"That is a lovely idea but I do not have my passport with me nor do I have enough money to buy a ticket"

"Neither do I" Genevieve replied with a half-smile *"But it was a nice to think that we could just escape all this trouble and be somewhere alone together. I have never flown on an airplane before. Have you?*

"Yes I have" Benoit replied. *"My parents took my sister and I away for holidays quite often. We were very lucky."*

Benoit walked up to the café counter, took a tray and slid it along the rail. He selected two baguettes, one filled with tuna mayonnaise and one with brie and then he ordered two Café Crèmes. He paid the cashier at the till and then carried the tray back to the table.

"Cut the baguettes in half Gennie and then we can both have one piece of each one."

For the next ten minutes they just eat an drank in silence. Suddenly Benoit said:

"Gennie do you think that we should just give them what they want?"

"What do you mean? Give them the film?"

"Yes"

"Why?"

"Because if we don't one of us or both of us could get seriously hurt or worse"

Genevieve thought for a minute or two and then drained the rest of her coffee before saying:

"No Benoit I do not. I don't see us as romantic heroes or anything stupid like that but these men are cold-blooded killers. They may very well have killed before and could well do so again. Yes. We must be very careful but I fundamentally believe that the right thing to do is to hand

*the film over to the media or some other responsible
organisation so that they can be brought to justice"*
    Benoit smiled and leaned over and kissed her hard on the
lips.
    *"I am proud of you" he said "I agree but I just had to
know that you definitely felt the same way too."*

    Benoit did not really like airports. He didn't really know
why but he had always done so. Perhaps it was something
to do with the combination of transience, of everyone being
in a hurry, of being involved in their own 'bubbles' with no
one really wanting to be there but all putting up with the
fact that the airport was a means to an end; of getting where
they wanted to go. He watched as the people passed by and
wondered who they were and where they were all going.
The whole scene seemed a very long way from the protests
on the streets of Paris. Not just protests he reminded himself
but death on the streets of Paris. He shivered at the memory
of the images that he and Genevieve had seen earlier as he
had turned the handle of the editing machine in the little
attic space. These people, here however, were all very well-
off, either businessmen, film stars orjust wealthy
individuals. After all flying was not a cheap method of
transport and the thought came to him as to what Genevieve
might now be thinking after he had said quite casually that
he had flown *"quite often."* He silently rebuked himself for
making such a callous remark.

    An hour later Benoit walked out of the café and bought
a newspaper from the kiosk a few meters away. He then
bought two more coffees from the Café counter and
returned to the table where Genevieve was sitting looking
after the two suitcases.
    "Things are really spiraling out of control" Benoit said
as he looked up after reading the front page of the paper. *"A
sit-down strike started yesterday at the Sud Aviation plant*

near the city of Nantes. Evidently the workers locked the management in their offices and their action is now being copy-catted by many other factories and manufacturing plants all over France."

"What do you think is going to happen?" Genevieve said *"Do you think that there will be a general strike?"*

"I think that that is a distinct possibility. I cannot see this thing ending soon unless the government makes some big concessions which they seem very reluctant to do. They just believe that repression is the answer but I think that it is just getting too big for that. I really don't know Gennie."

The afternoon passed slowly. Every now and then Benoit would pat the inside pocket of his jacket just to check that the film tin was there and all of the time he scanned the flow of people coming in and out of the airport for any sign of their pursuers. He lit a cigarette and lent back in his chair and just lost himself in his thoughts for a few moments. So much had happened in the last few days and weeks. How different his life had become. He was still in shock at the sight of the wrecked apartment and its implications and it was only now that it was all starting to sink in.

"Would they ever be able to move back in? Could they ever restore it back to how it had been? Could they ever escape from these people who were pursuing them?

So many things raced through his mind at the same time and then with relief he settled on one image. He was lying on the ground making love to Genevieve in a remote part of his parent's estate, his dogs lying nearby, sky larks flying overhead and autumnal leaves dropping from the tress all around them. He smiled and stubbed the butt of the cigarette out in the ash tray on the table and when he looked up and saw that Genevieve was fast asleep with her head resting on her arms on the table.

Chapter Eleven

It was a few minutes before seven in the evening when Benoit and Genevieve knocked on the front door of Marco and Marie's apartment. They had taken the Métro from Antony station and alighted at Port Royal without having to change lines. The apartment was situated in Rue des Boulangers, number 71 which was only a few minutes' walk from the Cardinal Lemoine Métro station. They were both tired from carrying the suitcases around all day and they were relieved when they found that the lift was working in the apartment block and that they did not have to climb the stairs to the second floor.

The door opened after the first knock and it was Marie. Her face was still covered in bruising but the angry purple had now started to give way to various shades of yellow.

"Come in" she said and embraced them by kissing both of them on each cheek.

"You can put your suitcases over there" she said pointing at the corner of the room and she closed the door and Benoit noticed that she slid the chain through the loop. Did she always do that or was she now being extra careful he thought.

"Sit down please and I will get you a drink. Marco is in the kitchen as he is cooking tonight. He said it is an old family recipe so I expect that it will be some kind of pasta but he is keeping it a secret."

"Sounds delicious. I am really looking forward to it" said Genevieve

"Yes it really is very kind of you both" added Benoit

Marie opened a bottle of red wine. And poured out three glasses, handing them round. *"This is Chianti as Marco insists that everything is Italian tonight"* she said with a smile.

Just at that moment Marco came out of the kitchen into the lounge

"Welcome my friends" he said *"It is great to see you here and I hope you are able to get some rest after everything that you have both been through"*

"That is so kind of you Marco but we can only stay here for one night and must leave in the morning because we do not want to bring any trouble on you. The people who are chasing us are professional and very serious and we now know what they are after." Benoit stated

Marco sat next to Marie on the sofas and poured himself a glass of red wine,

"I am not going to propose a toast" he said *"Because I just don't think that any of us have anything to celebrate right now. What did you mean by you know what they are after?"*

Benoit looked at Genevieve who just nodded. He then turned to Marie and said

"I expect that Marco has told you everything that has happened in the last few days?"

"Yes" she replied taking a sip of wine *"I am so sorry about your flat.it was beautiful and you had both put so much work in to it. We will help you restore it"*

"Thank you so much" said Genevieve *"We are so lucky to have friends like you two"*

Benoit looked at Marco with a glum expression on his face *"Right now it is not the flat that I am worried about"* and he got off the sofa and walked to the corner of the room and opened his suitcase. He took out the cine film editing machine and set it up on the coffee table and plugged the lead into the socket in the wall.

"I would like to show you something." He then went to his jacket that was hanging behind the front door and unzipped the inside pocket and took out the film tin.

Marie looked at Marco and he just shrugged his shoulders.

"Do you remember Marco when you suggested that I start to make a film record of what is happening on the streets of Paris right now?"

"Of course. We were in your apartment a few weeks ago when you showed us the film that you had made of Genevieve."

"Yes that is right. Well this is the footage that I took at the mass demonstration last Friday. It was taken a few hours before Marie was attacked by the police."

Marie and Marco got off the sofa and sat on the floor around the coffee table as Benoit loaded the film spool onto the left-hand side of the machine and threaded the film through the slot and into the empty spool on the right-hand side. He then switched the editing machine on and the small screen lit up.

"Marco please could you turn a couple of lights off as it will make the small screen easier to see"

Marco turned off a couple of table lights just leaving one on in the far corner of the room and sat back down on the floor next to Marie. Benoit started to turn the righthand handle slowly and the film sprung into life on the screen. The film clearly showed the massed crowds and the placards and banners. Clouds of tear gas sometimes blurring the clarity but they could still see missiles and projectiles being thrown at the phalanx of riot police lines in front of the crowd. The film jumped as the crowd moved but Benoit had done well to keep it focused high above his head giving a clear field of vision of what was happening. A few seconds later the crowd had surged forward but were repelled by the advancing police who were swinging their batons above their heads indiscriminately straight onto the unprotected protesters. Then the camera turned to the left to see a large detachment of CRS charging out of a side alley and just laying into the fleeing protesters who were now trapped in a pincer movement. But it was clear to everyone watching that this wasn't about crowd control or management but a direct and indiscriminate attack carried out with a level of violence that was hard to conceive.

"Bloody hell!" Marco exclaimed

"Keep watching" Benoit replied as he continued to turn the handle of the editor.

The camera then clearly focused on a small group of riot police who were attacking two people who were laying on the street having stumbled as the crowd had started to retreat from the two-pronged assault. As they lay there not moving or struggling, they were set upon by two members of the CRS who just rained blows on them with their batons. Blood could clearly be seen pooling over the cobble stones from the open wounds on their heads. Immediately the police can be seem pushing the crowd back aggressively swinging their batons to create a clearing around the two motionless bodies. It happened in an instant but one of the officers who had been beating them started to stand up and for a few seconds, time seemed to freeze and his face was perfectly framed in the middle of Benoit's camera lens and then a few seconds later the film went blank.

Marco said nothing but just got off the floor and switched a couple of lights back on and Marie went and sat back down on the sofa.

"Mon Dieu" she uttered *"Are they dead?"*

"I think so" said Benoit

"But there has been no mention of it in the press" Marco said

"And I don't think there will be" Benoit replied *"I think that they would want to cover this up which is why they are so desperate to recover this film."*

"You have just filmed a double murder" Marie said not quite believing what she had just seen.

Benoit unplugged the editor and rewound the film on to its original spool and replaced it back in the tin and then zipped it back into the inside pocket of his jacket. Marco retreated into the kitchen and they could all hear some pots and pans banging around as Marie poured out three more glasses of wine and opened another bottle.

"We have brought two bottles" Genevieve said *"They are in my case but they are French"*

"It really doesn't matter" Marie replied *"I doubt if Marco is in a mood to be particular after watching Benoit's film"*

Ten minutes later Marco brought out a beautiful Lasagne in a large oval dish and placed it on some cork mats on the coffee table. He then re-entered with a bowl of green salad and some sliced pieces of baguette as Marie placed four plates and some cutlery on the table.

"Help yourselves everyone. This is Grandma Spirelli's favourite dish" Marco said

A half an hour later they were all sitting on the sofa and the two old arm chairs smoking and listening to Leonard Cohen on the record player. The sombre music and haunting lyrics of *'Sisters of Mercy'* seemed to perfectly fit the mood that pervaded the room.

Eventually Marco turned to Benoit and said:

"What are you going to do?"

"Well we clearly cannot stay here" longer than tonight. *We will leave first thing in the morning"*

"You don't have to do that" Marie said turning towards Genevieve

"Yes we do." Benoit replied *"As I said earlier these people are serious and obviously will stop at nothing to cover their tracks. I have a feeling that these aren't the first killings that they have carried out"*

"But where will you go?"

"Well we obviously cannot go to the police" Genevieve stated

"We will go and get my car and drive out of Paris and find somewhere to lie low for a while. Maybe we will go and stay with my parents and find a way to get this film to the newspapers" Benoit said with more confidence than he felt inside. Deep down he was scared now. More scared than he had ever been in his life but he could not let Genevieve know that. They were fugitives. Running away from an unknown, violent and ruthless foe.

"You could always just give them the film" Marie said

"Yes. We could" Benoit said and then thought for a moment before he added *"But that would be letting these people get away with a double murder. Would that make us accessories to murder? I do not know I am not a lawyer but I do know that these men are vicious thugs who clubbed to death two defenceless people in cold blood and I am not sure that I could live with myself for the rest of my life if I just capitulated to them but you are right it is always an option. Gennie and I talked about it a lot this afternoon."*

Marco stood up and slapped his friend on the back

"We will have one more drink and then we will all go to bed as it has been a long day for all of us"

"Good idea" Genevieve replied.

The next morning, they got up early and Marco said that he would accompany them to get the car and carry Genevieve's suitcase for her. Benoit and Genevieve embraced Marie *'adieu'* and the three of them made their way to the Port Royal Mètro station taking the short journey to Cluny La Sorbonne and then changing to Line 7 to go to Place Monge and then take the short walk to Rue Gracieuse where the car was parked in an underground car park.

As the train pulled into the station at Maubert Mutualité station Benoit said:

"Come on Marco. Let me buy you breakfast at Chez Henri's. That way Gennie and I do not need to stop and get any food for a couple of hours which will hopefully get us out of Paris"

"OK good idea."

As the three of them crossed the Boulevard St. Germain, they saw Bruno and Yvette and they stopped to talk to them for a few minutes. Yvette was wearing a loose -fitting kaftan-type top which was covered with vivid colour in an explosive design emanating from the centre. Benoit had never seen anything like it but Marco said *"Have you tie-dyed that top yourself?"*

"Yes I have. Do you like it?"

"Yes I do very much. I saw a lot of people wearing clothes with similar designs when I was in London last year"

"We are now making them in small quantities at the Atelier Populaire and selling them to raise money to fund our poster production. I love the design. It demonstrates freedom of expression. I have decided that no one will restrict what I wear with rigid conventions anymore."

"Do you think they are now a couple?" Genevieve mused aloud

"Could be" Marco replied

"She is a pleasant and intelligent girl and if they are then I am pleased for Bruno but she is just so intense!" Benoit added

"Perfect match" Genevieve said with a smile.

Ten minutes later they were all seated around an outside table with Henri standing over them ready to take their order but just as they were thinking what to have, he said:

"Strange thing happened yesterday afternoon. Two serious looking men in black leather jackets came into the café and started asking questions about where they might find you. I have never seen them before and they hardly

144

looked like friends of yours. I told them I did not know where you were and so they left saying that they would be back"

In that moment Benoit knew that he had made a terrible mistake by coming to the café.

"What an idiot I am" he said to the others *"It is obvious they would have followed us here over the last few days. Why did I not just stop and think things through?"*

"Oh merde" Marco said suddenly as he looked up from the table and saw a man in a black leather jacket cross the Boulevard St. Germain and start to walk towards the café. He was only about one hundred metres away.

"Quick Benoit. You must leave now. They are here. I will look after your suitcases. Go now! Henri can you let them out the fire door at the back of the Café and I will explain later? Go hurry my friend and stay safe."

Without another word being spoken Benoit and Genevieve got up from the table and quickly followed Henri through the café and out to the back through the storeroom and at the end was a fire escape door and Henri lifted up the latch and swung open the door which led into an alley behind the café.

"Merci Monsieur" Benoit shouted back as they ran down the alley as fast as they could.

They ran out of the alley and back on to Boulevard St. Michel but away from the Place Maubert. After they had walked quickly for about five minutes, they saw up ahead the distinctive blue sign with the word 'TAXI' written on it in white letters. They were in luck there were two taxis waiting there so they stopped and caught their breath. They got into the back of the taxi and asked the driver to take them to the Rue Gracieuse and he dropped them off at the entrance to the underground car park. The traffic was light so the journey only took about ten minutes. Benoit was confident that they had not been seen coming out of the alleyway behind the café.

They descended down the stairs into the car park which were covered in graffiti and still stank of stale urine and was poorly lit. When they got to the level minus two, Benoit opened the heavy red fire door and they made their way to their parking bay. The blue Citroen Deux Chevaux was exactly as Benoit had last left it and he just hoped that the battery would not be flat. They quickly unlocked the car and got in and Benoit was delighted when the car started up on the first try. He gently reversed out of the parking bay and carefully manoeuvred the car around the tight corners and large concrete pillars of the car park and then up the first ramp and then up the second ramp and out into the street.

"Where are we going to go" said Genevieve

"I am not sure yet" Benoit replied *"But we have got half a tank of petrol which will take us quite a long way before we need to stop. We will go south through the southern suburbs of Paris until we can pick up the RN 7. Do you think you could light a cigarette for me?"*

Genevieve took a packet of cigarettes out of Benoit's jacket which was lying on the back seat together with his lighter and lit the cigarette and handed it to Benoit who took it and placed it in his mouth and then opened his window a little to let the smoke out. They drove for the next hour making slow progress hardly saying anything to each other. Both lost in their own thoughts. Although he really did not want to, Benoit had decided that the only option open to them, was to go home and stay with his parents for a while in St. Emilion. They would never find them there and he could explain to his parents that they were escaping the troubles in Paris as they did not want to be caught up in them. After all the university was closed anyway. He would explain all this to Genevieve when they had managed to get out of Paris and on to the RN 7.

146

"Le circulation est très mauvais aujourd'hui?" Genevieve suddenly said, breaking the silence that had existed between them.

"It is bad every day Gennie" Benoit replied *"Paris now desperately needs a major ring road to be built"*

"Benoit" Genevieve said suddenly a few moments later *"I need to tell you something important"*

"What?" Benoit replied suddenly feel a jolt of anxiety in the pit of his stomach.

"I am really scared. I have never been in a situation like this before"

"Nor have I Gennie and to be truthful I am scared too. I was putting a brave face on at Marie and Marco's last night but I really think we should just get away for a while and keep our heads down."

He took his right hand off the steering wheel and reached over to her grabbing her left hand and squeezed it as hard as he could as an act of reassurance.

"Where can we go that will be safe?" she enquired.

"I do not think that we have any other option than to go and stay with my parents although I do not want to but no one will ever find us there and we can just tell them that we are escaping the troubles and violence in Paris as we do not want to be caught up in it."

"OK. That is a good idea but I do not think that they like me very much"

"Why do you say that?"

"Because of my background"

"That is not true Gennie and anyway I don't care anymore about what they think. I have my own life to lead now" and he reached over and squeezed her hand once more and she just turned her face towards him and smiled.

Benoit started to study the traffic signs in more detail. They had made slow progress and had only travelled about eight kilometres and were now in the suburb of Boulogne-Billancourt and on the way to Clamart and then on to

Fresnes where he planned to join the main A road near Orly Airport where they had been the day before. But the traffic was just getting worse and worse and eventually they were just crawling in first gear and then they came to a complete standstill.

"I think that there has been an accident up ahead" he said *"Can I have another cigarette please?"*

If Benoit had been regularly checking his rear-view mirror over the last half an hour, he would have noticed the black Peugeot car gradually getting closer and closer behind them until it was only two car lengths away with only a small red Fiat and a silver Renault 4 between them. But Benoit had been caught up in his own thoughts and had not had to concentrate very hard on driving because the traffic had been moving so slowly. After five minutes the traffic had still not moved at all and Benoit said:

"I think I will turn the engine off for a bit in case the old girl overheats"

Just as he said those words a large man in a black leather jacket got out of the black Peugeot 204 two cars behind them. He quickly and silently walked up the passenger side of the Fiat and Renault in front of him and then with enormous speed and strength lunged forward and ripped open the passenger door of the blue Deux Chevaux.

"What the....?" Benoit uttered but it all happened so fast, the man leaned over the terrified Genevieve and punched Benoit hard in the face and then grabbed Genevieve who was now screaming, out of the car. Without any hesitation he just half frogmarched, half dragged her back to the Peugeot behind and threw her into the back seat with huge force and as he slammed the rear door and climbed into the front passenger seat, the driver was already undertaking a three-point turn and within seconds was heading in the free-flowing traffic in the opposite direction.

With blood pouring from his nose and mouth, Benoit got out of the car but only to see the black Peugeot 204 accelerating away back down the road that they had been crawling along for the last half an hour.

"Are you alright Monsieur" said a stylish petite blonde lady who had got out of the Fiat behind Benoit and at the same time a man came running towards him from the stationary Renault.

"What just happened there" he shouted *"It all took place so fast!"*

"I fear that my girlfriend has just been kidnapped" Benoit said quietly taking out a handkerchief from his pocket and wiping his mouth and then holding it against his nose.

"We must call the police now" said the man from the Renault

"I don' think that there is any point" Benoit replied unintentionally rather sarcastically

"Why not"

"Because those men in the black Peugeot 204 are the police."

Benoit got back into the Deux Chevaux and started the engine and he too, made a U turn and filtered into the traffic going in the opposite direction. The man from the Renault just looked at the stylish petite blonde lady and shrugged his shoulders and returned to his car. Benoit knew that he had no chance of catching up with the black Peugeot because they had a huge lead over him and they were in a much faster car so he just drove slowly and as he did so he felt the tears start to roll down his cheeks.

"Oh Gennie! How stupid of me. We should have just given them the fucking film. Now what am I going to do" and he shouted to no one at the top of his voice *"Just please don't hurt her."*

An hour later Benoit was nearly back at the Rue Gracieuse but before he reached it, he stopped at a petrol station to buy some cigarettes and on instinct he decided to fill the tank with petrol. He drove on, entered the underground garage and parked the Citroen in his designated parking bay and exited the car park noticing once again the stink of stale urine on the stairs but he didn't care. He had something that he needed to do and do quickly. He walked quickly towards the Mètro station at Place Monge, taking care to avoid going on to the rue de la Clef where their flat was located. He stopped on the way at a tobacconist kiosk where he bought a pack of tissues and a small bottle of water. The man in the kiosk was small and rotund with a spindly moustache that had the ends of it twisted together and waxed on each side and he was wearing a striped waistcoat with the buttons straining at the front because of his enlarged stomach but he had a big friendly smile

"Are you alright monsieur" he asked with a tone of genuine concern as he stared at Benoit's face which was streaked with tears and congealed blood.

"Yes, I am fine thank you. I slipped on the stairs in the underground car park and fell on my face on the concrete"

"Ah yes I can quite understand. They are always filthy with discarded rubbish and stink of piss" the man in the waistcoat replied as Benoit wandered off and leant against a wall. He pulled out some tissues and wetted them with the water from the bottle and wiped his face the best that he could without a mirror and then he used a couple of tissue to dry himself off. He stuffed the rest of the tissues in his jacket pocket and then patted the inside pocket to check that it was till zipped up and the film tin was still safely inside.

"Stupid bastards" he muttered to himself as he realised that his jacket had been on the back seat of the Citroen all the time and if they knew what it contained, the man in the

150

black leather jacket could have just grabbed it instead of taking Gennie.

Benoit entered the Métro at Place Monge and walked up to the large map of the Paris Mètro on the wall and pretended to be working out his route which on this occasion he actually was. He kept glancing around but could see no evidence of anyone watching him but these bastards were clever he thought. How on earth had they tracked Gennie and him down in the car? How did the know exactly where and when they would be there? He would have to sit and think this through later but for now he had a much more important task to do. Besides he thought now they have Gennie they will perhaps stop following me for a while and I am sure they will contact me and threaten me when they are ready.

He descended down to the platform and took the train on Line 7 all the way north to the station at Opéra. He got out of the train and sat on a bench on the platform checking all of the passengers who also alighted from the train but there was no sign of the kidnappers. He then just sat for a few minutes remembering that a few months earlier, Gennie and he had come here and got out at this station and strolled around the magnificent Gallerie de Lafayette on Boulevard Haussman with its wide range of brands that are available at the store to suit all budgets, from ready to wear to haute couture. The architecture of the store was Art Nouveau, with a remarkable dome and a panoramic view of Paris that has made it a tourist attraction of the French capital city and Genevieve had been enthralled by it. After they had wandered around the store for a couple of hours, they had come across a small bistro behind the huge department store and had enjoyed a romantic candlelight dinner which Benoit had been delighted to discover hadn't been too expensive. It had been a brilliant evening.

151

Five minutes passed before he stood up and he realised that his eyes were moist again so he took one of the remaining tissues out of his pocket and dried them. He then slowly walked along the platform and followed the route to the platform for Line 8. He didn't have to wait long before a train arrived and he got on it, once again he glanced up and down the platform to check there was no one pursuing him. He made the short one-stop journey and alighted at the next station which was Madeleine. He left the train, walked along the platform, climbed the stairs and exited the station. As he did so, he looked back once again to check if he was being followed but he saw no one that gave him any concern and his eyes settled for a moment on the large ornate iron sign at the entrance to the station with white lettering saying *'Passage Public Métro'* set against a vivid red background. This sign, Benoit knew, was the original one dating back to fifty years earlier when the station had first opened as part of Nord-Sud company line between Porte de Versailles and Notre-Dame-de-Lorette.

Benoit walked into the Place de La Madeleine and stood before the façade of the venue he had come to visit. Ten years earlier he had visited L'église de la Madeleine as part of a school trip to Paris and it had had a lasting effect on him. He was not sure why because they had visited many famous churches and landmarks on that trip but L'église de la Madeleine had remained a special place for him ever since and it was no coincidence that it was here that he came today to do what he had to do. For a few moments, he stood still in front of the magnificent edifice of the church in its commanding position centered at the end of the Rue Royale. It had been built in the neo-classical style and its appearance was not typical of a religious building as it was in the form of a Greek temple without any crosses or bell-towers. Napoleon wanted it to be a pantheon in honour of his armies. Benoit knew that it was one of the earliest large neo-classical buildings to imitate the whole external form of a Greco-Roman temple, rather than just the portico front. Its impressive fifty-two Corinthian columns, each twenty metres high, are situated around the entire building; giving it a rather majestic aspect. On the pediment there is a high relief that represents the last judgement of Christ. Benoit just stood and stared up as he had done ten years earlier. He had often thought of bringing Genevieve here but it was just one of those things that he had not got around to yet. There was no denying it, the façade of the church was truly stunning.

He climbed the steps and paused just before he passed through the large bronze doors which bore reliefs representing the Ten Commandments, turning around to check if he had been followed but once again could not see anyone who gave him any concern. He entered into the church and could immediately hear that someone was playing the pipe organ and the music filled the entire interior of the building. The church had a single nave with three domes over wide arched bays, lavishly gilded in a decor inspired as much by Roman baths as by Renaissance artists. At the rear of the church, above the high altar, stood a statue by Charles Marochetti depicting Saint Mary Magdalene being lifted up by angels. The half-dome above the altar was frescoed by Jules-Claude Ziegler, entitled *The History of Christianity*, showing the key figures in the Christian religion.

The interior of the church was dimly lit but near the entrance there was a large table with a significant number of lit votive candles providing additional light form the flickering flames that emanated from them. Benoit walked quietly down the central nave glancing left and right and upwards, all the time looking for an ideal safe place to hide the tin containing the developed film. After about ten minutes he returned to the place that he considered to be the best. He looked around him. At the moment there was no one to be seen or heard. He quickly took one of the congregation chairs and stood on it stretching upwards as far as he could without losing his balance and secured the tin in place with some very strong tape. Once he was happy that the tin was sufficiently concealed, he walked out of the church, down the steps and crossed the Place de La Madeleine and down the Rue Royale towards the River Seine, deep in thought. He walked aimlessly through the Place de la Concorde with its two fountains and central Egyptian obelisk decorated with hieroglyphics. There were as usual lots of people in the public square, tourists, Parisians, and street entertainers but most all, as in the rest of Paris it was dominated by traffic. He walked on and sat down at a small street café on Rue Rivoli. He ordered a beer 1164 and lit a Disque Bleu cigarette and once more he felt his eyes moisten up.

"Merde" he said to himself *"What am I going to do?"*
He drained the beer and quickly ordered another.

"I really am out of options" he thought *"I cannot go to the police because I cannot be sure that they can be trusted. I cannot call my parents because they will not be able to help and I really do not want to involve anyone else because they could be endangered too."*

After wandering along the bank of the Seine for a few hours, he finally decided that he had no one to turn to for advice but Marco. Marco, he realised had become in the last few months the closest person he had ever had that could be called a 'best friend.' For some reason he still felt a little distant from Marie. She did not seem to emanate the same warmth and empathy as Marco. Benoit could never really put his finger on it and he had discussed it with Genevieve on a number of occasions who had just said:

154

"It is because she is a Parisian. She comes from a middle-class family and that is the way that they are. What more is there to say?

So later that afternoon he found himself knocking on the front door of Marco's apartment that he had only left much earlier that morning. Marie opened the door:

"Hi Benoit" she said *"What are you doing here? What has happened to your face? Where is Gennie? Marco is not here at the moment he decided to go to Chez Henri to see what was happening and catch up on things."*

Five minutes later Benoit was sitting on one of their old arm chairs smoking a cigarette and telling Marie everything that had happened."

"Mon Dieu Benoit. This is really serious now. Please go and talk to Marco but I think you need to make contact with them and give them the bloody film"

"Thanks Marie. I will go and talk to Marco"

Benoit left the apartment hoping that he had not been followed there but he was certain that he had not been followed all day. He entered the Mètro and alighted at Maubert Mutualité station and walked into the Place Maubert and towards Chez Henri's. As he approached, he could see that the café was busier than usual and that all of the tables outside were full. Three of the tables had been pushed together and about a dozen students, mostly boys but he did recognise Yvette who was with another girl, were all drinking beers and talking animatedly and some were huddled around a transistor radio. Bruno caught his eye and waved him over:

"Hi Benoit. Come and sit down with us and celebrate" he said in a loud voice. He had obviously consumed a fair number of beers already thought Benoit.

"What are you celebrating?" Benoit said only half interested as his eyes scanned the other tables looking for Marco.

"Earlier today the revolutionary student movement has occupied the Odéon theatre, the cultural symbolic heart of the bourgeoisie. From now on the theatre will become a centre for revolutionary cultural and social activity."

"Congratulations" Benoit replied *"That is exciting news. Have you seen Marco?*

"Yes. He is inside talking with Henri"

Benoit walked away from the group and entered the café which too, was full and very smokey. He saw Marco standing at the bar talking with Henri. They did not see or hear him approach until he tapped Marco on the shoulder.

"Benoit!" He exclaimed *"What are you doing here? What has happened to your face"* as he stared at the split and swollen lips of his friend and the large and swollen bruising on his right cheek

"I need to talk to you urgently" Benoit replied quietly but seriously.

Marco could see the strain and anxiety in his friend's eyes and turning back to Henri he said *"Please can I have a 1664 for Benoit. And another for me. I will settle up with you later. Come on we will go outside. It is very smokey and noisy in here"*

Just as they walked out of the café carrying their beers, one of the group around Bruno who had been huddled around the transistor radio suddenly jumped on to his chair and shouted excitedly:

"The Renault factories at Cléon and at Flins have been occupied and more occupations are taking place all the time. We are now a mass movement that cannot be stopped"

"What is the problem mon ami and where is Genevieve?" Marco said as they sat at a table that had just been vacated by two students.

"*The bastards have got Gennie Marco*" Benoit just blurted out, his eyes welling up once more

"*What!! Calm down and tell me what has happened.*"

"*Oh hell!*" exclaimed Marco when Benoit had finished telling him what had occurred earlier that day "*It is just unbelievable. Where is the film tin now?*

"*I have hidden it*" replied Benoit wiping his eyes with the last remaining tissue in his pocket.

"*Where is it hidden?*"

"*It is probably better that you just don't know*" Benoit said matter-of-factly.

After a few minutes Marco said:

"*Benoit. You have to make contact with these people and give the film to them for Gennie's sake*"

"*I know but that isn't what she wanted*" Benoit said and told Marco what they had discussed at Orly Airport Café the day before.

"*Yes, I understand that but this situation changes everything Benoit*"

"*You are right. I do not know how to contact them but they are probably watching me and will make contact very soon I am sure.*"

"*You must come back to our apartment again tonight Benoit*"

"*That really is very kind of you but I do not want them to follow me to your apartment otherwise your place will probably get trashed as well. I do not want to get you involved. Marie has been through enough already.*"

"*Are you sure*"

"*Yes*"

"*Where will you go then?*"

"*I will go back to our flat and start cleaning up. It doesn't matter if they come there because I am not going to run away anymore.*"

"*Ok. Let's stay here and have a few more drinks and have something to eat first.*"

157

" Good idea" Benoit said and he got up and went inside the café returning a few minutes later with two beers and a menu and placed them on the table.

Suddenly there was another huge cheer from the group around the three tables and someone shouted *"A number of naval shipyards have now been occupied as well. Vive la revolution!"*

"Henri says that the Special tonight is really good. It is one of Veronique's best dishes"

"What is it?"

"Boeuf Bourguignon which has been cooking slowly all afternoon with dauphinoise potatoes and green beans"

"Magnifique" replied Marco *"I'll go and order us two plates"*

An hour later after they had finished their meal and drank a large carafe of Henri's house red wine, they paid their bill and left the café and crossed over the road and headed towards the Mètro station. Suddenly a strong arm grabbed Marco from behind and wrapped it around his neck *"Don't struggle or I will hurt you"* said a well-built physical man in a black leather jacket and as Benoit turned around to see what was going on he recognised the man as the one who had punched him in the face and snatched Gennie from his car earlier in the day. Before he could say anything, another man in a similar black leather jacket stepped out from where he had been hiding behind a parked van and Benoit froze. Time seemed to stand still for what appeared to be ages but in fact was merely a second or two and Benoit realised he was now staring in the face of the man whose face had been so perfectly framed in his cine film that he had taken the previous Friday.

"You have caused us a great deal of trouble mon ami. But this situation will end now. We have your girlfriend and she will not be harmed provided that you hand that film that you took last week over to me now"

"What film?" Benoit replied

"Don't play games with me. That time has run out" and just to emphasise the point he punched Benoit in the stomach causing him to double up and nearly vomit.

"Hand it over now" the man said quietly but with real menace in his voice

"It is not here"

"Where is it?"

"I have hidden it earlier today" replied Benoit straightening up but with one hand clutching his *stomach*

"OK this is what is going to happen. Jacques you can release him now, he will not give us any trouble. If he does you can break his neck. You will meet us at 8.00pm tomorrow, Friday night in the northern part of the Bois de Boulogne. Adjacent to the Jardin d'Acclimatation you will find a large statue of Louis Daubenton where we will exchange your girlfriend for the film. You can bring your friend here with you but no one else. Place the film at the bottom of the statue and then move away but stay close by so that you can be seen. We will be watching you. If you fail to turn up or give us the wrong film something very nasty is going to happen to your girlfriend which will involve body parts."

To emphasise the point, the big man removed a large flick knife from his inside pocket and sprang open the blade and then closed it again.

Benoit went pale and thought that this time he would vomit as bile rose up into his throat but he fortunately managed to swallow and keep it down and just stared at the man with the unshaven face and the menace in his eyes.

"We will be there" he said meekly and then the two men just walked casually away.

But Benoit knew that he had just stared into the face of a cold-blooded murderer whose visage had been so perfectly framed in his cine camera lens a few days earlier and he felt his own blood run cold.

Chapter Twelve

"No one is following us Alain you can slow down now" said the man in the passenger seat of the black Peugeot 204 to the driver. Genevieve was in the rear with a large and powerfully-built man who had in the last few minutes bound her hands together in front of her with rope so that she could not grab the door handle.

"If you scream or make a noise, I will gag you tightly" he said as he held up a piece of white linen cloth that he had pulled from the pocket of his black leather jacket. *"Do you understand?"*

Genevieve just nodded gently and tears started to roll down her face and she stared out of the window at the passing buildings as they travelled back towards the centre of Paris. No one in the car said anything and Genevieve was left with thoughts just racing through her mind; none of them good and her mood became blacker and blacker.

"What are they going to do to me? Will they kill me? Will they rape me? The thoughts just kept going around and around in her head and then she thought of Benoit. She had seen him get hit hard in the car just before she was dragged out. "What would he be thinking and doing now. He would be desperate" and the tears just kept on rolling down her cheeks and still no one spoke inside the car

They had been travelling for some time now, they had crossed the river and had passed near to the Gare du Nord and were still heading North. After another fifteen minutes or so they entered the district of Saint Denis and the driver slowed down and turned into a side street. The man in the passenger seat wound down his window and lit a cigarette. The area was completely different to the Latin Quarter. There were a significant number of North Africans, Algerians mostly, Genevieve thought walking on the pavements. Shops lined the roadside, many with Arabic writing on them, vegetable and fruit sellers with stalls that spilled out on to the pavement. They passed a café where men were sitting outside drinking coffee and smoking shisha pipes. The flavoured tobacco smoke passing through water at the bottom making the water bubble rhythmically as the smoker drew on the pipe. Through the open front window, she could smell the distinctive sweet flavoured tobacco and hear the strains of African or Middle Eastern music that she was not familiar with.

"This place is looking more and more like Algiers everyday" the man beside Genevieve suddenly said out loud.

"That should make you feel at home Jacques" the driver replied with a smile

The large man beside Genevieve didn't reply but simply grunted. Five minutes later the car slowed and pulled into a rough patch of ground and stopped alongside some other cars that were parked there. The two men in the front got out of the car and the one who had been in the driver's seat waited while the big man got out and beckoned Genevieve to follow him and then he took her by the left arm whilst the large man had her right arm and they marched her towards a grey metal door on the side of the adjacent building. The man from the passenger seat then unlocked the door and they all followed him up a steep staircase that led to a front door of an apartment at the top which obviously lay across the top of the women's dress shop with its bright and vibrant coloured fabrics below.

They entered the apartment which was at first glance looked gloomy and was sparsely furnished and Genevieve

161

was pushed down on to a hard-backed wooden chair which one of them had placed in the middle of the room. The large man then undid the rope around her wrists and rebound her hands behind her back to the chair and then secured her ankles to the chair's front legs.

"How dare you kidnap me and take me here" she said with a strength that surprised her *"What do you want from me?"*

The man who had been in the passenger seat of the car whom she later learnt was called Jean-Pierre, who also seemed to be the leader of the group walked towards her after closing the apartment door. He had an unlit cigarette dangling from his mouth and a look of menace in his unshaven face. Without hesitation he suddenly backhanded her across the face almost knocking the chair over.

"A few house rules" he said without removing the cigarette that was still dangling from his lips *"You only speak when spoken to. If you answer our questions fully without lying, we will let you go but if you do not there is a lot more of that to come. Do you understand?*

Genevieve just nodded meekly., her face stinging and a little blood trickled from the corner of her mouth. The big man, Jacques then stood up and went behind her and tied her mouth with the white linen cloth in a tight gag which prevented her from speaking anyway.

The one called Jean-Pierre then looked over at the big man and said

"Make a pot of coffee Jacques and Alain and I will go out and get some food."

When the two of them had left the apartment and she heard the lower outer door slam shut she looked around the apartment. It was quite small. She was in the main room which served as a lounge, dining room and kitchen as well. There were two doors off the room which she presumed were bedrooms and a door to a small bathroom. It was shabbily decorated, smelt of stale food and tobacco and hadn't had a good clean for a while. Jacques was in the kitchen area making the coffee and Genevieve stared at the wall and realised that she had never felt more alone and more scared in her whole life. She shivered involuntarily and the ropes binding her to the chair cut into her wrists and she winced in pain and her eyes misted up once more.

Ten minutes later the others returned with baguettes, cheese and ham and fresh tomatoes which they placed on the small dining table. The three of them sat down around the table and started to cut up the bread and hand it round completely ignoring her. They started to speak in a low voice, barely more than a whisper and she could only make out the odd word.

A while later they got up from the table and disappeared into the two bedrooms. When they returned, they were wearing black trousers and black boots and the partial uniform of the French CRS police. Jean-Pierre looked towards Jacques and nodded and Jacques walked behind Genevieve and untied the gag in her mouth. He then stood in front of her and said:

"Listen this is what is going to happen. My friends and I have to go out on shift now to control more of your riotous and unpatriotic colleagues and socialist drop-outs. When we come back at 6.00pm pm we will have a little chat. Another friend of ours is coming to baby sit you. He is a member of the CRS as well and he also earned a rather nasty reputation overseas so do not mess with him. Just tell us what we want to know and then you will not be harmed. We will then take you to a place tonight at 8.00pm where we will exchange you for something that your boyfriend is going to give us and then that will be the end of the matter. Do you understand?

"Yes" Genevieve replied quietly. *"Can I go to the toilet?* She enquired.

163

"Yes but no funny business. There is no hiding place. Nowhere to run to"

Jean-Pierre once again nodded at Jacques who undid the ropes and escorted Genevieve to the small bathroom and stood outside the door and when she reappeared escorted her once more to the chair in the centre of the room and retied the ropes and replaced the gagging cloth in her mouth. Five minutes later the doorbell rang and Alain went down the stairs to answer it and was followed back up by another man. Compared to the others he was a bit scrawny and had a pock-marked face and when he saw Genevieve, he smiled revealing yellow stained and crooked front teeth.

"This is Albert" Jean-Pierre said *"He will just sit with you but please do not mess him around as he has a short temper"*

The three of them then said something to Albert who just smiled and nodded and then they left the apartment. Genevieve was more frightened than ever now. She really did not like the look of the newcomer. He had a sly glint in his eye and she noticed that whist he was sitting on the sofa smoking he was constantly looking over at her and she shivered once more causing the ropes to burn her wrists a second time. However, she was confident that Benoit would hand the film over to them tonight and then hopefully they could forget about this whole nightmare and carry on with their lives but she had some doubts about all of this. Still it was only about eight hours to wait.

A few hours passed and although nothing had been said, Genevieve felt that there was an increased tension in the apartment. Albert was almost chain smoking and he kept staring at her and seemed to be coming more and more uneasy. She did her best to avert his eyes but she was feeling increasingly emotionally uncomfortable. She was physically uncomfortable too as the ropes were binding into her wrists and her legs were starting to feel numb. She tried

164

to wriggle her hands and feet just a little to try and loosen the binds but also to ease her discomfort. Suddenly she noticed that the man was standing over her with a smug grin on his face.

"Do you want to be let lose for a while ma Cherie? He said with a sickening smile which exposed his rotten teeth and Genevieve thought that she might vomit there and then.

"If you play ball with me. I will play ball with you" and he leant forward and stroked her face and then her hair and he removed the gag from her mouth. Genevieve tried to recoil from his touch but was unable to do so but every sinew in her body went rigid.

"Such beautiful blonde hair. Your boyfriend is very lucky."

"Just stay away from me you revolting man" Genevieve shouted.

But Albert just smirked and bent down and untied the ropes securing her ankles to the chair and then released her arms from the back of the chair but still kept her wrists bound behind her back. He then pulled Genevieve up out of the chair and tried to kiss her but she lashed out with her foot catching him in the groin and he reeled back.

"Now that is not very nice and I will have to teach you a lesson in manners" and he pushed her towards one of the bedrooms grabbing the gag once more and thrusting it in her mouth and then forcefully threw her onto the bed causing her to wince in pain as she rolled off balance and unable to steady herself with her hands hit her head on a wooden side table.

Albert then quickly removed his jacket and unbuckled his belt and jumped on top of her as she wriggled and squirmed under him. She could feel his hands all over her body and the smell of his foul body odour and bad breath as he started to pull at her clothing.

Then just as she was starting to lose the fight, she heard the exterior door down the stairs slam shut and a few seconds later the door to the apartment opened. Jacques took one sniff of the air and screwed up his face and he looked at the ash tray on the table and saw the remains of three roaches and rolled-up reefer cigarettes and he said without turning round:

"What a stink! That is a nasty little habit that you picked up in Alegria Albert"

Jacques turned round sensing that all was not right and he then saw the empty chair in the middle of the room and the sounds of a struggle coming from one of the bedrooms. He rushed into the room and pulled Albert off Genevieve and punched him hard in the face:

"You dirty little weasel. I would avoid Jean-Pierre if I were you" and he manhandled him down the stairs and out of the front door. Jacques re-entered the apartment and saw Genevieve standing there with her blouse half undone and tears streaming down her face. Jacques removed the gag and untied her hands and said:

"Go into the bathroom and clean yourself up a bit"

When she emerged from the bathroom, he re-tied her ankles and secured her to the chair once more but left her hands free for the moment,

"Would you like a cup of coffee?" he said. It was all he could think to say. Although he was a hard and sometimes very violent man, he had never violated a woman in any way in his life and he despised those who had.

"Yes please" Genevieve replied weakly *"Just black with no sugar."*

After she had finished the coffee, Jacques rebound her hands behind her to the chair but he did not replace the gag in her mouth because she was completely silent. Genevieve had simply retreated within herself as she had sipped at the hot black coffee. She had said nothing and just sat on the chair staring into space utterly traumatised. In the space of just a few days her life had completely spun out of control and it was as if she was living a nightmare in a parallel universe.

An hour or so went past and she had not said a thing and Jacques had opened some windows in the room and sat at the table drinking a bottle of beer and reading a day-old newspaper. The tears gently flowed once more and ran down her face and dropped onto her blouse which she had refastened but two buttons had been ripped off. She thought of Benoit. He was so different to any other boy she had ever been out with. A year ago, she would not have given him a second look but she had started to tire of the party crowd and those on the far left. It had been so exciting in the first year of university and her father had been delighted that she was engaging so much in left-wing politics. But she had already started to find them a bit arrogant and negative. She had ended a relationship with a boy called, Stéphane, one of her group after a couple of months in the second term of the first year. Initially it had been exciting, having illicit sex in the dormitory but after a while she had tired of him because he was boring. Yes, they talked politics but his viewpoint seemed very narrow to her and they never did anything or went anywhere except to the same student venues. Most of all she found him a bit depressing and he never made her laugh or lifted her spirits. Benoit, however, was mysterious. He was tall and classically good looking but a little awkward in social company but she had liked that. She allowed herself a slight smile when she thought of their first night in bed together and how clumsy and awkward, he had been but he had been a quick learner she thought. She had been surprised how quickly they had grown together over the next few months and she could never have imagined that she would ever have moved into a flat with him but now she would not have it any other way. She whispered his name to herself;
"Benoit."

Jean-Pierre was in a foul mood when Albert opened the door of his grimy apartment in the rather run-down suburb of Aubervilliers at about 6.30pm that evening. Albert tried to close the door but Jean-Pierre was much faster and put his boot in the way stopping the door from closing.

"That was not very friendly Albert now was it? "he said in a low menacing voice.

"What do you want" Albert replied *"I did what you requested earlier on today"*

"Oh yes you did mon ami but you also attempted to do a bit of private work yourself with my captive and in my apartment. That is not good."

"But jean-Pierre........" Albert replied but Jean-Pierre raised his hand to cut him off.

"Now listen to me you little weasel." And he leaned in close to Albert's face and said in not more than a whisper *"Have you forgotten how I pulled you out of that burning car after you crashed it and carried you away to safety in Algiers just before the soldiers arrived? Now you can repay me twice. There will be no third time Albert. Do you understand mon ami"* and he patted Albert's cheek with his gloved right hand, turned on his heels and walked back to the black Peugeot that was parked on the street with Alain in the driving seat. Albert closed the front door quickly with a racing heart beat and a dry mouth.

Chapter Thirteen

Benoit arrived back at his flat at about 9.00pm. He had decided after he had parted with Marco and thanked him for his support, to walk the rest of the way home. He opened the door of the flat and was met with the now familiar mess. He switched on the lights but left the blinds open and opened the windows to air the two main rooms. He had not bothered to check if he had been followed and he was sure that there was no one watching outside now. It was now a question of what would happen tomorrow evening at 8.00pm in the Bois de Boulogne.

He set about clearing up the flat starting with the bedroom first. He moved the mattress back on to the bed and remade the bed by spreading out the sheets and covers. He then put the clothes back in the wardrobe and put the drawers back in the chest and started to replace the contents. He then replaced the ornaments that had been around the room. Some were broken so he picked up the pieces and carried them through to the kitchen and put them in the bin. There were also some broken photograph frames that had been on the bedside table so he put the frameless photos back where they belonged and swept up the glass fragments and put them in the kitchen bin as well. At least one room was back to normal he thought and closed the bedroom window and the blind and closed the door behind him as he went back into the lounge.

"What a bloody mess" he said to himself surveying the devastation in the lounge but he was far too tired and

emotionally shattered from the day's events to do anything more about it now. So, he collapsed on to the sofa and then remembered that most of the stuffing had been pulled out and hit the wooden frame hard. *"Bastards"* he said quietly. He reached for the crushproof packet of Disque Bleu from the pocket of his jacket that he had discarded earlier and lit a cigarette and found the two empty wine bottles that had been on the table and the two candles that had fallen out of them and set them upright on the coffee table and switched out the main light carefully avoiding the pool of oil from the smashed lave lamp on the floor and carpet.

"Oh Gennie" he murmured softly *"Where are you? How are you? "I know you must be frightened but I will sort it out tomorrow. I promise."*

The record player was laying on its side on the floor still plugged in so he righted it and sorted through the pile of records that had been strewn across the floor some out of their sleeves and some now broken. However, he managed to find what he was looking for; *'The Freewheelin' Bob Dylan.'*

He then went into the kitchen and found a half empty bottle of wine with the cork still in it and the bottle intact. He couldn't see any wine glasses that had not been smashed so he found an intact coffee cup and went back into the lounge and put them on the coffee table next to the two candles that were burning brightly. He then switched the record player on and loaded the twelve-inch vinyl record and sat down gingerly this time on the sofa. Miraculously the record player had not been damaged and Benoit felt himself relax a little as the gentle rhythmic melody and gentle lyrics of freedom of *'Blowin' in the Wind'* started to drift over him. He poured some red wine into the coffee cup and drank it but by the time the track *"A Hard Rain's a-Gonna Fall"* started to play he had already fallen fast asleep.

The next morning, he awoke quite early because the sun was streaming through the window with the blinds not having been pulled down the previous evening. He got up and made some black coffee and had a shower in the shared bathroom on the landing and then he found some clean clothes and got dressed. There was no food in the kitchen and what had been in the cupboards was still spilt all over the floor. He was not sure what would happen that evening but he just had to get Gennie back safe and sound and he prayed that she had not been harmed already but he had to be as ready as he could be for all eventualities.

Ten minutes later he was back up in his attic space and he found what he was looking for – a spare film tin that was identical to the one that he had hidden in L'église de la Madeleine the afternoon before. He then found some red-coloured intro film which was used to put at the front of a cine film so that this was threaded through the projector so if it got jammed it would be this and not the actual film that might get damaged. Then he found some pieces of exposed and developed film that he had discarded from the final copy of the film that he had made about Genevieve around Paris about six weeks ago. He spliced these segments of film together and then he found the film that had about thirty seconds of rioting and police response from a previous film. He held the film up to the light and selected the footage that contained this part and separated it and then spliced it to the front of the film footage about Genevieve and right behind the red-coloured intro film. He then rewound it onto a spare spool and placed it carefully in the empty film tin and put it in his pocket. He turned out the light and closed the hatch and came down into the lounge.

He carried all of the rubbish and debris that he had swept up, down the stairs and put it in the large dustbins at the rear of the apartment block. Unfortunately, the lift wasn't working again so he climbed up the six flights of stairs up to the third floor. He closed the front door of the flat and walked over to the record player and saw that Bob Dylan was still on the turntable so he put it on again and made some more coffee and sat on the battered sofa and smoked a cigarette just staring into space and letting Bob Dylan's lyrics and melodies wash over him. He knew that they would be able to get the flat back to where it was without too much difficulty and expense. Another secondhand cream rug, some more black photo frames and the ornaments that had been damaged. But somethings could not be restored. Firstly, the lava lamp and secondly and more importantly, the sense of security and privacy that had been violated and would be lost forever. But none of that mattered now. His only concern right now was that Genevieve was released safe and sound.

Chapter Fourteen

Benoit and Marco arrived at the Bois de Boulogne arriving there by Mètro and getting out at the Porte Maillot station. They walked along the Boulevard Maillot on the northern edge of the famous park which had once been royal hunting grounds but had been ceded to the city of Paris by the Emperor Napoleon III to be turned into a public park in 1852. Benoit nervously looked at his watch. It was 07.45pm; fifteen minutes till the agreed meeting time for the exchange. The film in exchange for Genevieve back safe and sound. His heart was beating fast and he was sweating as they walked along the Boulevard in silence. Marco was leading the way. He had kindly offered to check out the exact location of the statue earlier that afternoon so they would not get lost in the huge public park which consisted of over two thousand acres.

"Calm down mon ami" turning to look at Benoit behind him *"We are in perfect time. It is only a five-minute walk to where we are going"*

Benoit just nodded and patted the film tin zipped into the inside pocket of his jacket. They were following the signs to the Jardin d'Acclimatation which was a popular amusement park with rides, play areas, horseback riding, workshops and events but it was closed at this time of the evening. The statue of Louis jean-Marie Daubenton, the famous French naturalist was situated adjacent to the venue. Marco then turned left and entered the park and soon they could see the large glasshouses of the Jardin d'Acclimatation in the distance in front of them. It had originally been known as *Jardin Zoologique*

173

d'Acclimatation, where plants and animals from the colonies could acclimatise to France's weather conditions but that was now all in the past.

A few minutes later Marco stopped and pointed at the statue

"There it is Benoit" he said *"You go and place the film as they instructed and then we will go and sit over there"* and he pointed to a bench about ten metres away behind the statue and facing one of the glasshouses. Benoit checked his watch again, his heart now racing. It was now 07.55pm. he walked quickly up to the large statue and placed the film canister on the bottom of the statue on the white stone plinth and then walked back to where Marco was waiting on the bench. He looked around, there was no one in the near vicinity. About fifty metres away a couple were walking hand in hand farther along up the path in one direction and in the other a man was walking a dog but he too, was about fifty metres away from them. Benoit nervously took out a crushproof packet of Disque Bleu cigarettes and his lighter and lit one and then offered the pack to Marco who politely declined. He stared at the glasshouse in front of them and smoked the cigarette. Suddenly he was aware of a noise behind him and he saw a man at the base of the statue

"How the hell did he get there without us seeing him" Benoit said but Marco just shrugged his shoulders. They both got off the bench and stood up facing the man in a black leather jacket and dark glasses. The man said nothing for a moment and then he turned around and pointed to a group of trees and from behind them stepped a large man also in a black leather jacket and dark glasses and he held Genevieve by the arm. Benoit could not see her clearly but she looked OK and he thought that his heart would melt. He could feel it pulsing in his neck and his mouth was dry. He stubbed the cigarette out on the floor with his foot and

watched as the man bent down and picked up the film tin from the foot of the statue.

It was however, just as Benoit had suspected; the man would not accept the film that Benoit had placed at the base of the white stone plinth of the statue in good faith. He was far too wily for that. Marco reached out and took hold of Benoit's arm indicating that he should just stay completely still.

"You had better not have cheated on me mon ami for your girlfriend's sake"

"Of course not" Benoit said without blinking *"That is the film. You can check it"*

"Oh believe me I most certainly will. I have not survived this long by trusting anyone other than my closest friends."

He opened the tin and took out the spool and unclipped the end of the film and then carefully stretched out about a half metre of film.

"What is this" he shouted *"It is just blank red tape. Did you think that you could deceive me with this!"*

"No wait" Benoit relied anxiously *"That is what is called an intro tape which is attached to the film so that it is fed through the projector first so if there is a jam the actual film does not get damaged. Pull it out about another half a metre and you will see the film."*

So, the man pulled out another half a metre of film and let the initial metre of film dangle down to the floor as he held up the first few frames of the developed film to the light. Even though the images were small and the light was now not good at 8.00pm, he could clearly make out scenes of rioting and police baton charges.

"OK mon ami" and he turned and shouted at his friend who was holding Genevieve *"Jacques you can let her go. Come on let's get out of here. This mission is terminé. Alain is waiting in the car for us."*

"Just wait a couple of minutes Benoit" Marco said as they watched Genevieve walk slowly towards them and the two men walked off in the other direction. Then Benoit just broke free of Marco's hold on his arm and ran towards Genevieve and threw his arms around her neck and just hugged her to him never wanting to break the embrace.

"Oh Gennie. I just don't know what to say" he said as tears welled up in his eyes.

Genevieve placed the forefinger of her right hand on to his lips and just said *"Sssch"* and then kissed him firmly on the mouth and they walked hand in hand to where Marco was standing at the foot of the statue. Marco embraced Genevieve by kissing her gently on both cheeks and then said:

"Come on its all over. Let's go for a drink. Marie is waiting at Chez Henri for us."

They all walked back to the Porte Maillot Mètro station and took Line 1 to Châtelet and then to Jussieu and then to Place Maubert. As they crossed the Boulevard and walked into the square and towards the café Marie, who had been sitting at an outside table got up and ran towards her friend and embraced her firmly.

"Thank God that you are safe" she said *"This nightmare is finally over"*

They sat and ordered two large 1664 beers for Marco and Benoit and two large glasses of white wine for Genevieve and Marie.

"Are you celebrating mes amis" Henri said when he brought the drinks to the table

"We most certainly are" Benoit said

"But there is not much to celebrate right now" Henri replied rather solemnly *"Paris will be paralysed tomorrow with a huge strike. The Mètro will be closed. It will be very bad for business."*

"Oh yes there is" Benoit replied

"What?"

176

"Life" Benoit said enthusiastically and raised his glass to toast his friends whilst Henri just walked back into the café and shook his head.

Bruno was also celebrating with a large and boisterous group outside the café. They had pushed three or four tables together and were huddled round drinking copious amounts of beer and then one after another was standing up and giving a two- or-three-minute speech which was either cheered noisily with lots of applause or with a chorus of 'boos' and encouragement to sit down.

"What are they all celebrating?" Benoit said

"I don't know" Marco replied *"I will go and find out"*

So he got up from the table where they were sitting and went over to the group and said to Bruno *"Hi. What is going on?"*

"Well a few of us have been allocated a speaking slot for the 'Assemblées Générales' tomorrow night and we are rehearsing our speeches."

"Who has been allocated a slot"

"Me, Pierre. Nancy, Yvette and Paul who you don't know"

"What is yours about?"

"The future direction of the movement and how it can lead to the dissolution of the Fifth Republic and the return of true democratic government run by the people for the people"

"Well good luck"

Marco then wandered back to the other three and told them what was going on:

"We should go over and listen for a while one-night next week" Benoit said

"Good idea" Genevieve replied.

"I don't know anything about this" Marie said *"What is the 'Assemblées Générales'?"*

"It is a general assembly of the student movement which takes place in the grand amphitheatre in the Sorbonne

every night. I went for a couple of hours on one of the nights that you were in hospital last weekend. It was actually quite an amazing experience. I have never seen the amphitheatre so full. All the seats on the three balcony tiers were full so that means there must have been five thousand people in there."

"That must have been very atmospheric" Marie replied

"Yes it was. Very noisy but not chaotic! There were two flags, one black and one red, hanging over a simple wooden table on the podium at which the chairman sat to try and maintain order and keep things moving. I have to say it was very well organised."

"That is some feat actually" Genevieve chipped in *"I have been in there when meetings of only ten per cent of that number have broken up in utter chaos."*

"The loudspeaker system seemed to ensure that everyone heard what was going on" Marco continued *"From what I could tell each speaker was granted about three minutes but some were allowed more if the audience demanded it. It was pretty obvious that the audience exerted a significant degree of control on the platform and on the speakers and an interactive experience developed very quickly. Positive and well thought through speeches were listened to intently and loudly cheered at the end but those that were regarded as being useless, rambling or downright idiotic were given short shrift."*

"interesting" Marie said *"Yes I would like to go too one night but I am glad it is not going to be tomorrow"* and she looked over at the sight of Bruno once more on his feet speaking loudly and now swaying on his feet a bit unsteadily.

A few minutes later Benoit took a large sip of his beer and announced:

"Tomorrow Gennie and I have decided that we are going to Cancale in Brittany for a few days to keep our

heads down and have a rest and get over the trauma of the last week. You are both welcome to come with us if you would like to?

"Why Cancale?" Marco enquired

"Because my parents have a holiday home there. They have owned it for years. When my sister and I were young we used to go there a lot but I have not been there for a few years. I know where they keep the key and I also know the lady who keeps an eye on the property for them" replied Benoit

"How rich are Benoit's parents?" Marie whispered in Genevieve's ear.

"Very" she replied.

"That is about four hundred kilometres" Marco said *"There will be a strike tomorrow and everywhere will be closed and we may not be able to get any food or petrol."*

"I have a full tank of petrol and it will only use about thirteen litres to get there and the tank holds twenty litres and I am sure that one or two small local shops will be open on the coast. They always are. It is a long way from Paris up there not just in distance but in culture and attitude."

"That is a great idea" Marco said *"It would be good to get out of Paris for a while. It is very kind of you to invite us."*

Marco then got up and went inside the café to order another round of drinks. Does anyone want some food?" he said looking back from the café entrance.

"Can you bring the menu" Genevieve shouted *"I'm really hungry as I have not eaten all day"*

Ten minutes later they were all eating plates of oeufs et frites et jambon.

"It was the right thing to do Benoit" Marie suddenly said

"What was" he replied

"To give those thugs the film. At least it is all over now."

Benoit did not say anything but just turned quickly to glance at Genevieve who made an imperceptible nod.

After a few minutes she said quietly *"Benoit gave them a film but not the film"*

"What do you mean?" Marie said quizzically and with a little anxiety in her voice.

"Benoit made up a dummy film with just a little footage of a previous day's protest but not the footage that was taken on Friday 10th May"

"That was very clever and very courageous of you Benoit" Marco said taking a large sip of the beer

"Or very reckless" Marie said quietly

"You do not have to come to Cancale if you do not want to" Genevieve said to her friend *"We do not want to put you in any danger. We just want to do what we think is right"*

"What is that exactly?" Marie replied

"Those men are cold-blooded killers of two people who were our age. We don't even know if they were male or female but we think they were a couple. Their parents will never know what happened to them. I am sure that those CRS bastards will have disposed of the bodies somewhere and so the parents and close family members will never be able to bury them and grieve for them and have closure. Their lives will be taunted forever in the hope that one day they will return. The parents and the victims all deserve justice. Benoit and I decided that we could not live with ourselves if we didn't try and achieve this for them after what we have uncovered."

"You have done the right thing my friends. It was very brave of you and you have also told us and we have a choice whether to join you tomorrow or not but I think that we are in this too deep with you now anyway." Marco said *"I am sure that we will both see you tomorrow morning at the garage."*

180

Not long afterwards they paid the bill and walked back to their respective apartments. Instinctively Benoit kept checking behind them to see if they were being followed but there was no one there. When they entered the flat Genevieve said *"I see that you have started to clear up. Well done. We will get it back to how it was next week when we return"* She walked over and touched her favourite glass and chrome coffee table *"I see that this has still survived. It was obviously meant for us."*

Just as Benoit was about to turn off the lamp that was beside their bed Genevieve said *"Wait Benoit there is something I need to tell you."*

"What" he replied

"In the apartment in Saint-Dennis, one of the men tried to rape me"

Benoit could hardly believe what he had just heard so he just swallowed hard a few times and then pulled her close to him and wrapped his arms around her and he felt her warm wet tears dropping on to his chest and so he held her tighter still.

The following morning, Saturday 18th May, Benoit and Genevieve got up got up early and made their way from Benoit's flat to the underground garage at Rue Gracieuse where Marco and Marie were waiting for them. They descended down to the garage and found the blue Citroen in its normal place and Benoit unlocked the car and Marco put the bags in the boot and they drove out of the garage. It was an eerie feeling as they started to drive out of the city at about 7.00am The normal traffic, even at this early hour of the morning would have been very busy indeed with commuters trying to get to work and Parisians going about their daily business but the streets were virtually empty and every Mètro station that they passed was closed. All the shops were closed except for one or two independent convenience stores and tobacco kiosks and there were still some street cafés that were serving coffee and le petit déjeuner. They were to learn later that the strike that had previously been confined to the private sector now extended to all public services as well and two million workers across France were now on strike.

An hour or so later and they were making good progress because the traffic in Paris had been so light. Marco was on Benoit's left in the front passenger seat and Genevieve and Marie were on the back seat. They had not spoken much in the car mostly because everyone was exhausted from everything that had happened the day before but clearly there was something else. Suddenly Marie broke the silence by saying:

"I am sorry if I was a bit negative last night but I agree you both have done the right thing and justice needs to be done if you can make that happen. We obviously cannot bring that couple back but we can give their parents some closure. To be honest last night I was scared. I am not as strong as you two are and I am amazed at how you have managed to deal with everything that you have both been through. I think being beaten up by the police has completely knocked all of the confidence out of me and I just don't seem to have managed to get my composure back yet. What do you plan to do Benoit?"

"When we get back to Paris from Cancale next week I will retrieve the real film from where I have hidden it and then I will endeavour to get it to a responsible newspaper whom I can be confident will not suppress it but expose the information and give it to the right sections of the police and justice system to pursue. We must have faith in our institutions or we have nothing left and there will be anarchy. There will always be 'rotten apples' but I am confident that the majority are law-abiding and decent human beings."

"Who do you think would be the right recipient? Marco enquired

"I have been thinking about that a lot Marco. I do not want to make a political point here. It is just about making sure that justice is done and more importantly to be seen to be done. So I believe that 'Le Monde' is the most appropriate."

"Why do you think that" Marco said

"Because 'Le Monde is a newspaper of record which means that it has a large circulation throughout France and who's editorial and news-gathering functions are considered authoritative. I checked it out the other day, its headquarters are on the Rue des Italiens in the ninth arrondissement of Paris. The building is unmistakable because of the giant and impressive historic clock on its façade"

"I read somewhere that its circulation has reached eight hundred thousand since the riots and demonstrations have started so it certainly has the readership" Marie said.

"I think that is a good choice Benoit" Marco said *"Perhaps over the next few days we can discuss a strategy of how you can get the film to the right person safely."*

After two hours of driving they were clear of the northern suburbs of Paris and were by-passing the outskirts of Rouen. They decided to stop and found a small café open so Benoit parked up the Citroen. It was a lovely sunny morning with a clear blue sky and they sat outside the café and ordered four café cremes and a selection of croissants, pain au chocolats and baguettes with butter and strawberry jam. When they had finished eating Benoit passed round a crushproof packet of Disque Bleu cigarettes but only Marco accepted one and the two of them sat there smoking in silence. Genevieve had left the table and started to walk around to stretch her legs and then she turned back and beckoned to Marie to join her.

"I want to tell you something in confidence Marie"

"OK what? Have you decided to split up with Benoit?"

"No definitely not! Completely the opposite I am more committed to him than ever"

"Then what then?"

"When I was a hostage in that dingy flat in Saint-Dennis one of the men tried to rape me"

"Oh mon Dieu!" Marie replied and put her hand to her mouth involuntarily. *"He didn't succeed, did he?"*

"No thank God. One of the others returned early off their shift because the streets were relatively quiet and he pulled him off me, punched him and threw him out of the flat. The man was awful. He was scrawny and dirty looking with yellow-stained and rotten teeth and his breath smelt when he tried to get on top of me. It was disgusting and the thought of it still makes me sick now."

"Does Benoit know?"

"Yes I told him last night"

"Maybe you should talk to someone about this Genevieve. There are people who can help you get over this"

"I'll see when we get back to Paris but I don't want to make a fuss and I certainly don't want anyone reporting it to the police."

"Try and forget about it for the moment and just enjoy the next few days. I think that we all need to have a few days of rest and normality to recuperate."

"Time to get going" Benoit shouted as he and Marco got up from the table and left the money under an ashtray to pay for the breakfast that they had all eaten.

They all got back into the blue Citroen but just before they set off Benoit said:

"Would you like me to open the roof a little as it is such a nice day?"

"Great idea" Marie said *"We'll let you know if it gets too windy."*

184

So, Benoit got out of the car after unbuttoning the canvas roof from inside and then carefully rolled it back and secured it with the tapes that were on it. They continued driving and eventually reached Caen, the port city on the Normandy coast. Much of the city had been destroyed in 1944 during the Battle of Normandy during the allied invasion of Europe in the second world war but it had now been rebuilt and had become a thriving fishing and ferry port.

An hour or so later and they entered the town of Cancale.

"Why did your parents buy a house here Benoit?" Marie enquired leaning forward in the seat so that she could be heard above the wind noise coming from the open roof.

"I am not too sure" Benoit replied *"Because they bought it when I was very young but I think because it is a very picturesque town and is a very tranquil place to be by the seaside and my mother is a great lover of seafood. Cancale is known as the 'oyster capital of Brittany' and they are absolutely delicious. The taste of the sea."*

"I have never tried oysters before" Genevieve said shouting above the wind noise *"They are not common or very popular in Toulouse"*

"Then you are in for a treat" Benoit said and he turned round quickly to smile broadly at her *"You know that they are the food of love"*

"What do you mean?" she replied

"They are a renowned aphrodisiac" Benoit said and looked at Marco beside him and winked.

Genevieve turned to Marie and just raised her eyebrows and her cheeks were a little flushed.

The house that belonged to the Dufort family was an impressive three-storey stone-built house alongside the port; la Houle. It had a commanding view looking out to sea and then over to the Baie du Mont-Saint- Michel.

185

Benoit pulled up outside the house and parked the car in one of the two parking places and got out and stretched out his arms and took a deep breath of the fresh salty sea air.

"C'est magnifique ici. We are a long way from Paris and molotov cocktails and tear gas here."

"Wow Benoit. I can see why your parents love it" Genevieve said as she looked out across the port and the rows of pretty houses, shops, cafes and restaurants.

"I don't think the strike has affected this place too much" Marco remarked

"I didn't think it would" Benoit said. *"Wait here for a few minutes I have to visit Madame Dupré."*

"Who is Madame Dupré?" Genevieve asked quizzically

"Ah you will see. Come with me Gennie. She is a larger than life lady in all respects. She has looked after the house for my parents for years. We will only be five minutes." Benoit said turning to Marco

"No problem. We will sit on that wall over there" Marie said pointing at a low brick wall on the edge of the harbour. It was low tide and there were a number of fishing boats both large and small either tided to the harbour wall in the port or stranded temporarily on the sea floor as the waters had receded.

Benoit and Genevieve walked down the harbour front road and stopped outside a small florist's shop that was open and had baskets and buckets of flowers and plants outside. Benoit opened the door and a little bell rang out. A few seconds later a lady came out through some hanging strands of a ribband plastic curtain from the back of the shop wiping her hands on a green apron that was tied around her substantial mid riff. She was short probably only about one and a half metres and very rotund with a big mop of curly red hair and rosy plump cheeks. When she saw Benoit she just cried out:

"Mon petit! I have not seen you for a few years and how you have grown. What a handsome young man." And she rushed forward and cradled Benoit to her ample bosom as he bent down to embrace her and Genevieve thought that she would suffocate him.

"And this must be your beautiful new young lady that your mother told me about in her last letter." She said when she had finally released him and Benoit could breathe again.

"Yes I am Genevieve"

"We have come with two friends to stay at the house Mme Dupré just for a few days. Probably until Tuesday so three nights only, I think. Please don't tell my parents that we are here or they will ask all sorts of questions."

"No problem Benoit" and she touched the side of her nose twice with her finger *"Une liaison secrète. Très bien. What it is to be young. There is plenty of clean bed linen and towels in the storage cupboard. Things are not good in Paris right now ae they?"*

"No they are not. These are strange times Madame which is why we wanted to come here for a few days to get away. I will not need the key Madame as I know where the spare key is hidden."

"OK Benoit. It is lovely to see you and to meet you Genevieve. Please come and say au revoir before you go back to Paris." As they departed the shop, she turned towards the back of Genevieve and gave Benoit a slight nod of the head and a big smile.

"She is indeed a formidable woman Benoit. I thought she was going to smother you!" Genevieve said with a big smile as they walked back beside the harbour wall to where Marco and Marie were sitting. *"There is a shop open over there where we can get some food and provisions for this evening. The old town of Cancale is located up on the hill above the port and we can go and explore that in the morning."* Benoit said.

187

Five minutes later they were back at the car outside the house with the shopping that they had bought. Benoit unlocked the Citroen and announced:

"Come on. Let's get our bags out of the car and I will show you all around the house."

Chapter Fifteen

The Dufort's house in Cancale was a magnificent building. It had been built towards the end of the nineteenth century of large granite stone blocks that had become weathered over the years by the constant exposure to sea water and the elements. It had a commanding view out to sea and all along the harbour front and had large, shuttered windows at both the front and rear of the house. The shutters had been painted a misty blue colour that matched the large front door which Benoit had unlocked for them after retrieving the spare key that was hidden behind a water butt in the font garden. The house was a three-storey construction with two bedrooms and a bathroom on each of the first and second floors. On the ground floor there was a substantial lounge, dining room, kitchen and utility room and a large cellar that was accessed down some steep stairs through a door in the kitchen. Benoit had shown them all around the house after their arrival on Saturday afternoon and Marie had said that she could hardly believe that this was a 'holiday house.' Even more so because it had been so beautifully and tastefully furnished in a combination of a rustic and seaside French style with pastel colours and striped fabric sofas and light French oak antique furniture throughout.

"Wow! Is that what I think it is" Marco called out. He had wandered on into the dining room whilst the others were still in the lounge and was staring in awe at a large oblong painting on the wall which had been done in a panoramic style. It showed numerous gondolas and

gondoliers on the Grand Canal in Venice with the beautiful Venetian architecture lining the sides of the canal.

"Unfortunately, it is not a Canaletto" Benoit said as he entered the dining room and saw Marco staring at the painting. *"But it has been in the family a very long time and it is believed to have been painted by one of Canaletto's students in a similar style so it has a value of its own but not in the stratospheric range of a genuine Canaletto. I have always loved it even as a small boy. It is just so vibrant and atmospheric."*

"it is truly wonderful mon ami and makes me feel very homesick" Marco said with a smile as he turned to face Benoit. *"Thank you for bringing us all here."*

"You are very welcome. I just hope that we can all have a bit of respite after everything we have been through and the good news" Benoit said as he patted Marco on the shoulder *"My father always keeps a well-stocked cellar here!"*

"Sounds great to me. A little food, some wine and an early night for us I think."

It was the following evening on Sunday and they were all sitting in the dining room around an elegant old French oak dining table in the House of Benoit's parents in Cancale. Genevieve and Marie had cooked them a superb dinner of a chicken liver starter and a duck confit main course. Benoit had retrieved two bottles of Chateau Grand Vue 1965 red wine from the cellar under the house and decanted them into two cut glass ship's decanters which he had placed on a side table in the dining room. He had gone down to the cellar with Marco descending the steep staircase that led from the kitchen once the entrance door had been unbolted. They had taken candles with them because Benoit had explained that there was no electricity down there. Benoit found some other candles that had been placed in old wine bottles and lit those from the one he was

190

carrying. The light flickered off the brick walls creating long dancing shadows as Marco looked around the cellar. There were cobwebs everywhere and a few pieces of furniture and the length of one wall which must have been five metres long and two metres high was covered in wine bottles in black wrought iron racking. He had never seen anything quite like it in his life.

"This is amazing Benoit. How many bottles are there here?"

"I honestly don't know but there must be a few hundred I would have thought. The vast majority are from our vineyard and are racked in descending years."

Once Benoit had selected what he was looking for they extinguished the candles in the old wine bottles and ascended the stairs back into the kitchen and the light and Benoit bolted the door behind them.

They were now eating a selection of cheeses, Camambert, Brie, Pont-l'Évêque and the blue strongly flavoured sheep's cheese, Roquefort which was Benoit's favourite. Benoit poured the remains of the red wine from the second decanter equally amongst the four glasses and then went out into the kitchen carrying a packet of coffee.

"This is Blue Mountain" he said *"It is without doubt the best coffee in the world and it is my father's favourite and he drinks a lot of it. Probably too much."*

"Where does it come from" Marie asked

"The Blue mountains in Jamaica" Benoit replied.

"It tastes so good because its unique mild flavour and complete lack of bitterness which is what makes it so popular and consequently so expensive. Gennie would you mind making us a pot whilst I will see what I can find in my father's cocktail cabinet" He was back a few minutes later proudly holding up a three-quarters full bottle of Remy Martin brandy.

"Look what I have found" he said with a big smile.

"Do you think that we should drink it? Won't your father mind. We have already drunk two bottles of his red wine and an expensive packet of his Blue Mountain coffee?" Marie enquired.

"He won't even remember that it was here" Benoit replied *"I expect that there is another one in the cellar anyway."*

Marie just said *"Ok"* and looked across at Marco and raised her eyebrows.

"Genevieve in that cabinet over in the corner there should be some cut glass brandy glasses." Benoit said pointing in the direction of an old French oak corner cabinet with a lead-paned glass window door to the upper half and a plain door to the lower half; standing in the dining room.

Genevieve returned with the glasses and Benoit opened the bottle and poured out four generous measure which he handed round and then standing up he raised his glass and said *"A toast to a brilliant French meal and thank you to the cooks"*

The others all stood up and raised their glasses to join in the toast.

Marco then pulled out a crushproof packet of Gauloises cigarettes from his pocket and passed them around but only Benoit accepted one and then he leaned forward and lit the cigarette with the flame of the candle burning in one of the elegant glass candlesticks on the dining table and signalled for Marco to do the same. He then took a long smell of the brandy having raised the glass to his nose and swirling the liquid in it slightly. He smiled remembering the aroma and took a long sip; holding the brandy in his mouth for a while to gain the maximum flavour and then enjoying the burning sensation as he swallowed it down. He then looked across the table at Marco and said:

"We are in a period of great struggle in our country and everything and everyone is very serious but do you think

that all the participants have genuine and sincere motivations?"

"That is a very hard question" Marco replied. *"Initially when it was just the student movement; then it would have been a simpler question to answer but now there are so many actors and sections of the population involved that I cannot believe that there is a consensus of motivation and direction."*

"Well start with the student movement then" Benoit urged.

Marco took a large sip of his brandy and then put down the glass gently and having thought for a few moments said:

"I believe that most of the students in the movement for change and involved in the protests and demonstrations do share a set of common ideals. They want a fairer society and to many that means a socialist society but not everyone so you already have a fractured movement. But I expect that the majority of the student movement do want a socialist society of some kind."

"Would you include yourself in that analysis Marco?" Genevieve enquired.

"Good question. I, like many people want to improve the world in which we all live. I would like to see an end to famine, war, unemployment, and pollution and a fairer distribution of wealth in society but I do not necessarily agree that this can all be achieved by getting rid of the capitalist system"

"I think our thinking is very much aligned mon ami" Benoit said taking another large sip of his brandy. *"I understand that to many Marx and Marxism offer a straight forward and essential analysis of the capitalist society in which we all live but I struggle with two things. Firstly, that the Marxist dialectic can be a simple panacea to all of the issues and problems within society when they are so disparate and complicated and second, many of the institutions that have been created were hard fought for by our forebears and many have provided stability and economic growth"*

"Such as?" Marie interjected

Benoit thought for a moment and then said:

"The equilibrium and balance that has been achieved by the introduction of a semi-presidential or dual-executive system"

"Please explain" Marie asked reaching for Marco's packet of cigarettes but lighting it with a lighter from her pocket.

"A semi-presidential system or dual executive system is a system of government in which a president exists alongside a prime minister and a cabinet, with the latter being responsible to the legislature of the state. It differs from a parliamentary republic, which we had previously and collapsed after the Algerian crisis, in that it has a popularly elected head of state. He or she is more than a mostly ceremonial figurehead, and from the presidential system in that the cabinet, although named by the president, is responsible to the legislature, which may force the cabinet to resign through a motion of no confidence."

"In that way we achieve the separation of powers which also supports a fully independent judiciary" said Marco.

"Exactly" Benoit added.

"That sounds very good in theory" Marie countered *"But I don't believe that that is what we are experiencing right now"*

"I agree with Marie" Genevieve said putting her glass back down on the table after taking a large sip. *"We have a president who is too arrogant, too aloof, has too much power and is too authoritarian and too conservative so where are the checks and balances now?"*

"I agree Gennie but that is the fault of de Gaulle and some of the rather sycophantic members of government rather than the system itself."

194

"You said that you were struggling with two things" Marco said *"What is the second?"*

"The second one is this. I am not totally convinced that the workers of France, the proletariat, are committed to radical change. They have serious grievances yes but I believe that the working class particularly, are at heart quite conservative. Their major concerns are not societal and structural change but rather closer to home. They are more concerned with wages, job security, levels of investment and a greater involvement in factory decision-making."

"I think you are broadly right" Marco said taking a final swig of the brandy that was left in his glass. *"But I do not think it is as simple as that because I don't think that the workers themselves speak with one voice."*

"What do you mean? Marie said

Benoit got up from the table and walked round it pouring out everyone another *generous measure of Remy Martin as Marco continued:*

"Well firstly, of the fifteen million workers in France, only about twenty per cent belong to a trade union and secondly it seems to me that the trade unions cannot agree on a clear strategy that they can all unite behind. For example, it would appear that the CGT are concentrating on traditional 'quantitative demands' whilst the CFDT seems to want to give priority to 'qualitative' demands for union freedom and to control by workers over employment policy and investment, while salary claims take second place."

"Interesting analysis" Benoit said as he took another large sip of brandy.

"I would be really grateful if someone could explain to me in relatively simple terms what is Marxist dialectic?" Genevieve said quietly *"I have never really understood it when it was discussed on the course."*

"Heavy stuff for a Sunday evening" Marco said *"But I believe that dialectic is a discourse between two or more people holding different points of view about a subject but wishing to establish the truth through reasoned arguments."*

"How does that relate to Karl Marx then?"

"I think I can explain Gennie. I did a lot of reading in my first year because I didn't have any other distractions" and he looked at Genevieve and winked. *"I am far from an expert but I hope this helps. Dialectical materialism is a philosophy of science and nature based on the writings of Karl Marx and Friedrich Engels. Marxist dialectics emphasizes the importance of real-world conditions, in terms of class, labour, and socioeconomic interactions. Marx's own writings are almost exclusively concerned with understanding human history in terms of systemic processes, based on modes of production (broadly speaking, the ways in which societies are organised to employ their technological powers to interact with their material surroundings). This is called historical materialism. More narrowly, within the framework of this general theory of history, most of Marx's writing is devoted to an analysis of the specific structure and development of the capitalist economy."*

"That was the simple explanation was it?" Genevieve said sarcastically

"This is enormously complicated particularly after a fair amount of red wine and brandy" Marco added *"But I think I can help by summarising the discussion for you Gennie. Benoit said that he struggled with the thought that Marxist dialectic can be a simple panacea to all of the issues and problems within society. I agree with this because many people say that we cannot understand capitalism without considering Marx. It is true that Marx wrote a lot about economic crises but that does not mean that every economic downturn proves Marx right. I am sure*

that there is a lot to be learned from studying Marx but there are also many other, more contemporary writers and thinkers as well, both economists and those who are not technically economists but whose work and ideas have important implications for economics and modern society."

"Bravo Marco! Well said" Benoit stood up and clapped his friend and raised his brandy glass in a salute.

"Very impressive Marco" Marie said and leant over and kissed him on the cheek.

The following day towards midday they all headed out of the house and walked along the harbour wall of Port Houle. The wind was strong this morning blowing in from the sea and both Marie and Genevieve had tied scarves around their heads.

"Where are we going?" Marie asked struggling to be heard above the wind.

"We are going to sample one of the best culinary delights in France. Second only to your duck confit of course!" Benoit replied. *"Follow me"*

Benoit led them to the far end of La Houle harbour to the *Quai Administrateur Thomas.* Past fishing boats that a few hours before had landed their catch. Sitting on the wall were a number of fishermen wearing blue smocks and faded denim kepis talking amongst each other animatedly and almost all of them with the ubiquitous Gauloises cigarette dangling from their lips. It was here at the Quai that the oyster market was situated and they were soon surrounded by baskets of freshly picked flat and pacific oysters set out on the vendors' stalls. *"Do we all want one"* Benoit asked They all nodded." Benoit bought a plate of six oysters which the vendor expertly sliced open with a knife and placed half of the oyster shell, containing the oyster on to a stainless-steel plate that had six hollowed out areas to contain the half shell and a central space for a lemon wedge. Benoit then took one off the plate and squeezed a little lemon juice on to it and lifted the oyster shell to his mouth and slurped it down and then relishing the flavour on his palette he said *"Perfect. The taste of the sea."* And he handed the plate round to the others. Genevieve, who was the only one of the group not to have tasted an oyster before was a bit nervous and apprehensive but she went ahead anyway and took one from the plate.

"Delightful" she exclaimed.

"What flavours can you taste?" Benoit enquired

"Salty, sweet, minerally and then citrus all at the same time."

"I think it was the French poet Léon-Paul Fargue who said 'Eating an oyster was like kissing the sea on the lips" Marco said

Marie turned to look at smiled broadly and said *"That's really nice Marco."*

"There's an extra one for the two cooks" Benoit said offering the plate back to Marie and then to Genevieve.

They left the market and Benoit led them on a walk along the coastal footpath that was once used by customs men on the look-out for smugglers. The path gave them some fantastic panoramic views across the Bay of Mont Saint-Michel that was punctuated by the rhythm of the tides, flocks of gulls and other birds wheeling across the sky on the strong wind which blew hard against them and made their eyes water.

"This is wonderful Benoit" Marie shouted above the noise of the wind.

"Not an aroma of tear gas anywhere" Benoit replied laughing.

Later that evening they were sitting in the lounge of the house in Cancale and listening to various records that they had brought with them on Benoit's parents' state-of-the-art radiogram. They had decided that after the gourmet meal that they had had the night before that as this was their last night at the house before returning to Paris in the morning, they would just have a simple supper. Marie had cooked a huge saucepan of Moules-frites and slices of baguette to soak up the beautiful juice of white wine, parsley, garlic, olive oil and crème fraiche and she had divided it all out into four large bowls and put the frites on a large flat serving dish so that they could all share them.

"It just doesn't get any better than this" Marco said

"I agree" Genevieve added *"I am so glad that you went back to the market at Quai Administrateur Thomas after our coastal walk to buy the fresh mussels Benoit"*

"So am I. There is something so special about the mussels here. It is the freshness straight from the sea without having to be transported anywhere. They grow them on ropes just outside the harbour." As he said that he got up and went into the kitchen and came back with a chilled bottle of Muscadet white wine and four glasses. Marie and Marco had insisted on buying two bottles of the wine because they didn't feel comfortable drinking any more of Benoit's father's wine. Benoit poured out the wine and they all shared a toast and ate in silence as the pile of mussel shells grew larger and larger on another large flat dish that Marie had put on the coffee table in front of them.

Later, after they had cleared away the plates and dishes and Benoit had replenished their wine glasses, Marco and Benoit smoked a cigarette each whilst the girls were tidying up the kitchen.

"What do you think you will do at the end of the summer term after you have graduated?" Benoit enquired knowing that Marco was in the third year whilst he and Genevieve were still in their second.

"You are assuming that the university will reopen and that we will be able to sit our exams"

"Yes of course I am"

"I am not sure yet" Marco replied *"I have been giving it a good deal of thought. I do not think that I will stay in France and particularly not in Paris. A lot will depend on what Marie wants to do"*

"Do you think that you will stay together?"

"I hope so but we haven't really talked about it. I would like to return to Italy."

"Where exactly are you from?" Benoit enquired

"I was born and brought up in Lombardy in the north of Italy and we lived in various places but my parents have now settled in a city called Pavia which is about forty kilometres south of Milan which is a very nice area and to be honest I miss it quite a lot"

"What do your parents do?"

"My father is a lawyer and my mother is a schoolteacher. There is just me and my older sister, Louisa who started in the fashion industry in Milan and has now moved to London. She has done really well for herself."

"What would you like to do?"

"That is a hard question mon ami and one I have given a great deal of thought to over the last couple of years. I am good at languages as you know and can speak fluent Italian, French and English but is there a market for a multi-lingual qualified sociologist?"

Benoit burst out laughing and stubbed out his cigarette in the large cut glass ashtray that was on the light French oak coffee table in front of them.

"And what about you Benoit? I expect that your father will want you back at the *Chateau when you finish at the Sorbonne."*

"Yes he will expect me to return to Saint-Émilion but I am not sure that I am ready for or indeed even want that life. Tell me Marco why is it different for my sister Monica? Why is there no expectation of her and she is free and even encouraged to pursue her career in medicine? And then there is Genevieve." Benoit sighed and poured out another

glass of wine for himself and Marco and accepted another cigarette that Marco offered him.

They sat in silence for a moment and then Benoit got up and put a record on the radiogram. He chose '*Strange Days*' *by The Doors* and sat back listening to the opening track of the same name.

"*Do you know Benoit I think that I would quite like to get involved in the Italian media industry. There are a lot of very successful youth-orientated magazines focusing on fashion and music which I would particularly be interested in. My sister has been dating an Italian man for about three years now and he is quite senior at the company that owns the Italian music magazine called 'Giovanni' and he has already indicated that they may be willing to take me on for a trial period because of my English skills which would enable me to work in Britain or America as well as in Italy.*"

"*That sounds really exciting Marco and I think that you would be well suited to that environment. Where did they say that you would be based?*"

"*Milan.*"

"*So what does Marie say that she would like to do?*"

"*That's the problem. She hasn't said anything and every time I raise the subject, she just dismisses it saying something will turn up. Marie was born and brought up in Paris. She knows the city and she is a true Parisian. Do you know what I mean by that?*"

"*I am not sure. I know that they have a reputation for being a bit snobby and stand-offish and a sort of arrogance. Is that what you mean?*"

"*In part. A lot of that is just myths and clichés but with all things there are some grains of truth in them. Marie has elements of all of that, she is headstrong, determined and very fashion-conscious. She can make ordinary casual clothes look very stylish just by the way she wears them or the accessories she adds to them. Have you noticed how she*" *often wears sunglasses even on a cloudy day? But at the same time, she can be quite dismissive and impetuous. Paris may be one of the prettiest cities in the world, but having been born and brought up there has certain drawbacks. First of all, Paris has one of the highest population densities in Europe. Consequently, its residents are faced with constant traffic jams, crowded streets, and packed public transport. In the end, perhaps the apparent coldness of Parisians is above all a way to protect themselves from any agitation and the infernal pace of life in the city?"*

"I know what you mean about Paris and Parisians. Whatever happens next year I will not stay in Paris either. So how does all that manifest itself in her?"

"I love all of those facets of Marie's character. It is what makes her who she is but it does seem to mean that she doesn't seem to be able to slow down and consider things."

Jim Morrison was singing '*When the Music's' over*' as Marie and Genevieve walked back into the lounge. Genevieve was carrying the second bottle of chilled Muscadet which she passed to Benoit together with the corkscrew and asked him to open it.

Benoit refilled everyone's glasses and said:

"Thank you all for coming to stay at the house in Cancale. It has been a lovely few days' break with you. I have enjoyed it a lot and I had forgotten how much this place means to me and the memories of my childhood that are here but tomorrow we will travel back to Paris. I wonder what the situation is like there?"

"I hope that those men have finally gone away" Marie said

Benoit looked at Genevieve and he felt a knot in his stomach and he knew that she would be feeling the same way. They had managed to put their experiences temporarily behind them but now it was going to be back to their new reality once more.

The following morning, they all awoke fairly early and after breakfast cleared the house and repacked the car.

Benoit said "I will just go and say goodbye to Madame Dupré and let her know that we are leaving. Do not worry too much because she will change the beds and clean the house thoroughly the way that she knows that my mother likes it to be done."

Ten minutes later he was back.

"So you escaped with your life then" Genevieve said laughing

"Only just!"

They all got into the Citroen as Benoit locked the front door and relocated the key back in its hiding place behind the water butt. He then closed the black wrought iron garden gate which clanged loudly as it connected with the railings, climbed into the car and started the engine.

Chapter Sixteen

Jean-Pierre had gone absolutely apoplectic when he discovered that he had been duped and the film that they had exchanged their hostage for was not the one that incriminated him and probably Jacques as well. He had decided just as a precaution to have the film checked by someone he knew that worked in a police film laboratory and he had discovered that the film contained about thirty seconds of footage from a demonstration that took place before Friday 10th May and the rest of the footage was of their previous captive at various sight-seeing spots around Paris.

"I have had enough of these games Jacques" he had said as he threw the film tin against the wall in the Saint-Dennis apartment above the North African women's clothing and fabric shop. *"No one puts one over on me. We will now go in hard and they will know what is to double cross former members of the OAS."*

He was glad now that he had instituted his other insurance policy, that of ordering Albert to do a stake-out of the apartment in the rue de la Clef every other night to determine when they were in residence; just in case of an occurrence like this.

"They do not know who they are dealing with. I have not survived so long in enemy territory to be outdone by a couple of college kids."

It was Albert's third night on watch outside Benoit and Genevieve's flat in Rue de la Clef. He had already spent a number of hours leaning against the wall and hiding in the shadows on Sunday and Monday night looking for any sign of activity at the window on the troisième étage – third floor window. It was now 8.00pm on Tuesday evening when he saw a young man approach the entrance to the apartment building. He slunk back into the shadow of a recess in the wall opposite and stubbed out the cigarette that he had been smoking. He waited in silence and then a few minutes later a light went on and started to shine brightly through the third-floor window before a blind was closed that dimmed it considerably.

On their last evening in Cancale Marie had invited Genevieve to stay at their flat the following evening because she had arranged to go out with two other girls that they knew from the university for a girls' evening at an Italian restaurant near to their apartment in Rue des Boulangers. So when they arrived back at the underground car park in Rue Gracieuse and Benoit had parked the Citroen back in its place, they had gone their separate ways and Benoit had walked back to their apartment alone stopping at a café to have quick meal of jambon et frites and two cold 1664 beers en route.

"Got you" said Albert and he turned and walked quickly up the street to where he had parked his motor scooter and he started it and began the ride back to Saint-Denis to report to the man who had ordered him to stay on watch.

Benoit had not slept well that night perhaps because he was not used to sleeping on his own particularly after having such a convivial few days with Genevieve at the family house in Cancale. He had got up at 7.00am and made some coffee and decided that as Genevieve wasn't due back until lunchtime that he would walk over to Chez Henri's and catch up with what was going on and what he had missed out on over the last few days. He would have to walk because the Mètro was still on strike. Just as he was about to put his jacket on and leave the apartment, he heard an enormous commotion going on in the landing outside, further up near the entrance to the lift. A woman was shouting and screaming and a dog was barking wildly and then yelping and a man was shouting loudly and swearing. Benoit opened the door quietly and peered out. At the far end of the corridor he could see his neighbour, Madame Charpentier remonstrating with a tough-looking man in a black leather jacket who evidently had got into the lift with her at the bottom just as she had returned from taking Charles, her little dog for his morning constitutional walk. The dog had attacked the man in the confined space of the lift and had bitten his leg and as the lift had got to the third floor and she had opened the grille the man had lashed out and kicked the dog hard.

Benoit moved quickly. He opened the door gently and then clicked it shut behind him and tip-toed to the other end of the corridor and as quietly as he could he lifted the bar of the fire escape and leaving the door open behind him descended as fast as he could down the black iron spiralled stair case. He reached the ground at the rear of the apartment block and walked quietly down the alley way and into the street and glanced quickly back. Leaning against the door of a black Peugeot 204 that was parked at the side of the road in front of the apartment building was a man in dark glasses and a black leather jacket. Just then the other man who had kicked the dog, came running out of the building, shouting and pointing at the man across the street and at another man on a motor scooter a few yards further down the road.

Benoit acted instinctively and with adrenaline pumping through his veins he ran down the Rue de la Clef and crossed over Rue du Fer à Moulin and then down Rue Scipion and then turned right onto Boulevard St.-Marcel.

He was breathing hard now and sweating and he dived into the doorway of a large men's clothing store. He stared back down the street furtively with haunted eyes like a hunted wild animal. His breath was coming in huge gasps. *'Maybe I am not as fit as I thought I was'* he said to himself. Then he saw him, the scrawny-looking man on the motor scooter as he came around the corner and started kerb crawling slowly up the street towards where he was hiding, his face turning from left to right scanning everything in front of him. Benoit turned away and stared into the shop window pretending to be viewing something of interest and held his breath. He stared into the large pane glass window and watched as the motor scooter passed slowly by him just a few metres away. He let out a deep breath and then walked quickly back up the street from where he had come but then walked swiftly across the Boulevard and straight into a tobacconist's shop as a large man in a black leather jacket walked around the corner out of Rue Scipion. *"Where the hell has he just come from?"* Benoit whispered to himself. He bought some cigarettes and a newspaper and walked out of the shop, lit a cigarette and opened the paper and held it up to his face and buried his head in it pretending to read something avidly. He made the occasional glance over the top of the paper and then sauntered back down the Boulevard and turned left into a side street and then he saw the Mètro station *Les Gobelins* in front of him. He ran down the steps into the ticketing area and followed the signs to the platform for northbound platform of Line 7 as he did not need to wait to buy a ticket because he always carried his monthly pass in his wallet. He stood on the platform and walked past everyone else who was waiting there to the far end of the platform for two reasons. One, so he could see anyone coming down the stairs and on to the platform and two, so that he could get into the first carriage and then be able to get out quickly at wherever he decided to alight the train and be the first to get to the exit staircase and away from the platform and out of the station. He waited anxiously and just stared ahead of him at the large advertisements on the curved wall of the tunnel on the other side of the track. There was one with the front cover of the latest 'Vogue' fashion magazine, with a close-up of a pretty model wearing a very chic black and white zebra-print hat that looked like a wrap-around. On the righthand side of that was a poster of a classic painting of two glamorous Parisian young women of the Art Deco era with the overprinted slogan of *'There's nothing in the world like Dubonnet'*. On the left-hand side of the 'Vogue' advert was a large black and white poster with a striking photograph of a glass bottle with a label on it with the writing 'No. 5 CHANEL PARIS.'

The train arrived a few minutes later and Benoit got in but not before anxiously checking down the waiting line of passengers standing at the edge of the platform. He sat down in the half empty carriage on the pull-down seat by the door so that he could get out quickly unhindered if he needed to. His mind was racing,"*Where do I go? What do I do? This whole situation has become a nightmare. I rather naively thought that this would all be over when we came back from Cancale.*"

With no clear thoughts in his head, Benoit just decided to stay on the train unless he saw a threat which he was glad that he hadn't and about forty minutes later the train arrived at the last station on the line; *Poissonière*. Benoit got off the train as soon as the doors were released and without turning, headed straight for the exit stairs and out of the station. If he had turned around, he may have caught sight of two men in black leather jackets and dark glasses exiting the train from the last carriage and pushing their way roughly through the other passengers alighting on to the platform. After leaving the station Benoit turned left and then crossed the Rue de Maubauge and through a myriad of small streets till he ended up in the Quartier Pigalle; famous for its neon-lit red-light district and eclectic nightlife; from the 19th-century cabaret Moulin Rouge to glamorous bars and restaurants. He found a café and sat down at an outside table on the street and ordered a coffee and smoked a cigarette, half glancing at the newspaper he had still been carrying with him. He looked all around at the crowds that were in the area. Pigalle had a bit of a sleazy atmosphere Benoit thought but it was also exciting and vibrant and the people he was now watching seemed to reflect that. They seemed carefree not bound by convention carrying on a tradition that had pervaded the quarter since the late nineteenth century. His senses were on the highest alert. His eyes darted everywhere, scanning every face in the passing crowd.

"Are you alright monsieur?" The waiter asked as he placed the coffee that Benoit had ordered on to the table. *"You have the face of the fox who is trying to evade les chasseurs."*

"I am fine. Thank you but you don't know how accurate a description that is"

The waiter just shrugged his shoulders and walked to the adjacent table where someone had called him over.

Benoit took a sip of the coffee and lit another cigarette. He had no idea if he had evaded his pursuers - *les chasseurs.* He suspected that he hadn't. Whether it was just paranoia or not, he had this constant feeling of being watched, of his every move being observed. After all these men were professionals and probably highly trained and experienced in surveillance and pursuit. He felt like the mouse being played with by the cat. He just could not live like this anymore. First thing in the morning he would retrieve the film tin and take it to the newspaper offices in Rue des

Italiens and hand it over for the personal and immediate attention of the News Desk Editor.

Benoit had been right. He was being watched. Unseen by him fifty metres away, one of *les chasseurs* was speaking into a wall-mounted public telephone whilst another had 'eyes on' the target, Benoit sitting smoking and drinking at the café table. Fifteen minutes later Benoit asked for the bill and left some money on the table and walked off.

For the next hour or so he just wandered through the small streets of Montmartre passing bars, restaurants and cafes all full of smiling people eating, drinking, smoking and full of life. It was a beautiful sunny spring day in Paris like the scene that had been captured so marvelously by the French Impressionist painter, Pierre-Auguste Renoir in his famous painting of *1876 'Dance at le Moulin de la Galette'* painted in La Butte Montmartre where he lived at the time. He passed by the bottom of the steps leading up to Basilica de Sacré-Coeur and intuitively just started to climb up the two hundred and seventy steps. He paused at the top to catch his breath and stared up at the absolutely stunning architecture of the nearly one hundred-year-old church. He decided not to enter the church as there was already a queue of people, mostly tourists, waiting at the entrance, so he just turned around and gazed out at the magnificent panoramic vista of the Parisian landscape laid out before him from the highest point in the city.

After a while he descended the steps and wandered on and found himself in the Place du Tertre, the small, café-lined cobbled square which was the hang out for buskers and artists painting portraits or drawing caricatures of visitors and tourists. Benoit knew that during the belle époque, it was frequented by Van Gogh and Picasso, and there are still touches of the incredible art scene that once thrived here. He had meant to come here with Genevieve but they had never done it. They must make time for visiting places like this together.

"Genevieve" he whispered "Where are you? *You must be wondering where I am?"*

A huge cloud of melancholia descended over him and then the clouds over his mind blackened further because just entering the square Benoit saw a large man in dark glasses. He wasn't wearing his ubiquitous black leather jacket but Benoit recognised him instantly. It was one of *'les chasseurs'* that Genevieve had told him was called Jacques. Benoit had also seen him at the statue in the Bois de Boulogne, he had been the one holding Genevieve. His pulse quickened and he darted into a café. He picked up a menu and pretended to be studying it carefully but glancing up every few moments. When he saw the man pass by the entrance to the café, he put down the menu, exited the café and started to walk out of the square. He had to get away but how? He walked quickly on through the increasing crowds in the Montmartre swollen by the good weather. Then he noticed that he was passing by the entrance of the Luxour Palias de Cinéma. He looked up at the advertising board and saw that it was showing the recently released film by Stanley Kubrick '2001: A Space Odyssey' with French subtitles. The next showing was in half an hour so he went inside. He bought a ticket at the booth and entered into the dimly lit theatre passing a sign which said that it had opened in 1921. Even though there was only a low light, Benoit could see that the interior decor of the theatre had an Egyptian style which he didn't know but had been influenced by the film *'Cleopatra.'* He chose a seat towards the rear and slid down in the seat to make himself as invisible as possible. There were only a few other people inside as far as he could tell and the atmosphere was hushed with people speaking in whispers.

Ten minutes later the curtains were drawn back automatically and the projector was turned on and a powerful beam of light cut through the darkness revealing the clouds of cigarette smoke in its path. The advertisements started and some more people came in but there was no sign of the large man; Jacques. Two and a half hours later Benoit emerged from the Cinema and into the bright sunlight and he shielded his eyes until they became accustomed to the light. He decided to find a café to get something to eat and as he walked along the distinctive opening fanfare of Richard Strauss; '*Also sprach Zarathustra*' was still ringing in his ears. He stopped at a café and went inside not wanting to be too visible. He ordered a 1664 beer and a cheese and ham omelette and frites. He ate the food greedily realising that he had not eaten anything since the previous evening. He had been thankfully distracted by the film. It really had lived up to his expectations and what everyone had been saying about it but now he was back in reality again and the dark mood that had descended on him earlier was back. '*Where could he go now? Where could he sleep tonight?* He couldn't go back to the flat or maybe he should, to warn Genevieve that she may be in danger again. He put his head in his hands for a few moments; his mind in complete turmoil. He paid the bill and left. He looked across the street and he could barely believe his eyes but there he was again, leaning against a wall, smoking a cigarette. It was the large man in dark glasses; Jacques, *'le chasseur.'*

Benoit walked quickly down the street and then broke into a trot but he felt too full to really run. He didn't look back. He didn't need to as he knew he would be there. There was simply no way that he could shake off these people. As he jogged down the street, he saw a bicycle leaning against some railings outside a shop. Benoit had never stolen anything in his life but he was desperate now and he wasn't really stealing it as he had no intention of keeping it. He was just borrowing it or that is how he would justify his actions if he ever had to. He jumped on to the bicycle and started pedalling furiously avoiding the pedestrians who were constantly crossing the road right in front of him often completely oblivious to his presence causing him to ring the bell furiously rather than to slow down.

Benoit did not look behind him he just kept going. He hadn't ridden a bicycle for over ten years but he rode it hard now bouncing over the cobbled streets of Montmartre until he reached the intersection with Rue Caulaincourt where he slowed down and waited for an opportunity to cross. He saw a break in the traffic and started pedalling across the main road. Suddenly he sensed a movement behind him and there it was accelerating really fast; a motor scooter which was just a blur in his peripheral vision but as he went past, the rider stuck out a foot and kicked him hard. Benoit instantly lost balance and the bicycle veered out of control and collided with some large commercial refuse bins that were standing at the side of the road awaiting collection. He collapsed in a heap both dazed and winded.

"Are you alright monsieur?" a man on another bicycle shouted as he stopped alongside Benoit.

"Yes I am fine thank you. I just lost my balance somehow."

"That is because that crazy scooter rider lashed out at you. They are a liability in this city. They go too fast and where are the police when you want them? Heh?"

"Why did he do that"

"I don't know monsieur. Maybe you just got in his way. They are impetuous and always in a hurry with no consideration for anyone else."

Benoit got to his feet and lifted up the bicycle *"Thank you monsieur I will be OK now"*

Benoit leaned the bicycle against one of the large refuse bins and looked at it. There was no real damage just a few scratches and the mirror on the handle bars was bent and the glass cracked. Benoit felt a huge pang of guilt about the damage and the fact that he had stolen the bicycle in the first place but all of those thoughts vanished in an instant as he saw the large figure of Jacques in his dark glasses start to walk quickly towards him. He was about fifty metres away and narrowing the gap rapidly. Benoit had no choice. He just abandoned the bicycle and ran across the intersection dodging in between the two lanes of traffic. When he reached the other side he just kept running and within a few minutes he had reached the large imposing gated entrance to the Cemètiere de Montmartre. Benoit ran in through the gates but just before he did so, he glanced behind him but couldn't see the pursuing figure of Jacques, so he was confident that no one could know for sure that he had entered the cemetery. What Benoit was not aware of however, was the fact that this was the only cemetery in Paris that had never added additional entry points to the grounds as the years had gone by. This meant that he was potentially trapped.

He stopped running and walked slowly to catch his breath. He was surprised to see that the cemetery was quite busy. Montmartre Cemetery was one of the first garden cemeteries in France and plants and greenery grow everywhere amongst the graves and trees hang low over the grave sites and it had a wonderful peaceful and serene ambience particularly on a lovely Spring afternoon Benoit thought. So perhaps it was not so surprising that it was a popular place to visit by both the loved ones of the residents and the tourists who visited Paris. Benoit decided to secrete himself in the shrubbery behind a mausoleum structure that obviously contained the remains of a wealthy person or people. He looked at his watch, it was nearly four in the afternoon. He had noticed as he ran through the entrance that the closing time of the cemetery was 6.00pm so he decided that he would just rest up here for about two hours and then leave just before the gates were locked. It would be a relief even if it was only for a couple of hours, to have respite from this mad and macabre game of hide and seek. Benoit wasn't squeamish but he did not relish the thought of spending the night in a graveyard or of being discovered by a grounds man and being handed over to the police.

Across the city, Genevieve was getting increasingly concerned. She had arrived back at the flat at about 12 noon to find that Benoit was not there and he hadn't left a note although she could see that he had been in the flat earlier and overnight. She was just making a cup of coffee when there was a knock at the door. She opened it and was faced with a very distressed Madame Charpentier, her neighbour.

"Please come in" Genevieve said *"Whatever is the matter?"*

"Those horrible men were back. You know the ones that were looking for you and Benoit a few days ago"

Genevieve felt a sickening feeling growing in her stomach.

"I had just arrived back at the apartment block after taking Charles for his morning walk and I got into the lift and one of them came bursting through the front door and got in next to me. Charles took an instant dislike to him and started barking madly and the man made a movement with his hand and Charles bit him on the ankle. He is only a small dog so it can't have hurt that much but the man went crazy and started ranting and raving at me. When we got to the third floor and I opened the grille gate, he followed me and kicked out at poor Charles who let out a huge yelp. It was really upsetting."

"Is he OK now?" Genevieve asked sympathetically

"Yes I think so. He is asleep in his basket at the moment. It is just all so distressing. Who are those horrible bastards anyway.?"

"They are dangerous men Madame Charpentier. I will tell you all about them another day but you are well advised to keep out of their way. By the way have you seen Benoit?"

"Yes he was in the flat last night and when I was remonstrating with that bastard who kicked Charles, I saw Benoit slip out of your flat rather surreptitiously and then go out of the fire escape. I don't think he wanted to be seen by that man."

"No he wouldn't" Genevieve replied quietly with real concern in her voice.

That was five hours ago and there was still no sign of Benoit. She went into the bedroom and repacked her overnight bag. She decided that she didn't want to stay in the flat on her own as they may come back for her and the thought of being held prisoner again in the dingy flat in saint-Dennis almost made her gag. She had no choice but to go back to Marie's and ask if she could spend another night on the sofa. She scribbled a quick note to Benoit and left it on the glass coffee table propped up against an old wine bottle with an unlit candle in it and a few minutes after that she was walking down the Rue de la Clefs and back towards the Rue des Boulangers.

He must have dozed off because when Benoit awoke and looked at his watch, it was now 5.30pm so he got up from where he had been sitting in the shrubbery and walked slowly back to the entrance. The cemetery was nearly empty now and the visitors had all left. He kept turning around and checking behind him to see if he was being followed but he couldn't see anyone. As he approached the entrance gates, he took out a cigarette and lit it and just stood to one side of the path and waited. A couple of people passed by him on their way out but there didn't seem to be anyone else around so he took one last pull of the cigarette and then stamped it out on the floor and put his hands in his pockets and walked very quickly out of the gates and onto the main Rue Caulaincourt. He didn't look around or to either side but just kept his head down and walked briskly. As he did so he took out his wallet and looked inside. He only had one ten franc note left but he thought that that would be sufficient for what he wanted to do.

About five minutes later, he found what he was looking for; a taxi stand. There were no taxis waiting at it but neither was there a queue so the next one would be his. He just hoped that it would be soon. Fortunately, a taxi pulled up beside him quite soon and he jumped into the rear seat. He gave the address to the driver and leaned back in the seat.

He had been chased all day. He was now both mentally and physically exhausted and he didn't mind admitting it to himself; scared. He could now only think of one place to go that he felt that he would be safe and that no one else knew about. It was the last place that he wanted to go but he had completely run out of options and he knew that he was now in very serious trouble indeed. Perhaps fatal trouble. He didn't think that these men would just settle for getting the film back now; they probably wanted to tie up all the loose ends and get rid of the photographer as well. He could very well end up like the bodies of the two murdered students who had been killed on the demonstration on 10th May that had he captured so well on his film. *"How ironic would that be?"* He thought.

Chapter Seventeen

Genevieve knocked on the door of Marie and Marco's apartment in Rue des Boulangers after climbing the stairs because their lift had broken down again. The door was opened quickly by Marco who said:

"Hi Gennie. What are you doing here?

"Can I come in please?"

"Of course. What is the matter.? Please sit down"

Genevieve sat own on one of the old arm chairs and just burst into a flood of tears and uncontrolled sobbing just as Marie came into the room from the bedroom who rushed up to her saying:

"Gennie what is it? What is wrong?" She took a clean tissue from the pocket in her jeans and handed it to her *"Here. Wipe your eyes?*

"Thank you" Genevieve said and wiped her eyes and face. She let her breath slow down and said:

"It's Benoit. He's gone. He's not at the flat and he hasn't left a note or anything."

"Don't worry Gennie. He's probably gone out for a drink or a catch up at Chez Henri's or something." Marco said reassuringly.

"No. I know he hasn't. I know he is in trouble."

"How can you know?"

"Because Madame Charpentier who lives next door had an altercation with a man in the lift earlier today and her dog bit him and the man kicked the dog and she recognised him as one of the men who had been asking her about Benoit and I a few days earlier"

"It's them isn't it? Marie said quietly.

"It has to be" Genevieve replied. "Who else could it be. Well anyway evidently Benoit heard all the commotion and slipped out of the flat quietly and ran down the fire escape at the end of the corridor to escape but she is convinced that the man followed him soon after as soon as he realised what had happened."

"Presumably there would be others outside" Marco added glumly.

"And now they must have him" Genevieve said and started sobbing again. "I know that they are going to hurt him. I am sure even if he hands over the film they will not stop there. Madame Charpentier said the man was extremely rough and violent and incandescent with rage and she had been really frightened."

"Oh merde" Marco mumbled.

"Maybe it is time to go to the police now" Marie said

"Perhaps you are right"

"Even if you do. What are they going to do? Where do they start to look for him assuming that they will do that anyway? If those men have Benoit then you do not know that they will harm him as long as he hands over the film" Marco interjected. "I think you should stay here this evening. If Benoit does return to your flat. he will know that you are here and come over. I will go back to the flat with you in the morning and if there is no sign of him then we will discuss what we are going to do. OK?"

"Come on. Let's all go to the bar over the road and have a drink and get something to eat." Marie said handing Genevieve another tissue.

"I am not hungry" she said

"Well, just have an extra drink then" Marie replied laughing forcing Genevieve to smile weakly.

Benoit got out of the taxi near the Trocadéro and paid the driver noticing that he had very little money left now in his wallet. He was in the sixteenth arrondissement which he knew was a very expensive and exclusive neighbourhood and the least populated part of the city. He walked down the Rue Benjamin Franklin and then turned right into the Rue le Tasse. This was obviously a very upmarket residential street with large belle époque style apartment buildings, some behind large black wrought iron gates but all with a clear view of the Eiffel Tower. He walked a little further and found the number of the building that he was looking for. It was a very grand building indeed. He went up to the impressive front door and rang the bell. The door was opened almost instantly by a doorman wearing a green and gold braid uniform and he was ushered inside and escorted up to the concierge desk.

The concierge looked at Benoit taking in his rather disheveled appearance and said rather condescendingly:

"Comment puis-je vous aider monsieur?"

"I would like to have the key to apartment number twelve please monsieur" Benoit replied quite matter-of-factly

The concierge looked down at the Registry Book and replied *"I am sorry monsieur but I can only release the key to that apartment to Monsieur Dufort"*

"But I am Monsieur Dufort "Benoit replied showing him his 'carte nationale d'identité' which he had taken out of his wallet.

"Yes you are" the concierge said looking at the card "*But you are not Monsieur Philippe Dufort.* I *need the permission of Monsieur Philippe Dufort to release the key to the apartment."*

"Then please can you can call him on the telephone"

"Certainly Monsieur" and the concierge looked up the number in the Registry book and dialled the private business number of Benoit's father and the phone rang in his study in the chateau.

Philippe Dufort was in his study smoking a black Sobranie cigarette with a large glass of cognac on the table in front of him and wearing his favourite burgundy coloured velvet jacket and a light blue cravat. His glasses were half way down his nose as he had been studying the latest financial statements from the vineyard.

"Dufort" he said and then he just listened saying *"I see"* a couple of times and then he said *"Please can I speak with my son?"*

The concierge handed the phone over to Benoit and then stepped back from the counter.

"Benoit?"

"Yes father"

"What are you doing there trying to get the key to my apartment?"

"I am in some trouble father" Benoit said quietly

"What trouble?"

"I will explain everything tomorrow father but please don't worry"

"How did you know about the apartment?" Philippe enquired

"Monica found a letter addressed to you at this address on your desk a while ago and a concierge invoice and she told me about it"

"Did she tell your mother?"

"No. I told her not to"

"Très bien Benoit."

"Look father I don't care why you have got an expensive apartment in Paris and you have not told my mother. Let's just say it is a private investment matter but I need to have somewhere to stay for a night or two"

"Very well Benoit. Please pass the telephone back to the concierge."

A few minutes later Benoit was in the lift taking him up to the third floor as he had been directed by the concierge who had still given him a stern look when he handed over the key noting that he had no luggage with him. Benoit knew very well why his father had this private exclusive apartment in Paris but he was not going to discuss it with him tonight and certainly not in front of the concierge. It could all wait for another time. He walked along the thickly carpeted corridor and arrived outside apartment number twelve. He put the key in the lock and opened the substantial door and entered into a hall area. He then walked on and entered the lounge.

The room was beautifully furnished. Heavy ornate blue drape curtains hung at the long windows, held open by thick gold braid 'tie backs.' There were two matching blue velour sofas with silk cushions with a gold and blue oriental style design. Paintings adorned the walls and the French oak planked floor was covered with a large blue and gold oriental rug and a glass chandelier hung from a central ornate plaster ceiling rose. There was a small dining table and four chairs at the other end of the room, an antique mahogany card table and some side tables with ornate lamps and shades. A doorway off the lounge led into a well-fitted kitchen but one that was too small to eat in. Benoit walked back into the hall and discovered a bathroom with a shower over the bath and a toilet and another door off the hall led to a small spare bedroom and the last door opened into the master bedroom with an ensuite shower room and toilet. This room too, was ornately furnished with a large king size double bed with a quilted burgundy-coloured silk bedspread and matching scatter cushions. Paintings adorned the walls of this room too and a small chandelier hung from the plaster ceiling rose that matched the one in the lounge.

"Very tastefully decorated father" Benoit muttered to himself as he walked back into the lounge and collapsed onto one of the sofas suddenly feeling absolutely exhausted. He took a crushproof packet of Disque Bleu

cigarettes out of his pocket and lit one using the glass lighter that was on the card table in front of him that was placed next to a matching ash tray.

"What a day" he said to himself. *"This cannot continue, I will not be able to evade them much longer. First thing in the morning I will retrieve the tin with the film in it from the l'église de la Madeleine and take it to the offices of Le Monde in Rue des Italiens and hand it over at the front desk with an instruction that it should be taken immediately to the chief editor."*

As he sat there his thoughts returned again to Genevieve. He knew that she would be worrying about him and she may even have spoken to their neighbour, Madame Charpentier which would have made her worry even more. But there was absolutely nothing he could do about it. He could not return to the flat now. They would find him very quickly so he just stubbed out the cigarette in the ashtray feeling a huge sense of frustration and helplessness. This feeling of desperation would have increased significantly if he knew that a scrawny man with rotten teeth had followed the taxi in which he had arrived here at a safe distance on a motor scooter and was now parked fifty metres away up the road. The man had removed his crash helmet and was standing at the side of the road casually smoking a cigarette and glancing at the entrance to the grand apartment block every now and then. He waited for over two hours and when Benoit had not come out of the building, he put on his crash helmet and drove off heading north in the direction of Saint-Dennis.

After a while Benoit wandered into the kitchen and opened the fridge. There was no food in it at all but there were a couple of bottles of Sancerre so he took one out and found a corkscrew in a drawer and a wine glass in a cupboard and poured himself a generous measure of the white wine. He took a large gulp of the wine and put the glass down and started to open the cupboards in search of any food. Eventually he found one with some tins and packets in and he settled for a tin of foie gras and an unopened packet of savoury biscuits. He opened the foie gras and the biscuits and put them on a plate together with a knife from the cutlery drawer and took them into the lounge and put the plate on the card table. He then returned to the kitchen, topped up his wine glass and went back into the lounge and sat on the sofa. The wine proved to be a good match for the foie gras as its acidity cut through the fattiness of the paté delivering some lovely flavours.

A while later Benoit wandered into the bedroom and opened some cupboards and found a fresh bath towel and some of his father's casual clothes which were a little too big for him but would have to do. When he opened the top drawer in the bed side table looking for some socks, he saw some photographs inside. He picked up the one on the top and looked at it. It was a close-up of a glamorous tall blonde-haired lady in a broad brimmed hat holding a glass of champagne and smiling. He turned the photograph over and saw some handwriting.

"To Philippe"
Love
Valerie
Prix de l'Arc de Triomphe
Longchamp
October 1967

He replaced the photograph in the drawer without looking at the others that were there and closed it. He wasn't shocked or indeed that surprised by the fact that his father had a mistress. It was quote common in France particularly amongst middle-aged wealthy and successful people to have long-standing extra-marital affairs and he

224

was sure that his father had always been discreet and had always behaved with full consideration for his mother.

Benoit re-entered the lounge and poured himself another glass of the cold Sancerre wine from the fridge and sat back down on the sofa and glanced up at the gilt-framed antique mirror that hung above a faux fireplace with a beautiful and ornate plaster of Paris design over a wooden frame. He stood up for a moment and stared at his face in the mirror at one end of the room. He looked tired and drawn and he said quietly to himself:

"One way or another this has to end tomorrow" and then he just whispered her name: *"Genevieve"*

He then collapsed back on to the sofa and ten minutes later he had fallen fast asleep.

Jean-Pierre had been in a foul mood all day. He had exploded again earlier in the afternoon, still incandescent with rage about being duped by some 'bloody students.' Jacques and Alain said nothing but both knew that inside he was furious with himself and that the only way that he would get over it was to lash out with vengeful violence. They had seen it all before. However, when Albert showed up at the Saint-Dennis apartment later that night on his scooter, smiling exposing his rotten yellow teeth, and told him the news, Jean-Pierre had laughed out loud:

"All sins are forgiven Albert mon ami" and patted him twice on the right cheek.

Ten minutes later they were all sitting round the table in the dingy and smokey apartment drinking beer out of bottles.

"OK my friends. Tomorrow is the end game for this mission. We will settle it for good. I think that there is a very good chance that he will try and retrieve the film from where it is hidden and I am also sure that he has told no one else where he has hidden it so we will follow him and

wait our chance. The way I see it there are three options. We get the film and destroy it, we don't get the film but we dispose of him anyway and the film will almost certainly never be discovered or thirdly we do both" and he took a large swig from the beer bottle in his hand and grinned at his friends."

He then walked into one of the bedrooms and came back with his police-issue hand gun, a Manhurin MR73, a French made .38 calibre revolver. In his other hand he had a few loose bullets. *"I have had these a while so they will not have to be accounted for if we have to use them" h*e announced.

"Tous pour un" Jacques said raising his beer bottle in the air in a salute.

"Et un pour tous" replied Jean-Pierre

The following morning Benoit arose early feeling very stiff from his night on the sofa and he undressed and had a shower and found the best-fitting underclothes and a clean shirt he could from his father's cupboard and made himself a cup of black coffee. He was starving as he had only had the foie gras and biscuits the previous evening and he hadn't eaten all of it because it was so rich. So he decided he would leave and find something to eat on his way to the Place de la Madeleine. He had looked at a street map of Paris in his father's apartment before leaving and had estimated it would take him about half an hour to walk there and then he would retrieve the tin with the film in it and then make the fifteen minute or so walk to the offices of 'Le Monde 'in Rue des Italiens and then this whole episode would be over. He took the lift down to the ground floor and retuned the apartment key to the concierge, not the one who had been on duty the previous evening and a doorman opened the front door for him and he stepped out into the street. It was a bright day and Benoit took a deep breath of fresh air. This really was a beautiful part of the city. He walked back to the Trocadero and found a café and sat down and ordered a breakfast of a croissant and two rolls, ham, cheese and strawberry jam and a cup of black coffee.

But Benoit was not the only person to have got up early. The black Peugeot 204 was parked down one end of Rue le Tasse but there was no one in it. Jean-Pierre, Jacque and Alain had placed themselves strategically so that they could not be seen clearly but they all would have 'eyes-on' their target when he exited the apartment building. Albert was sitting on his scooter at the other end of the street just smoking and watching the people pass and pretending to be studying a street map of the city. When Benoit had left the building and made his way to the café in Trocadéro, they had kept in formation and were now just observing him and Albert had relocated to a new position at the side of the road. Twenty minutes later Benoit paid the bill and left the café and started to walk along Avenue du Président Wilson and soon he was in the Place de l'Alma where he stopped at a tabac shop and bar to buy some cigarettes and that's when he saw him. Jacques wasn't wearing a black leather jacket or the ubiquitous dark glasses but his formidable frame made him a familiar figure and Benoit recoiled in horror pretending to have forgotten to buy some matches just to give himself a few seconds to think. Benoit observed Jacques across the Place and he now assumed that the others would be here too somewhere. He was once again at the mercy of *les chasseurs* who seemed to be closing in on their prey.

Jacques knew that he had been seen and he immediately dropped to the back of the formation out of sight of Benoit and the others readjusted their positions. Benoit didn't know why he did it but he just panicked. Maybe he had finally had enough of this potentially deadly cat-and-mouse 'game' of hide and seek and he just ran. Which in hindsight was probably the most foolish thing to do but adrenaline just seemed to take over in a fight-or-flight response; an automatic physiological reaction that often occurs in response to a perceived harmful event, attack, or threat to survival.

Once Jacques had dropped back a little to be out of Benoit's sight, he then raced forward again to get ahead of him on the others side of the street. Seeing that Benoit had stopped running to look in a shop window and presumably take a surreptitious look at what was behind him, Jacques then crossed over the road. Jacques had effectively frog-leaped in front of Benoit and they were now on the same side of the road and he then dived into an apartment block doorway and out of sight once more. Seeing no one immediately behind him, Benoit started running once more and in doing so fell straight into the trap that had been laid. Just as Benoit was passing the doorway entrance of the apartment block, Jacques stepped out behind him and grabbed him firmly by his jacket. Somehow Benoit instinctively squirmed and struggled and he slipped out of the jacket leaving it hanging in Jacques' hands and he continued to run as fast as he could. He estimated that he could get to Place de la Madeleine in about ten minutes at this pace but how could he throw off *'les chasseurs'* to give him enough time to retrieve the tin with the film in it from its hiding place and evade them in order to get to the Rues des Italiens?

He was glad that he had got rid of the jacket as it was a warm day and he was sweating heavily now from the physical exertion of the run. There had been nothing of any significant value in the jacket and what did it matter now anyway he thought. He was now on Cours la Reine and running beside the river Seine and heading towards Place de la Concorde. Unknown to Benoit at this point, Albert had overtaken him and was sitting on the side of the road in the busy Place de la Concorde right now and Jean-Pierre was just about to join him leaving Alain and Jacques behind Benoit. The box was closing in on him fast although Benoit was unaware just how precarious his situation now was.

The Place de la Concorde was busy with both people and traffic. Benoit's mind was racing and his chest was heaving. How could he buy himself some time to keep out of their clutches until he had retrieved the film? Just as he slowed down an open sided single-decked tour bus stopped at a pedestrian crossing and as it pulled away again Benoit leapt on to the rear platform and caught hold of the guard rail and hauled himself aboard. Benoit patted his pockets and realised that he didn't have any money because his wallet was in the pocket of his jacket that he had now lost but fortunately the bus was quite full of people and the ticket collector was at the front of the bus and working his way back down to the end. When he got near to where he wanted to go, he would just have to jump off and run. The bus was heading north passed the Place de la Concorde and on to Rue Royale which Benoit knew would take him into Place de la Madeleine. Had he bought himself enough time? He really didn't know. The bus was moving slowly as the tour guide spoke to the passengers through a system of small ceiling-mounted loud speakers which were difficult to hear because of the traffic noise through the open windows and the open rear of the bus. Not that it mattered because Benoit wasn't listening anyway; he was just scanning the pavements on both sides of the road. But he failed to notice a scooter rider wearing dark glasses pass the bus and head straight on into Place de la Madeleine ahead of him.

The bus arrived into La Place de la Madeleine about five minutes later and the tour guide was describing the church and its history and as the bus slowed to the side of the road so that many of the passengers could take photographs,

Benoit leapt off the back platform and was pleased to see that the ticket collector was still only half way down the bus and hadn't noticed him at all. He walked up to the church, once again, mesmerised as always by its magnificent façade and then hurried up the steps, glancing at his watch as he did so. It was 09.45 which was fine because he knew that the church opened at 09.30 and there would be hardly anyone in it at this time. He entered into the church through the large bronze doors and his eyes took some time to adjust because the interior which was very dimly lit. There was some daylight coming through the three domes which are not visible from the exterior of the church and also coming from the pendant lights hanging from the ceiling. It was eerily quiet and he noticed that there were just three votive candles flickering on the table near the entrance which meant that either there was no one inside or only a very few people.

He walked quickly up the single nave of the church until he got to the location that he was looking for and he stared up. It was the statue of Jeanne d'Arc - Joan of Arc. He quickly dragged over one of the pew chairs and stood on it and stretched upwards, thanking once again that he was so tall. He felt with his hand and with great relief found that the film tin that he had secreted behind the upper part of the left leg of the statue and held in place with strong tape, was still there. He pulled it free and put in the pocket of his trousers but he was just about to climb down from the chair when a voice rang out in the dimness but Benoit could not see where it was coming from.

"Les chasseurs' had wasted no time and had caught him up quickly and they were informed by Albert that he had gone into the church just a few minutes before. Albert had parked up his scooter and he and Alain had gone to the entrance and were stopping anyone entering the church by

showing their CRS credentials and informing the only potential visitors so far, two tourists from Germany, that the church was closed temporarily whilst his colleagues were searching the inside for a very dangerous escaped criminal. Jacque and Jean-Pierre had hurried inside. Jacques had quietly moved around the edges of the interior walls so he would conceal himself as much as possible in the poor light and he was delighted to discover that there was no one in the church at all apart from the person they were ;looking for who was stretching upwards whilst balancing precariously on a chair and he had not seen or heard either of them. Jean-Pierre was concealed behind a stone pillar behind the statue.

"Throw me the film tin in your pocket or I will shoot you"

Jean-Pierre then moved out from behind the pillar and stood about three metres away from where Benoit was standing on the chair and pointed his gun directly at him. For a few seconds they just stood facing each other in complete silence in the dim light and then Benoit made a slight move indicating to Jean-Pierre that he was about to jump down and make a run for it.

"There is nowhere to run to mon ami. The entrance is guarded by two of my colleagues so just hand over the tin with the film in it."

Benoit just froze not knowing what to do and just staring at the gun that was pointing directly at him held in the outstretched hand of the man in front of him. Suddenly he felt a strong hand on his shoulder. Jacques had crept up quietly and was about to drag him off the chair. Benoit lost balance and fell to the stone floor of the church and as he did so the tin fell out of his trouser pocket and onto the stone-flagged floor with a small metallic clang. It rolled away on its edge for a few seconds almost in slow motion and then slipped through an old large black wrought iron grating set in the stone floor a metre or so away before anyone could move to get it. Jacques went over to the grating and got on his knees and peered down. It was very dark as he peered through the grate but he could sense that it was also deep and he could hear running water many metres down below the stone floor. It was obviously some kind of old drain that would probably eventually empty out into the River Seine flowing though the centre of Paris. Jacques looked up at Jean-Pierre and shook his head and got on his feet.

Jean-Pierre did not say a word but he kept the gun pointed at Benoit who was lying on the floor at the base of the Jeanne d'Arc statue. He then released the safety catch of the Manhurin MR73 revolver and a sinister smile came over his face:

"You have caused us a great deal of problems. As well as completing our exhausting shifts controlling riotous, traitorous and disrespectful students, we have had to spend a huge amount of time and effort chasing after you and your girlfriend. Perhaps we should tie up all of the loose ends now Jacques?"

Benoit thought that he was going to vomit, his heart was beating so fast in his chest that he thought it would burst and he was sweating profusely and he realised that he had just involuntarily wet himself. He tried to say something but no words would come out of his mouth.

Suddenly Jean-Pierre re-applied the safety catch on the revolver and returned it to the inside pocket of his jacket and said:

"Today is not the day you will die mon ami"

Then he turned and walked quickly back to the entrance of the church with Jacques following him behind closely but then he stopped for a moment and threw something on the floor. Benoit recognised it as his jacket which Jacques must have been carrying since he had slipped out of it a short while ago on Avenue Président Wilson. The two men exited the church and were glad to see that Alain and Albert were not with anyone else so they all walked down the outside steps of the church.

Benoit sat up and leant against the base of the statue and tried to take stock of what had just occurred. He had been a whisker away from losing his life and for what? Now even the film was gone. The men would get away with a double murder that the world would never know about. He buried his face in his hands and wept. A few minutes later he got up and sat on one of the pew chairs and did something that he had not done for a while. He clasped his hands together in front of him and prayed. He stayed like that for quite a time until he heard movement and hushed voices coming up the nave of the church. For one horrible moment he thought that the men were back and had changed their minds but when he stood up, he could see that it was just some visitors who had come into the church. He realised that he must look a mess so he hurried passed them, picking up his jacket on the way and made his way out of the church and back into the warm sunlight once again.

Chapter Eighteen

It was the afternoon of Thursday 24th May and Benoit and Genevieve were sitting with a number of others outside Chez Henri. It had only been a few hours since his traumatic experience in l'eglise de la Madeleine but he had insisted to Genevieve that after having a rest that he wanted to go out and already the experience was starting to fade like a bad dream. Genevieve had come back to the flat and was astonished to find Benoit back there having a shower. At first, she was furious with him, thinking that he'd been out drinking all night or something when she had been beside herself with worry but when she had heard everything that he had had to say she just embraced him and didn't want to let him go.

"Mon Dieu Benoit! I cannot believe what we have both been through."

"It is now over Gennie and we can get on with our lives"

"But those bastards will get away with murder"

"Unfortunately that would seem to be the case but we did all that we could. No one could have done more and we are lucky to have come out of this unscathed and still alive."

"It just doesn't seem right to me. There is no justice for those victims or their families." Genevieve said sadly.

There was already quite a crowd of people at the Café in Place Maubert avidly discussing the current political situation and the rising tension that was now prevalent throughout French society.

"There are now over eight million workers on strike in France" said Antoine *"The paralysis has spread out across the whole of France but Paris is still the epicentre"*

"What is more these strikes are not being led by the trade union movement" Bruno added *"They are being organised by the workers themselves who have put forward a broad and radical political agenda demanding the ousting of the government and President de Gaulle and attempting, in some cases, to take control of the factories. This is the real momentum of the revolution."*

"I agree" said Yvette who was sitting by his side. *"In fact, the reactionary CGT has tried to contain these spontaneous outbreaks of militancy by channelling it into a struggle for higher wages and other economic demands. They have demonstrated their true colour of being nothing more than government stooges."*

"De Gaulle is going to make some big television broadcast tonight" Antoine announced

"Do you think that he is going to resign" enquired Nancy

"Absolutely no chance" Antoine replied

"I agree" added Pierre *"If anything he is probably going to prepare the public for the possible intervention of the army. Troops will be placed on the streets and deployed to protect key communications centres like TV stations and Post Offices. I am convinced of it. He is a predictable animal and when an animal has his back to the wall, he can only react in one way."*

"Then they will be crushed by the overwhelming power of the revolutionary force of the people" said Bruno and Yvette nodded her head vigorously in support.

Ten minutes later Marco arrived with a couple of the days newspapers and pulled up a chair from another table to join the group. Benoit had already ordered some baguettes and coffee for him and Genevieve but when

Henri arrived at the table, he ordered a coffee for Marco as well. He sat sipping his black coffee and nibbling a piece of fresh baguette that he had torn off and put a knob of butter and strawberry jam on it.

Whilst the others were continuing their heated discussion he leant forward and took one of the newspapers that Marco had brought with him from the table in front of them. It was a copy of *Le Figaro*, the largest selling newspaper in France with a traditionally conservative right editorial line. Benoit stared at the headline which was confirming what Pierre had said a few moments ago that the government was preparing to deploy up to twenty thousand troops to take hold of Paris by force.

"I have bought some food Marco" Marie said as she approached the table a few minutes later carrying two carrier bags *"But the market wasn't nearly as busy as usual. Many of the stalls were not open because they cannot get any deliveries because of the strike."*

"Would you like to come to dinner tonight at our apartment?" Marco said turning towards his two friends.

"Yes, that would be very kind of you" Benoit replied *"Do you think we could go to that bar across your street and watch the de Gaulle broadcast on the television?"*

"Of course. Good idea. We can see what he has to say and have an aperitif"

"Ok great we will see you later at about 7.00pm." Genevieve said as she and Benoit got up from the table and walked hand in hand across the Place.

Later that evening the four of them were sitting at a table in the small bar in Rue des Boulangers. Benoit and Marco were drinking 1664 beer and Genevieve and Marie glasses of white wine. The television above the bar was tuned to the main news channel and the President was about to start his national broadcast. Half way through the President's address Marco turned to benoit and said:

"I just don't think that he understands what the mood of the people is. He is completely arrogant and seems to once again mix the so-called destiny of France with his own by usurping democracy with his own personal style of direct democracy"

"Effectively all he is saying" Benoit replied is *"Back me or sack me. He is saying that his way of reform was the only way out of the paralysis and the only way to avoid civil war and that choice can be made in a referendum later that year."*

The broadcast continued with de Gaulle saying:

"I am ready again this time, and above all this time- I need, yes, I need the French people to say what they want. And indeed, our Constitution wisely foresees the way in which it can do so. It is the most direct and the most democratic way possible – the referendum."

"If the people don't trust him to lead us out of this crisis now why would they give him the endorsement to do so later this year?" said a man sitting on bar stool next to Benoit.

"I think he is a deluded senile old fool" said another

"Come on" Marie said *"The supper will be ready soon"*

"Good idea" Marco replied *"I think there could well be more trouble after that address."*

They left the others in the bar to continue their debate about what the President had said and left the smoke-filled bar and back out into the street and walked slowly down to number 71.

Later that evening as Benoit and Genevieve walked back to their apartment through the streets of the Latin Quarter, he knew that Marco had been proved right. There was trouble on the streets of Paris and elsewhere. They could hear the sounds of sirens and big palls of smoke could be seen in the distance. They quickened their pace to get back to the Rue de la Clefs as soon as possible.

The following day Benoit left Genevieve to lie in bed later than she normally did and he walked to Chez Henri's for breakfast. Once more the signs of trouble on the streets from the night before were everywhere. Rubbish had been strewn across the roads from the big piles that had built up through the cessation of collections, remains of barricades and loose pavés were everywhere. When he got to the café he sat at a table on his own outside and ordered coffee and a croque monsieur. He loved the flavour of the hot toasted sandwich made with ham and cheese and béchamel sauce. When he had finished eating, he lit a cigarette and sipped his black coffee and listened in to the conversation of a group of four students whom he did not know at the table next to him and whom had obviously been on the streets all night.

He was to learn from their conversation that trouble had flared up within minutes of the President's speech ending on the television. Once again. the largest demonstration had been in Paris, where an estimated fifty thousand workers followed the traditional workers' route from the Place de la Bastille to the Place de la Republique. They had been cheered by crowds of spectators who lined the pavements. But violence soon erupted when students broke through police cordons guarding bridges across the Seine and armed with Molotov cocktails, they advanced on the French stock exchange, the Bourse, shouting *"The Bourse belongs to the workers!"* and *"Occupy the Bourse!"*

They had broken down the doors of the building and smashed windows, stuffing burning rags inside. As other groups of students on the street outside sang the Socialist revolutionary song, 'The Internationale', the Red Flag had been hoisted above the building. Police had used tear gas to

238

cut a passage for fire engines to get through but the rioters had made barricades of overturned cars and linked hands around the vehicles to stop firefighters from running out their hoses. By 2230 however, the fire was out, leaving the main floor of the stock exchange badly damaged but running battles between the police and demonstrators had continued into the early hours, with casualties numbered in the hundreds.

Benoit had just finished his coffee when Pierre, Antoine, Nancy and Marco arrived almost at the same time. Benoit accepted the offer of another coffee from Marco and then said:

"Thank you for last night. It was a really nice evening"

"Yes it was. It was a shame it was spoiled by that speech by an old bufffoon of a President" Marco replied with a smile. *"I honestly do not think he has any real conception of what has been happening in Paris and elsewhere in France over the last few weeks. He treats the citizens of this country with contempt. He thinks that the people will just give up their legitimate demands and dance to his worn-out tune once again."*

A week later on Thursday 31st May the four of them, Benoit, Genevieve, Marco and Marie were once again outside Chez Henri's drinking coffee, smoking and talking. As he had done lately Marco had brought a copy of *Le Figaro* newspaper with him which he had bought at a kiosk during their walk from Rue des Boulangers to Place Maubert. Benoit picked up the newspaper from the table after Marco had put it down and looked at the headline which was concerned with the large demonstrations that had taken place in Paris the day before. An estimated five hundred thousand people had turned up to march and protest, far more than the fifty thousand that the police had estimated would do so and they had been caught out and inevitably violence had flared up once again. Inside the newspaper on page three there was further coverage of the violence particularly in Paris and then a small column article caught his attention:

Paris
Wednesday 30ʳᵈ May

A convoy of CRS riot police was attacked as it sped along a motorway into Paris last night.
A group of protesters all dressed in black and carrying black anarchist flags were seen congregating on a motorway bridge and then a large chunk of concrete was dropped from the bridge which hit a speeding police van and smashed through the windscreen causing the driver to lose control. The van then careered off the motorway and down an embankment and overturned. Six CRS officers were seriously injured and two have been confirmed as being dead at the scene. The two deceased officers were named as 30-year-old Jean-Pierre Robert, married and 32-year-old Jacques Simon, single. The other injured officers are expected to eventually make a full recovery.

Benoit blew out his cheeks and took a large gulp of black coffee and then reached for the cigarette pack in is top pocket and lit one sitting back in his chair and stared out across the Place Maubert and the Boulevard and watched people going about their everyday lives buying and selling produce in the market for the next few days ahead but there didn't seem to be nearly as many stalls as usual.
"What is it Benoit?" "You look like you have seen a ghost"
"In many ways I think I just have" he replied and handed the newspaper to Marco pointing out the small article.

240

"Mon Dieu! That is them is it not?"

"Almost certainly" he turned towards Genevieve and spoke quietly in her ear *"Gennie it is finally over"*

"What do you mean?

Benoit took the newspaper that Marco offered him and showed her the article on page three.

"Yes. It is them" she exclaimed and tears welled up in her eyes and she put her face in her hands.

"It is Karma" Marco said quietly to her as she uncovered her face.

"What is Karma?"

"It is a term about the cycle of cause and effect. According to the theory of Karma, what happens to a person, happens because they caused it with their actions. It comes from both Hinduism and Buddhism and I believe that there is a lot to it."

"Please can you explain?"

"In other words. You are what you have done previously and what you have done will determine what you will do or happen to you in the future."

"A sort of natural justice" Genevieve said rhetorically.

"It is truly over then" Benoit said with more relief than he had intended to show.

During the day the government had appeared to be close to collapse but de Gaulle had remained firm, though he had had to go into hiding and had considered abandoning his position. However, after being assured that he had sufficient loyal military units mobilised to back him if it became necessary, he made a national radio broadcast early that evening, unable to use the television network because they were now on strike. Benoit, Genevieve, Marco, Marie, Antoine, Pierre, Bruno< and Yvette and a number of others were all huddled around a transmitter radio set outside Chez Henri where they had been all afternoon sensing that something big was about to happen. All of them remained silent as the President spoke:

"Men and women of France.

As the holder of the legitimacy of the nation and of the Republic, I have over the past 24 hours considered every eventuality, without exception, which would permit me to maintain that legitimacy. I have made my resolutions. In the present circumstances, I will not step down. I have a mandate from the people, and I will fulfil it.

I will not change the Prime Minister, whose value, soundness and capacity merit the tribute of all. He will put before me any changes he may see fit to make in the composition of the government.

I am today dissolving the National Assembly.

I have offered the country a referendum which would give citizens the opportunity to vote for a far-reaching reform of our economy and of our university system and, at the same time, to pronounce on whether or not they retain their confidence in me, by the sole acceptable channel, that of democracy. I perceive that the present situation is a material obstacle to that process going ahead. For this reason, I am postponing the date of the referendum. As for the general elections, these will be held within the period provided for under the Constitution, unless there is an intention to gag the entire French people to prevent them from expressing their views as they are being prevented from carrying on their lives, by the same methods being used to prevent students from studying, teachers from teaching, workers from working. These means consist of intimidation, the intoxication and the tyranny exerted by groups long organised for this purpose and by a party that is a totalitarian undertaking, even if it already has rivals in this respect.

Should this situation of force be maintained, therefore, I will be obliged in order to maintain the Republic to adopt different methods, in accordance with the Constitution, other than an immediate vote by the country. In any event, civic action must now be organised, everywhere and at once. This must be done to aid the government first and foremost, and then locally to support the prefects, constituted or reconstituted as commissioners of the Republic, in their task of ensuring as far as possible the continued existence of the population and preventing subversion at any time and in any place.

France is threatened with dictatorship. There are those who would constrain her to abandon herself to a power that would establish itself in national despair, a power that would then obviously and essentially be the power of totalitarian communism. Naturally, its true colours would be concealed at first, making use of the ambition and hatred of side-lined politicians. After which, such figures would lose all but their own inherent influence, insignificant as that is.

No, I say! The Republic will not abdicate. The people will come to its senses. Progress, independence and peace will carry the day, along with freedom.

Vive la République!
Vive la France!"

"I think that we are on the brink of a complete military lockdown and an imposition of martial law" Antoine said when the speech had ended and the radio had been turned off.

243

"I agree" said Pierre *"The gloves are off. He would not have made that speech so confidently if he did not have the full co-operation of the armed services of France at his disposal."*

"Where does that get us" Marco added

"I really don't know" Benoit replied

"We continue with the revolution comrades. That is the only viable option available to us." Bruno stated

"I think what we have just listened to is the last throw of the dice by a nearly eighty -year old benign dictator desperate to cling to power. But you cannot paper over the cracks for long and change will come to France" Antoine said philosophically.

The address was followed the next day with a carefully managed, but huge, counter-demonstration by De Gaulle supporters which blocked the Avenue des Champs Elysées. To the fury of the students and the more revolutionary workers, the trades unions accepted a generous, capitalism-preserving deal from the government: a ten per cent increase in all wages and a thirty-five per cent increase in the minimum wage, a shorter working week and mandatory employer consultations with workers. By early June, the strikes and the student demos had just gradually melted away. The reinvigorated forces of law and order were soon able to crush all that remained of the student revolt.

France had been saved and the Utopian society dreamt of by so many was cancelled, or at least postponed.

Chapter Nineteen

"So, what was it all about?" Marco asked Benoit a few weeks later at the beginning of July as they once again found themselves sitting outside Chez Henri in one of the last weeks of the term. *"Were we really just struggling against being corralled into a stifled education system that churned out fodder for capitalist institutions and factories but often with no employment prospects or the ability to have individual thought and creativity and forge our own direction? Or was it about the right to grow our hair as long as we want and to wear coloured trousers, and to have sex when we wanted or was it more than that?"*

Benoit looked pensive for a while and took a long pull on his Disque Bleu cigarette and blew the smoke out slowly in a long plume. He then stubbed the cigarette out in the white porcelain martini-logoed ashtray on the café table and looked up at his friend.

"Yes. It was all of those things and a lot more"

"What more?" Marco enquired

"You are right in many ways Marco in what you say. I think the whole events of the last few weeks were an enormous outburst of creativity and the desire for self-expression against a very rigid, authoritarian and reactionary society that had not yet evolved to embrace the modern world that we are moving inexorably towards. Just as a small example why should male students have to wear jackets, collared shirts and ties when students in other western countries are free to wear faded Levi jeans and clothing that identifies with a counter culture. The lyrics of

many of the Bob Dylan songs resonated with so many peoples' feelings of isolation and alienation?"

"But you are saying it is much more significant than that"

"Yes I am. It is looking like many of the students' demands will be met. For example, we will get a share in the universities' governance, overcrowding will be relieved, the curriculum will be modernized and most professors will be forced to change their teaching and assessment methods. These are all progressive results."

"But you are still saying that 'Les événements de Mai' as they are now being referred to are more significant. If so in what way?"

Benoit took a last sip of his coffee but it was finished already.

"Wait here. I will get us two more" Marco said.

When he had returned a few minutes later, Benoit continued:

"I think it was more significant because the people that have taken part will never be the same again. The protesters will feel that they were part of a new generational movement that was changing the old, encouraging sweeping reforms and being free to express themselves. They will always feel empowered and they will inspire future generations to challenge and question the status quo. But equally for the forces of law and order there has been a sea change too. The police have often been used as political actors carrying out the wishes of the state but what we witnessed during May here in Paris was that on many occasions, they started to act independently, following their own agenda and their own belief systems. If left unchecked this could lead to serious challenges for society in western liberal democracies and the tolerance of debate and alternative views and lifestyles in the years to come."

"Mmm interesting Benoit. We will see."

"Have you decided what you are going to do, now you have got your degree Marco" Benoit said after taking a large sip of his coffee and fishing out a crushproof packet of Disque Bleu cigarettes from the pocket of his jacket.

"Sort of" Marco replied with a tinge of sadness in his voice as he accepted the offer of a cigarette and lit it. *"I have decided that I am going to return to Italy. The magazine 'Giovanni' have agreed to take me on for a trial period of three months which is great news and I will be based in Milan. However, Marie has decided that she wants to stay here in Paris and look for employment. I am not sure what that will mean for our relationship as I cannot really see it working when you are so far apart and only see each other now and again particularly after we have been living so closely but we will see. What about you?"*

"It looks like the university will allow me to change my course in the final year to add a Politics and economics module to the Sociology which will allow me to do my thesis in that area. It will mean a lot more work but it is only for one year and I think that I will find it a lot more meaningful."

"That is good news Benoit. I am leaving Paris next week so we will have a good evening out before I go but, in any event, I would like to keep in touch and I will write to you when I have settled in Milan."

Almost twelve months later Benoit was sitting outside Chez Henri. He looked around him and recognised some familiar faces but there was a whole new crowd of students too who had not experienced the 'heady days' during the month of May the previous year. For a moment he wondered how much time he had spent sitting in this café and how much political and economic debate he had taken part in. It was almost like being in a parallel universe, being at the Sorbonne and participating in debate and discussion at this café. He had however, really worked hard during the past year and had achieved a good degree which he was delighted with. His relationship with Genevieve was still strong but they had both decided a few months ago to curtail their social engagements and study hard although Genevieve still socialised with Marie fairly regularly. A couple of months ago, Genevieve had persuaded him to accompany her for a few days to visit her parents in Toulouse and they had travelled down from Paris by train which had been a very long journey taking over six hours. Benoit remembered that on the way down he had been apprehensive about the reception that he might receive and initially he had been proved right to be so. Celeste Legrand had welcomed him with open arms and embraced him warmly taking in his physical presence and handsome features but Pierre had been cool and off-hand.

Later that evening, they had been having dinner together, all sitting around a table in the lounge / dining room and Celeste had brought in the main course in a series of lidded ceramic pots and placed them on the table.

"Sorry you will have to serve yourself if you can remember to do so as we have no butler to assist you" Pierre had said gesticulating at the dishes on the table and looking directly at Benoit. Genevieve and her mother both shot her father a severe disapproving look but Benoit simply quietly replied

"I cannot change my upbringing or my ancestry but I will shape my future Monsieur Legrand."

Benoit sipped at his coffee and then tore off a piece of croissant and dipped it into the dark black liquid and ate it as he remembered that very frosty atmosphere that evening. The weekend may have started badly but it did get much better and had ended rather well. Evidently Genevieve had stayed up till late talking to her father after he and Celeste had retired to bed.

"You behaved appallingly tonight father and I am really disappointed in you. You know nothing about Benoit, his politics or his worldview. You just judge him by your own simplistic and outdated views"

"How dare you. Who do you think you are talking to?"

"No. You listen to me or we are leaving first thing in the morning and you will not see me again for a long time. I have spent my youth having to put up with your rather myopic and jaundiced views on life. I have now received an excellent and broad education and have a far more balanced view of things."

"is that what we have struggled for bringing you up to see you so disrespectful?"

"Father I am not being disrespectful but I am a woman now and not your young little girl anymore. I lo...like Benoit very much and I am sure you would too if you could see beyond your prejudices and understand the real man and not what your stereo-typed view of him is. It is time that you got rid of this 'chip on your shoulder' that you have been carrying all these years. You must accept some of the responsibility for the industrial accident that you had. After all it was you who left the chuck key in the lathe all those years ago." Genevieve thought that at that moment she may have just gone a little too far as she had touched on the one taboo subject that was never discussed in the household and she held her breath waiting for the explosion which never came. Instead Pierre did not say anything for quite a while and then he stood up and went over to the sofa where Genevieve was sitting and sat down next to her. He then gently put his arm around her and drew her close to him and embraced her warmly.

"It is good to have you back home Gennie. We are both pleased about your academic success and you have indeed matured into a very modern and independent woman and I am really proud of you."

Benoit's thoughts returned to the present moment and he reached into the inside pocket of his jacket and pulled out an envelope that he knew was in there. It was addressed to him and he recognised his mother's handwriting and it had arrived at the apartment earlier that morning. He opened the letter and read to himself. It was dated a few days earlier:

"Dear Benoit
I am delighted that you have graduated and received your degree and done so well.

I am, however, writing to you with some sad news. Unfortunately, your father has suffered a heart attack a couple of months ago. We didn't want to tell you until you had finished your examinations. Fortunately, he has received excellent care and it was evidently only a minor one but it is a significant warning and he has had to make some big decisions about his lifestyle. He has had to give up smoking immediately and significantly reduce his alcohol consumption which I am sure that you can imagine he has not been happy about! He has also been advised that he should stop working completely. We have decided, therefore, to put the house in Cancale up for sale which I know that both you and Monica will be upset about. In addition, evidently your father inherited an apartment in Paris from an old aunt a while ago which he had been renting out and we have put that up for sale as well. With the proceeds we are intending to relocate to Antibes on the French Riviera – the Côte d'Azur because the climate will be so much more beneficial for him.

The issue as I am sure that you will now have realized is Chateau Grand Vue. When we both eventually pass away the Chateau will belong to

250

Monica and yourself and you can then do with it what
you wish but whilst your father is alive, he cannot
accept that it would leave the family.

Benoit put down the letter and lit a cigarette. He felt the
weight start to return to his shoulders and the old burden of
expectation and constraint start to return. A feeling he had
not experienced for some time now. He sighed and picked
up the letter once more:

"Your father and I would like you to come down
to Saint-Émilion next weekend to discuss the
situation. Monica will also be here at that time but I
suggest that you do not bring Genevieve with you.
Please can you telephone us in the next couple of
days.

Much love
Brigitte x

Benoit put the letter back in his pocket, left some money
on the table and walked across the Place to the Mètro
station deep in thought; so many issues swirling around in
his brain. He was not bothered about leaving Paris as he had
always intended to do so once his time at the Sorbonne was
over but returning to a very staid and privileged life in
Saint-Émilion was not what he had thought of doing at all.
And then there was Genevieve. He knew that Marco and
Marie's relationship had ended only a few months after he
had left Paris for Milan. Was his destiny to be in a gilded
prison in Saint-Émilion without her? He entered the Mètro
and walked automatically to the platform to take the
southbound train to Jussieu and then change trains for the
one-stop journey to the station at Place Monge. As he left
the station his thoughts went back to the events of just over
a year ago when he had been scared of his own shadow,

turning around every few minutes to see if he was being followed, pretending to read the Mètro line map and the sight of men in dark glasses moving towards him on the platform with menacing intent. He shuddered involuntarily and climbed the stairs out of the station and into the sunshine.

As he entered the flat, he could hear the sound of *'Good Vibrations'* on the record player which was filling the room with sound but somehow the music did not match his sombre mood.

"Are you OK Benoit? You look a bit down" Genevieve said as she looked up from a magazine she was reading whilst seated on the sofa.

"Yes. I am fine thank you. Would you like to go out for dinner tonight?"

"Yes. That would be nice but what is the occasion."

"Does there need to be an occasion for a man to entertain a beautiful woman" Benoit replied.

Genevieve smiled and stood up and put her arms around his neck and kissed him passionately on the mouth.

Later that evening they were seated in a Brasserie just off Boulevard St. Germain. They had chosen to have a starter of six oysters because Genevieve said that it would remind her of the marvellous weekend they had had in Cancale the year before. Benoit ate one oyster with relish and then his mind started to wander as he searched for the right words to say but eventually said:

"I received a letter from my mother today" and he then proceeded to tell her about her father and what the implications were for him. *"I realise that I owe my father a lot. He has supported me generously over the last three years that I have been in Paris and he accepted my decision about what course to take at university without making a fuss. Above all I accept that I do have a responsibility as a*

member of the Dufort family. You cannot just take what you want and reject the bits that you don't"

"*So what are you saying Benoit?*" Genevieve enquired looking straight into his eyes.

"*I suppose that I am saying that I will have to return to Saint-Émilion and take responsibility for the running of Chateau Grand Vue and the estate. However, I have decided that if I do that then I will only do it on my terms and my father will just have to accept that.*"

"*What are those terms Benoit?*"

"*That I will not live in that privileged lifestyle with showy and ostentatious wealth. I will have no servants and loyal workers on the estate will earn good wages and receive supplementary payments that are directly linked to the success of the business and the vintage that is produced that year. Furthermore, the business will be modernised without compromising the traditional techniques that have made the wine from the Chateau what it is but complementing them with new skills and technologies. However, there is just one thing..........*" And his voice tailed off and he averted the gaze of her eyes and stared at a large mirror on the wall.

Genevieve said nothing and then gently slid her hand across the table over the white linen tablecloth and grabbed his hand and squeezed it tight and without letting go she said quietly:

"*You don't know me as well as you think you do Benoit, do you? I knew that one day this situation would arise sooner or later and you want to know if I will come with you, don't you?*"

Benoit turned back from staring at the mirror on the wall and looking directly at her, nodded his head.

"*I made my decision over a year ago when I was gagged and bound in that dingy flat in Saint-Dennis and some man with rotten yellow teeth tried to rape me.*"

"What was that?"

"That I didn't want us to separate after we finished at university. A decision that has been reinforced by what I have seen happen to Marco and Marie."

"You mean that you would come with me?" Benoit said hopefully

"Yes but I would have to have some conditions too"

"Such as?"

"I am from a working-class background in Toulouse. I cannot live in a grand house like Chateau Grand Vue whether we have servants or not. It just doesn't sit well with me and it certainly would not with my father!"

"I agree with you. I have some plans for the Chateau. What if we turned it into a small, exclusive hotel with a superb restaurant that focused on gourmet French food that matched the Grand Vue wine? We could then have either an apartment in the house or there are some other properties on the estate that we could renovate. I would take responsibility for the winery and vineyard and you, the house and restaurant."

When he had finished speaking, he looked at Genevieve and there were tears running down her cheeks and she squeezed his hand harder not wanting to let it go.

"I am going down to stay with my parents at the weekend to discuss the situation and how things will work in the future and my sister Monica will be there as well. It will probably be for the best if I go on my own."

"No problem I quiet understand" Genevieve said as she reached for another oyster and gently squeezed a little lemon juice on it and then let it slide into her mouth and she once again relished the tantalising flavours of the sea.

"I wonder if these have come from Cancale?" She said

"Quite possibly" Benoit replied helping himself to another Oyster and the reaching for a glass of chilled Muscadet white wine that they were having to accompany the Hors d'oeuvre.

That Saturday evening Benoit was sitting in the dining room of the house in Chateau Grand Vue with his parents and his sister Monica. They had already had first course of wild boar terrine with cranberry jelly and toasted brioche and Charles was now pouring out everyone a generous glass of 1960 Chateau Grand Vue wine from one of the decanters that had been standing on the sideboard. When he came to Philippe, Brigitte said to Charles *"Remember just a half a glass please Charles"* and Philippe looked crestfallen for a moment. The cook had produced a wonderful Chateaubriand beef roast which was being served with a Bearnaise sauce and chateau potatoes and green beans. Philippe raised his half glass of wine and toasted his family:

"It is lovely to see you all here again together. I have had a long and very useful discussion with Benoit this afternoon which I would like to share with you."

It had indeed been a very interesting and surprising discussion that Benoit and his father had had sitting in his study and with no one smoking or drinking Blue Mountain coffee but just sipping chilled Badoit mineral water from cut glass tumblers that Charles had brought on a silver tray. His father had opened the discussion as Benoit had expected with a long almost formal speech about maintaining and respecting family traditions, loyalty and the pedigree of the wine and its reputation that the family had toiled so hard to build up.

But what had surprised Benoit was when he had said that he would return to the chateau to take over the responsibility for running the estate that his father started to visibly relax and a wide smile of what Benoit could only put down to relief came over his face as he had reached out and shook his son's hand firmly. So much so, that when Benoit had continued to say that he had certain conditions to his return, there had been no interruptions or objections and in fact for nearly two hours they had talked excitedly about the prospects for the Chateau going forward.

"This is a magnificent vision Benoit. Preserving the old and embracing the new that is built on a solid foundation" his father had said and then started to add ideas and suggestions which had had taken Benoit completely by surprise. *"I will help you draw up the detailed plans, timescales and a costed business plan to turn this vision into a reality"*

"There are a lot of points of fine detail to be worked out" Philippe announced after taking a large sip of his wine which had almost drained the glass and whilst Brigitte was saying something to Monica, he winked at Charles indicating to him to top it back up again. *"But Benoit and I have agreed the main points of the future direction of the Chateau and I have to say that nearly all of the ideas are his and his alone. I am very proud of him. Basically, Benoit will return home and over a handover period of about a year completely take over the management of the business. He will become the Managing Director. I will remain on the board as Chairman in an advisory capacity and Brigitte and Monica as directors and shareholders. We have also decided to appoint Didier Arnaud to the board as recognition for his loyalty and service to the family and to the business and also to ensure that the knowledge and pedigree of Chateau Grand Vue wine is protected and preserved for future generations. As such, again over a handover period, Didier's assistant, Bernard, who I understand has been working hard and learning fast over the last five years that he has been here will step up to the more senior role."*

"This is excellent Philippe" Brigitte said having just finished the last of her Chateaubriand.

"I will let Benoit explain some of the rest. Afterall they were all his ideas"

"Well as you know we have been producing the first growth Chateau Grand Vue for a long time here and just after the war we introduced our second wine which has also been very successful. But now I would like to introduce a third wine that is radically different to the other two and will be marketed with no obvious connection initially with Chateau Grand Vue. It will be a lighter, more modern wine, with less tannins and a lower alcohol content to appeal to a younger age group of less traditional wine drinkers. I believe that if we do this now, we will be ahead of the curve."

"I think this is a superb idea and I believe that the development of this wine should be given as a project for Bernard to manage as part of his development."

"Furthermore" Benoit continued *"It is likely that Genevieve will come and live with me here at the Chateau but neither of us wish to live in the grand house so we have decided to renovate one of the rundown properties on the estate. One or two of them are quite substantial and we can then restore it how we both would like it to be."*

"What about the main house?" Monica enquired.

"It would be my intention to transform it into an exclusive wine hotel, for discerning people to have residential courses on wine appreciation and tasting which would take place in part of the house that will be turned into the Chateau Grand Vue Wine School. The School will be matched with a small but very upmarket restaurant in which menus will be developed to pair with our wines perfectly. It would be my intention that Genevieve has a lead role in the development of the restaurant design and particularly in the development of a fantastic front of house service style for both the restaurant, the School and the hotel. The idea is to use our reputation to develop a brand that becomes synonymous with wine, food and service excellence. I am aware that Genevieve may lack the

culinary expertise to develop the menu content but we will have to work on that"

"*Do not worry Benoit.*" Philippe interrupted winking again at Charles to replenish his glass when Brigitte was not looking. "*After you left my study earlier, I made a call to an old friend, Paul Bocuse. Brigitte and I have been fortunate enough to have dined at his restaurant* L'Auberge du Pont de Collonge *in Collonges-au-Mont d'or near Lyons many times and it has become world renowned and we have become very good friends. Paul thinks our ideas are excellent. So much so that he would like to rotate one of his students at a time from his Culinary School to work with us on a six-month basis to develop the menu content and run the back of house operation.*"

"*This is incredible father*" Benoit said and Monica and Brigitte both added their own approval.

Philippe beamed and then added "*According to Paul many of his students are developing menus that are based on a more modern style of French cuisine which is not based on Escoffier and use new techniques and applications which he believes could pair with our new wine very well indeed. There is much work to do but we have the time. Brigitte and I have two properties to sell and one to buy. Before I suggest that we toast our new venture there is one further thing that I would like to say. I have also had a meeting with Charles just before we sat down for dinner. Charles has been a loyal member of our household for over fifty years as did his father before him and Charles has earned an opportunity to retire and has accepted my offer of a pension and the use for life of one of the small properties on the estate which will be renovated to how he would like it to be so he can be comfortable in his advancing years. Let us all toast the future of Chateau Grand Vue. Charles please fill all our glasses and ensure that you pour one for yourself. Bonne santé et succès à toutes nos nouvelles entreprises*"

Epilogue

Thomas Laurent was thinking deeply about the speech he was due to make in an hour's time at the Sorbonne university to a group of human rights activists, of which there was a branch at the university. However, the event had been publicised broadly both around the university and more widely across Paris in bars and cafés where posters and leaflets had been displayed and distributed. A large audience was expected to attend and Thomas was nervous. Over the last year, since he had qualified from the Sorbonne, he had applied for a junior teaching job at the university in the Politics department whilst he was finishing his post graduate qualification there and had been accepted for the position. He was already being seen as a 'rising star' in the department and was tipped to be able to stay there and work to fund his doctorate qualification and would then almost certainly be offered a full-time position. The speech was entitled *"Quis custodiet Ipsos custodes."* The phrase was from the Roman poet Juvenal which literally translated meant *'Who will guard the guards themselves'* or *'Who watches the watchmen?"* He was linking this theme to what had occurred during the disturbances in May the previous year and particularly to the police reaction to them and to the significant potential threat to liberal democracy and the freedom of speech and expression if this kind of unregulated repression was allowed to continue unchecked.

He was walking slowly after exiting the Mètro at Cluny La Sorbonne station. He came to a stop at the Boulevard St. Germain waiting for an opportunity to cross the road. When

259

he saw a break in the traffic, he stepped off the kerb and the last thing he remembered was the sound of an engine revving and a car turning right out of Rue de la Parcheminerie, accelerating at great speed and just appeared out of nowhere. Then everything went black and he collapsed onto the cobblestones of the road. Witnesses were to say later that it all just happened so fast and they couldn't get a good view of the driver's face because he was wearing dark glasses and a beret and also was wearing a black leather jacket that was buttoned up to the top but the car was definitely black and probably a Peugeot.

The driver of the car however, had never even glanced back in his rear-view mirror as he sped away from the scene saying quietly to himself:

"As Aristotle once said 'It is not always the same thing to be a good man and a good citizen'"

The following books are also by Tony Barnard...

The Sheffield Avengers by Tony Barnard

A story of supreme courage.

Two boys who grew up together in the district of Tinsley in Sheffield against a backdrop of the declining fortunes of the once world-beating steel industry. One indebted to the other from an early age and both with powerful ambitions. *The Sheffield Avengers* is the story of their development, their personal relationships with their families and their lovers, acts of supreme courage and the restoration of pride. 'Made in Sheffield' is a global endorsement of quality, strength and consistency that can apply to its people, products and a warship that carried its name.

Fast-paced and international in its breadth and reach. The Sheffield Avengers is a meticulously researched and compelling 'what if' story of the skill and courage of Britain's Special Forces during the Falkland's War in 1982.

Paperback: 212 pages
Publisher: PublishNation 2014
ISBN-978-1-326-08086-0

High Five in Jerusalem by Tony Barnard

A story of our times.
An epic tale of good overcoming evil, of light over dark and hope over despair.

Tarik Tanović was only fifteen years old when his father was murdered by a Serbian sniper in his home city of Sarajevo during the three-year long siege. The incident was to have a profound effect on his life as he struggled to come to terms with his loss and the senselessness of it all.

This is Tarik's story. A compelling account of his strive to overcome his demons, seek an equalisation of events, achieve catharsis and finally get on with the rest of his life.

Paperback: 219 pages
Publisher: PublishNation 2016
ISBN-978-1-326-86760-7

Pebbles in the Pond by Tony Barnard

A collection of short stories about the effects of human interaction like ripples spreading across a pond after a stone has been thrown in.

Paperback: 132 pages
Publisher: PublishNation 2018
ISBN-978-0-244-43528-8

Printed in Poland
by Amazon Fulfillment
Poland Sp. z o.o., Wrocław